NIGHT SOIL

Books by Dale Peck

Fiction
Greenville
Body Surfing
Shift (with Tim Kring)

Gospel Harmonies
Martin and John
The Law of Enclosures
Now It's Time to Say Goodbye
The Garden of Lost and Found

Nonfiction
Hatchet Jobs
Visions and Revisions

Children's and Young Adult Fiction
Drift House
The Lost Cities
Sprout

NIGHT SOIL

Dale Peck

Published by Soho Press
853 Broadway
New York, NY 10003

Library of Congress Cataloging-in-Publication Data

Peck, Dale, author.
Night soil / Dale Peck.

ISBN 978-1-61695-780-3
eISBN 978-1-61695-781-0

1. Mothers and sons—Fiction. 2. Teenage boys—Fiction.
3. Family secrets—Fiction. 4. Gay youth—Fiction. 5. Domestic fiction.
I. Title.
PS3566.E245 N54 2018 813'.54—dc23 2018004484

Interior design by Janine Agro, Soho Press, Inc.

Printed in the United States of America

10 9 8 7 6 5 4 3 2 1

For Lou Peralta

NIGHT SOIL

"High treason, when it is resistance to tyranny here below, has its origin in, and is first committed by, the power that makes and forever recreates man. When you have caught and hung all these human rebels, you have accomplished nothing but your own guilt, for you have not struck at the fountainhead. You presume to contend with a foe against whom West Point cadets and rifled cannon point not. Can all the art of the cannon-founder tempt matter to turn against its maker? Is the form in which the founder thinks he casts it more essential than the constitution of it and of himself?"

—Thoreau, "A Plea for Captain John Brown"

NIGHT SOIL

I
Night Soil

1

I tried to be a good boy. I didn't speak unless spoken to, and when I did speak I called men "sir" and women "ma'am." I said "Please," "Excuse me," and "Pardon our appearance while we renovate," placed my napkin in my lap when I sat down to eat, dropped my eyes when I caught people staring. By the time I was three I'd given up fingerpainting, used brushes instead, but only the ones my mother discarded, and only at the most distant edge of her work table. If I remember anything from my pre-school days it's this: my mother perched at the far end of those six rough-sawn planks whirling a disc of clay before her like a captain in her stern—a stern captain, I can't resist saying—while I gadded about the prow, a gaudy figurehead stabbing his brush against the canvas as though trying to slice it open. When I'd finally conceded that I couldn't make things any better—or, at any rate, that more paint would only make them worse—I closed my easel and ferried my supplies to the back of the apartment, where an enclosed porch hung off the kitchen in a crazy parallelogram, its floor slanting almost as much as its roof. I hooked my palette on one nail, hung my apron on another, then mounted a severed section of ladder (itself a rickety affair, its rungs twisting beneath my feet like a strand of DNA) in order to wash my brushes in an industrial-sized zinc sink nearly as deep as I was tall. Only after I'd cleaned and stowed everything did I go back for my painting. I was no one's idea of an artistic prodigy but as a critic I was more precocious, by which I mean that even at three, four, five years old I recognized that the colors and shapes I'd chosen to combine were as incongruent as peanut butter, jelly, and mayonnaise smeared on the same slice of bread, and after a glance down the table for a reprieve from my mother—who probably hadn't realized I'd left the room, let alone that I'd returned—I folded the wet canvas closed on itself, less like a sandwich than a book I'd abandoned, a story that could no longer pique even the most abbreviated narrative curiosity. Close the *Aeneid* after Dido "calls it marriage" and she and Aeneas stay together forever, if you never crack the cover again, if you can convince yourself that the story belongs not to posterity but to you. I wasn't that strong. I painted every day for three years until finally my mother stopped giving me supplies. Even then I pressed on, diluting my pigments and painting on the halved versos of discarded canvases, the images growing smaller and smaller and fainter and fainter, until at length the only thing they depicted was my desire, and its failure to fructify.

It's a dubious gift to be able to envision something without also being able to make it. One wants to say it's the teacher's burden, or the writer's, or the male of the species'—his "burthen" I suppose I should call it. No doubt my dilemma was made more palpable by virtue of being Dixie Stammers's son. My mother never paid attention to what people said about her work, cared only about what she made and how closely it corresponded to what she'd set out to produce. I'd be lying if I said I didn't internalize that lesson from the time I was tall enough to recognize myself in a mirror, or at least until my mother replaced all the mirrors in our apartment with oxidized substitutes that reflected little more than shadows. It's not just that I thought of myself as a terrible painter: I thought of myself as a failure. In this regard, at least, I was my mother's son, and a budding Academy man to boot: I was interested only in what I could make paint show, not what it might show me. I've never looked at clouds and seen anything other than water vapor, and I've never been bothered by this. The fact that dihydrogen monoxide molecules clot together in denser and denser masses until finally precipitating in any of a half dozen different forms (my favorite being virga, the rain that falls but never touches the ground) seems to me more worthy of study than spurious fantasies that tell you only about the viewer, not what he's looking at (although I suppose having a favorite kind of precipitation is its own projection, its own confession). They filled our heads with a lot of nonsense at the Academy, outdated, esoteric, idealistic fantasies that now seem as remote to me as the school itself, but one lesson that's been hard to shake is the idea that the world doesn't exist to elucidate you: you are the world's elucidation, the only proof of its existence you will ever truly know.

COGITO

SUM

is the inscription over the campus's front gate, I THINK I AM, the letters carved into an anthracite revetment mounted in a bluestone Gothic arch, as if truth were only as durable as the rock from which (into which?) it's chiseled. I'm pretty sure the tablet was just a goof on the part of my great-great-great-great-great-grandfather, yet it stands as a measure of Academy belief in the literal meaning of words that I never once heard master or novice suggest there might be more than one way to read Great Grandpa Marcus's bowdlerization. A carriage horse needs blinkers because it can't keep its eyes on the road, a parrot forgets the sun is out when a curtain is draped over its cage, but an Academy man acknowledges only *what is*, and is misled by neither camouflage nor distraction.

Maybe this is just a roundabout way of saying that I lacked any artistic talent as a child. But what I want you to realize at the outset is that abandoning my brushes was an ethical decision, not an aesthetic one. I gave up painting because I wasn't good enough—not good enough *for me* (or, for that matter, my mother), nor even good enough *for painting*, but good enough *for the world*. There were simply more worthwhile things I could be doing with my life. For example: cleaning, a venerable vocation central to the Academy's founding, and one that, in a house like ours, required a certain level of imagination to see how such a seemingly impossible task could be realized. Before she moved into our apartment my mother had lived in a six-bedroom mansion furnished with 150 years of family heirlooms. She claimed to have left most of that "Queen Anne garbage" behind, but our apartment was still crowded with sofas and chairs, bureaus and china cabinets pushed right up against each other like furniture in a junk shop. Ours was a house of pyramids, every reasonably flat surface stacked with boxes and baskets and bowls, tapering towers of pillows piled on foundations of folded blankets or yellowed newspapers and crowned by balls of yarn or rag dolls or smooth gray river stones, ziggurats of belted leather cases sporting vases filled with long-dead flowers or velveteen bags jumbled with tea lights and loose change and matchbooks and mismatched gloves. So there was no way the place was ever going to be neat. But it could at least be clean.

Such was my epiphany, anyway, when one day in my first year at the Academy I walked into the apartment and saw more or less simultaneously the encrustations of clay that the wheels of my mother's stool had ground into the floor and, hanging off the wall above it like a superannuated relic, an antique push broom whose straw bristles had been worn nearly to the nub. We'd been to the Lake that day. While the other boys stripped off their robes and jumped into the frigid water I sat on the bank and pretended to listen as Master McCauley told me for the tenth or hundredth time how my great-great-great-great-great-grandfather had made it "his life's mission" to "cleanse the waters" before me from the residue of a half century of coal mining, an act of "environmental largesse" from which the Academy had been born. Faint splashes came through the bathroom door, along with the sound of something classical sawing out of the radio my mother kept in the window ledge above the tub. I hung my gown on a hook next to her smock, pried the broom from the wall in a shower of plaster (it turned out to have been nailed in place) and, almost idly, began pushing its stubbled surface over the pale dried clay. I was thinking less about Great Grandpa Marcus or the crystal-clear waters of the Lake than about the bare smooth skin of my classmates as, one by one, in graceful dives or cannonballs or crookedly spoked limbs, they splashed off the end of the dock while I squatted beneath my tented robe like a thick-shelled tortoise who'd long since renounced aquatic life. The broom did little more than score staff lines across the clay's surface, so I grabbed one of my mother's palette knives and used it to shiv up the mess instead, turning it edgewise to score long-dried filaments from the gaps in the parquet. A dozen times I stopped and swept the sticky crumbs onto a square of old canvas and carried it back to the trash can on the porch. A trail of gray footprints marked my progress like the steps to a rhythmless, frenetic tango, but somehow I didn't think of them as evidence of the futility of my labor, but, rather, as proof of how hard I was working. In this regard, at least, I was Marcus's kin, though it would be years before I realized it.

I'm not sure how far I got that first day, but I was at it again the next, and within a month or two had worked out a method that was to serve me for more than half a decade. I set to as soon as I got out of nones or, if I'd been at the hospital that day, as soon as my taxi returned me from Wye. I realized pretty quickly I had to begin with the ceiling or all the dust I dislodged would settle on the floor I'd just cleaned, and so I started at the top, coaxing spiderwebs from high corners with a dry mop, feathering lint from Murano glass chandeliers and crown moldings, whacking curtains, dry-wiping picture frames and faded patches of wallpaper and wainscoting, until eventually I'd made my way to the floor. I scraped up the worst of my mother's clay first, then began shifting the furniture around like the pieces of a sliding puzzle in order to attack the smeared, scarred parquetry one latticed diamond at a time, scrubbing and mopping and buffing each exposed square with beeswax and sheepskin until the whole floor (or at least the minuscule portion that could be seen at any given moment) glittered like snakeskin and exuded a rich smell, leathery, fecund, warm.

I sorted the glazes by hue then, weeding out and washing the empties, turned the grayware in the windows so it would dry evenly, and concluded each day's labors by handwashing my mother's smock, which couldn't go down with the rest of the laundry because Mrs. Brown said the clay would gum up her machine—the only thing in Marcuse besides herself and Mr. Brown, she liked to joke, old enough to have watched Abraham Lincoln sign the Emancipation Proclamation on the evening news. The gray scum from a thousand unconscious swipes of my mother's hands across her lap had dried in a flaky circle as big around as a pizza, leaving the blousy garment looking like a snow angel that'd been gut shot. I cradled the corpse in both arms so the clay wouldn't crumble onto my clean floor, walked on tiptoes and tenterhooks all the way back to the porch, where I unceremoniously drowned the smock in the sink and ground the soiled cambric into a washboard until every last speck of clay had been abraded away. I rinsed the sink and refilled it then, added a quarter cup of phosphate-free laundry detergent and two tablespoons of caustic soda. The lye stung my skin like chigger bites, turning it a florid salmon that melded with my birthmark where it cobwebbed across the back of my left hand, and sometimes the skin split and bled along the seam between purple and pink. (For a few months when I was seven I thought that if I used enough lye my birthmark might actually peel off, but though the cuts grew deeper, and burned and bled for hours, the only thing that ever fell off were two fingernails on my left hand, after which I took to wearing rubber gloves.) When the smock was finally clean I wrapped it around a steam pipe in order to wring the water from it, braiding the two halves together like one of Mr. Brown's Easter loaves, then hung it on a hanger, shriveled but spotless, and needing only a pass with the iron before matins to complete its resurrection. Only then would I pull out a box of macaroni or rice for dinner, a jar of some sauce or other, salad vegetables to keep what Mrs. Brown called "the crickets" at bay. I set plates and forks on the table, stood a wine glass at my mother's place, a cup of psyllium husk at mine, and when Mrs. B. came upstairs with the groceries I accepted today's full bag for yesterday's empty one, upon which I'd written what we needed for tomorrow.

Sometime after that—an hour later or three, depending on how dirty she'd felt when she went in—my mother emerged from the bathroom to fix dinner. My mother claimed she didn't get out of the tub until Mrs. Brown had come and gone because she found our septuagenarian housekeeper "judgmental" and "abusive" ("If she didn't want to carry *one bag of groceries* up *one flight of stairs* she shouldn't have *taken the job*—and I said 'abrasive,' Jude, not 'abusive'") but the truth is she'd done her own time at the Academy, and took her ablutions as seriously as did I. From forehead to toenails she glistened with whatever oil or lotion she'd coated her body with that day, but beneath the waxy sheen her skin was nearly as piebald as my own, so blotched and pruned from three or four or five hours of scourging that it looked as if she'd been whipped. The impression was only heightened by her slow, almost limping gait, as though her joints, grown accustomed to the buoyancy of soapy perfumed liquid, had difficulty supporting her weight. Only when I was older did I realize her body was in fact still recovering from its potting trance. That her muscles, like a cyclist's, needed to be coaxed back to the quotidian tasks of walking, stirring, lifting, bending. We lived in the parlor-floor apartment above the Browns' bakery until I was thirteen, the entirety of our lives crammed into four railroaded rooms taller than they were wide, so that my mother often said we needed to find a way to mount our furniture on the walls, or just knock the whole damn building on its side. Century-old Victorian moldings had softened into an antique vision of an edgeless future, a swoopy Deco facade from the thirties or a fifties Airstream trailer, simultaneously optimistic and archaic. But though the apartment wasn't large by any measure, it somehow managed to house me and my mother and the usual array of domestic paraphernalia—knee chairs, yoga mats, bromeliads—plus her more esoteric collections and obsessions: her death masks (six) and shrunken heads (two), her Turkish birdcages and Soviet constructivist posters, her mobiles built from animal bones and spent shot and shell-casings from the Civil War, her complete set (1951–57) of ⌀ (the shape reminds me of a lemniscate or a vesica piscis, but it was usually called *Eclipse* by those in the know), a general-interest quarterly magazine composed solely of found photographs in the belief that, *verba docent exempla trahunt*, inexpensive cameras and instant developing processes would soon make orthography obsolete—or at least I think that was the rationale, the magazine's editors having left no (written) record to explain their motives.

Then there were her toilet articles: her ear candles and neti pots and eye drops and enema balloons, an array of dental implements that looked less like instruments of hygiene than props from a torture porn, although these latter—along with her facial scrubs and body washes, her shampoos and conditioners and gels, her heel creams and knee creams and elbow creams and hand creams, pumice stones, sea sponges, loofahs, ayate cloths, bath salts, sugar scrubs, argan and almond and flaxseed oils and aromatic essences and astringents and antiseptics—oh, and her douches, of which there were more varieties than there are, as far as I know, types of vagina, let alone vaginal irritation, a vene-real pharmacopeia arrayed across three shelves by scent, viscosity, and applicator shape and marked with a rufous smudge if they could be/had been used during menstruation—were less collec-tion than confession, the obsession with cleanliness exposing not so much a guilty conscience as a dirty one, a mind fascinated by filth, failure, transgression. And let's not forget the tools of her trade: her kilns (three of them, each the size of a safe in a gang-ster noir, though only two actually worked, the third being used to store clay in a temperature- and humidity-controlled envi-ronment), and shelf upon shelf of glazes and brushes and wooden dowels and wire scrapers and, presiding like a Druidic altar over everything, her work table, three sawhorses across which lay six scaffold-grade planks of Douglas fir, each two inches thick, six inches wide, and fourteen feet long. When it was set up the table dominated the apartment's double parlor, and on the rare occasions it was broken down it remained a presence, the planks being so long that the only place to put them was on the floor thirty inches below where they normally lay, so that it seemed you walked a wobbly bridge when you crossed from one half of the parlor to the other—the planks themselves were perfectly straight, but the floor beneath them curved like the ocean's horizon.

There was all of this, and there was, finally, what it all made possible. No, no, not *us*. People were uncannily unique in my mother's world, unknowable, therefore inconsequential. The closer they were to her the stranger they seemed, so that the only person more alien to Dixie Stammers than me was herself. No, I mean her *pots*, of course, tucked into every nook and cranny and spare cubic foot the apartment had to offer, stacked upside down in bulbous columns six, eight, twelve high or scattered about like spittoons or upended copper diving helmets (of which my mother also owned three). Dozens and dozens of those "modern miracles of Mesoamerican methodology" as *Art in America* called them, in the magazine's first-ever review of an "(anything but) conventional" pottery exhibition—or, rather, of a potter's work, since my mother neither showed nor sold her pots until after that review made her famous, just gave them to friends or strangers or let them pile up in cupboards and closets and corners. Really, she didn't care where her pots ended up or what they were used for or even if they survived. She cared only about making them. The word "process" was used a lot in that first article, though it's not a word I ever remember hearing her say, just as she never called them "vases," "vessels," or "urns" the way the review did, let alone "her work," "the work," or any other term that smacked of "artspeak," by which my mother (who hadn't graduated from the Academy, but was still the daughter of its fourth president, great-great-great-great-granddaughter of its founder) meant a certain type of exegetical legerdemain that consumed material objects with a Kantian contempt for the phenomenal. My mother had unambiguously rejected the Academy proscription against making the year I was born, but certain lessons were less pedagogy than pedigree. Though she didn't see anything wrong with combining "already existing materials" to create something new (as if someone somewhere—on the Tibetan plateau maybe, or in the Holy of Holies of the Salt Lake Temple of the Church of Jesus Christ of Latter-Day Saints—conjured matter out of thin air), she would do so only if what was made resisted "the false gloss" of culture. Thus she didn't call herself a "ceramicist" or claim to "sculpt with clay," and never accepted the title "artist" or even "craftswoman." No, my mother was a potter. She made pots, and the pots she made were nothing *but* pots. That was it. That was all. End of story.

BUT THE TRUTH is it was only the beginning, right—or why would I be telling you this? Why would you be reading? Not to be too self-effacing (that's a pun, and if you don't get it now you will soon enough) but you wouldn't care about me if I wasn't the only child of the woman who was, by universal acclaim, the most technically accomplished potter the world has ever known, the "divine" maker of 174 "unparalleled masterpieces of conception and execution," or one pot for every twenty-eight days of her working life. This quotient is, I know, entirely arbitrary—my mother once made three pots in as many days, and when we moved to the Field two and a half years passed during which she never once touched unfired clay (well, not in the house anyway). Then, too, she was about the least Moon Goddessy–type of woman you can imagine. But still, it's difficult to resist the lunar resonance, especially when it's so strongly echoed in the pots themselves, which start out as silver crescents and swell into pale orbs whose single off-center orifice compels your confession like a priest's cupped ear. The pots themselves took only a day to make—had in fact to be finished in about six hours or the clay became immalleable—but before my mother ever sat down in front of the slab of porphyry she used as her rolling surface she had first to make temper and grog, in preparation for which she visited a restaurant in Marcuse once a week, leaving with a bag of mussel shells she soaked in the porch sink overnight to get the adductor muscle to release its grip, then dried in one of the kilns and pounded into a fine black powder in a quartz mortar as big as a commode. This was temper; grog was the by-product of broken pots she ground into coarse meal the color of thunder-clouds, salt to the shells' pepper. She grabbed big messy handfuls at first (I always knew the days she'd spent wedging because the floor was as gritty as a beachside boardwalk), kneading them into Roman brick–sized slabs of clay, taking ever smaller amounts until finally she was adding the tiniest pinches of black or white powder, like a pastry chef seasoning her dough. She worked the clay for hours until it achieved some magical consistency she couldn't quantify with a formula, could only feel in her fingertips, then let it set ("It has to set, Jude, not sit. *Set.* My *God*, those ginkgos smell like shit today") overnight in the broken kiln, and the next morning, after eating the corncake rollup and drinking the cup of coffee Mr. B. always left outside our door, she lifted the great gray slimy egg from the kiln and pulled chunks from it with taloned fingers and rolled the chunks into ribbons on the jagged-edged sheet of purple stone at the western end of her potting table. The slight porousness of phaneritic porphyry— i.e., its absorptive capacity—was assumed to be as important as its mildly scabrous surface in working the clay, but despite the elaborate preparation and the rarefied nature of the props— the kaolin imported from the Peruvian Amazon at $34 a pound; the three-inch-thick slab of stone quarried from the same mine in Egypt from which were said to have come the walls of the

Porphyra, the birthing room of the empresses of Constantinople; the pair of diffused halogen lamps she moved around on their articulated arms like a dentist peering into an open mouth—she resembled nothing so much as a wild-haired little girl rubbing her hands back and forth, lips pursed, brow furrowed, palms madly rolling balls of clay into pencil-thin ribbons and then—somehow, mysteriously, miraculously—building the ribbons up into hollow globes that were (I'm sure you know this, yet it bears saying again, and again and again, and 171 times again) perfectly spherical and exactly the same size, every last one of them.

It was the former detail that first attracted interest in her pots but it was the latter that made her a sensation: the fact that she made spheres that were not just mechanically perfect but *identical*, like a latter-day Giotto auditioning for the pope, but working in three dimensions and duplicating the feat over and over again. All this without benefit of mold, compass, scale, or any other tool, including of course—especially—a wheel. She'd worked with wheels once upon a time, like every other woman who takes a pottery class at her local community center (in this case the Wye Wreck Room, where, in the wake of my mother's success, classes went from $175 for a two-month session to $1,500 for five weeks), churned out her fair share of the earth-toned kitsch you find at swap meets and garage sales, dabbled with Ming, Tang, and Song techniques, went through the inevitable Japanese phase ("Although I mean *really*, how can you take something seriously when chance is celebrated as 'realignment'"—index fingers curled into ironic quotation marks that could've cracked walnuts—"It's like it's impossible to—no, I said 're*fine*ment.' 'Realignment' doesn't make any sense, although neither does Japanese pottery if you ask me").

It was during a visit to the Metropolitan Museum in New York City that she was exposed to pre-Columbian pottery and "just fell in love with it." The color, the texture, but above all "the tension," which was something you could see if you knew how to look for it, but was best experienced when you held the pot in your hands—which, my mother said, she *had* to do, lifting a Panamanian Coclé-style infant's funerary casket from its velvet-lined base and cradling it in her hands for "all of three seconds" before she was surrounded by museum guards who acted like "they would've pulled out pistols if they'd been packing." A pot that's been shaped from semi-aqueous clay whirled around on a potter's wheel was, in my mother's estimation, not just inanimate but *dead* ("and plus formally it's about as challenging as dishing up soft-serve ice cream"), whereas a pot built from coils is held together by energetic valences that, a thousand years after they'd been rolled, still set her fingertips atingle the way coca shocks the lips. Trips to Oaxaca, Arequipa, and Tierra del Fuego followed as she experimented with different clays, different techniques, different shapes. What makes these journeys all the more remarkable is the fact that she was a teenager at the time, a sixteen- and seventeen-year-old girl gamely braving right-wing paramilitaries, left-wing banditos, and, "like, *no* Spanish" in pursuit of her craft. She spent more than a year fashioning increasingly complex biomorphic vessels that were, in the words of the *Art in America* critic, "tours de force in their own right"—flaccid bladders with intricately curled tubes that looked like hearts and stomachs with tangled lengths of artery and esophagus still attached—but it was only after she discovered she was pregnant that she hit upon her project. "He was so special, so unique," my mother told the critic, speaking of her unborn child as though it had been a thinking, talking being rather than a clump of cells multiplying in her thorax. "I didn't ever want to give him up. I wanted to stretch out the experience forever, to safeguard the miracle that was taking shape within my body" and that, by inference (although perhaps only the former miracle inferred it), had yet to disappoint her with its deviation from whatever image she'd had in her head of the heir to the Stammers heritage and the corrective to a century of misguided Academy philosophy. Dixie's math is a little fuzzy here, her story a little revisionist, if not simply self-serving. The humbler truth is that I cracked a piece out of number 1 when I was three, but instead of punishing me all she said was "Don't worry, honey, I'll just make another." That's how I remember it anyway (although even I have to admit it's hard to imagine my mother calling me or anyone else "honey"), but who's to say she hadn't started cooking up the idea years earlier?

Since you're reading this I assume you have at least a passing familiarity with my mother's work. No doubt you've heard how her pots were tested at MIT, which found that each is as perfectly round as a cannonball manufactured by a munitions factory. Each has an external radius (which is to say, measured from the center point to the outside of the pot) of 141.393 millimeters and a 96.0749-millimeter opening, with a mean weight of 5306.69 grams (the slight differences in mass were chalked up to variations in the temperature and humidity of the rooms in which the pots ended up, although no pot deviates from the mean by more than six grams, which is about how much a quarter weighs), and each is so perfectly balanced that when placed on a plinth no wider than the aforementioned quarter the pot not only doesn't fall off but its opening sits 23.4° off perpendicular—i.e., the axial tilt of the earth, which, recalling my earlier metaphor, makes the pots planet to their own moon.

You know that. Everyone who's ever opened an art journal or flipped through the weekend supplement of a major metropolitan newspaper knows that. What no one could figure out is *how*. People assumed there were casts, a laser sight, a wattle frame that burned away during firing, until finally my mother consented to let a film crew record her making three pots in three days just to prove she used nothing but her eyes and her hands, the slab of stone on which she pounded and rolled the clay and a bowl of water (itself the bottom half of a broken pot, the sight of which caused the documentary's director to catch his breath as though he'd been punched in the stomach) with which she occasionally wet her fingers. There she is in a soiled smock (I'd long since stopped washing them), braless, the birthmark outside the areola of her left breast (not a port-wine stain like mine, but a cafe-au-lait oval about the size of a penny that's been run over by a train) becoming increasingly visible as sweat sticks the fabric to her skin. Her loose skirt is pulled up and piled beneath the smock like "the miracle" she'd tried so hard to hold on to, her bare legs and feet rooted to the earth but increasingly rising up on toetips, first one foot, then the other, at first like a ballerina learning to dance on point but increasingly like a dance itself, an oeta or hula whose internal percussion was given voice by the sound of her heels slapping against the floor again and again. By that point her skin was so chafed from years of compulsive bathing it looked like she had prickly heat, but gradually the pink-speckled expanse of her thighs and arms and face grew more and more splattered with gray scales, until she resembled a reptilian hybrid caught mid-metamorphosis (though whether toward the human or away is anybody's guess). Her concentration was absolute. She didn't react to noises or movement, didn't eat or drink or speak or use the bathroom, didn't *ever once* look away from the thing she was making and kept at least one hand on it at all times, until, after more than five hours of pushing-pulling-scraping-rubbing-smoothing, she suddenly sat back, tipped the pot on its side, brushed a number on its weighted bottom, and lumbered like a zombie into the bathroom. Number 1 all the way through 174, each (before they were glazed anyway), identical and indistinguishable to everyone but her who, like the mother of twins, could tell one from the other at a glance or, blindfolded, just by picking it up. The director of the film told her that her prices were going to double after she pulled that trick but he was wrong. They quadrupled.

(It was right about the time the film was shot that I came to believe my mother actually *had* given birth to twins, or, at any rate, conceived them. Academy science, being purely empirical, relieves the tedium of its self-imposed limits by a fascination with atypical physical development, be it congenital, experiential, or habitual. No doubt I would've been required to exhibit myself like DeVon Jones and his lactating nipples had my last name not been Stammers, but there were still ample opportunities for display, the October swim being required of all novices, the training going on year-round. Then there was the annual nude self-portrait, for which a fully mirrored carrel—floor and ceiling in addition to all four walls—was constructed, and from which issued a steady stream of drawings displayed in Stammers Hall throughout the fall; and although, as I said, I have no real artistic talent, I could still indicate the extent of my birthmark clearly enough, so that even from fifty or a hundred feet away the lone blotch of color glowed like a beacon on a wall full of darkly shaded kouroi. And so anyway, when I was twelve and discovered the interrelated phenomena of mosaicism, chimerism, and vanishing twins [the terms came from a magazine in my doctor's office, by the way; genetic theory at the Academy didn't go much past Mendel], I became obsessed with the idea that my birthmark wasn't actually *mine*—that it was in fact vestige and vengeance of a sibling I'd murdered and consumed in my mother's womb. This isn't quite as fanciful as it sounds, since, in the first place, many port wine stains, mine included, affect only one side of the body, and, as well, extensive hemispheric nevus flammeus is often associated with one or another of these anomalies. And my mother was a twin, and there were two other sets in the family tree—all fraternal, as it happens, and of mixed sex, which left me with the less attractive fantasy of murdering a sister rather than a brother who might have challenged my claim to the Stammers kingdom. Cain killed Abel, after all, not one of the unnamed daughters Eve begat after Seth: killed him because God preferred Abel's blood offering to Cain's grain, which is kind of ironic when you think about it, if not simply grotesque, since God got bored with the whole sacrifice thing four thousand years later and, after accepting his son's life, banned the practice in its entirety. The Ottoman sultan Mehmed III, on the birth of his first son, had nineteen of his brothers strangled with silk cords in order to ensure a smooth succession; the Mauryan emperor Aśoka was said to have killed no fewer than ninety-nine brothers as punishment for their role in the wars following their father's death—another irony, since it was Aśoka who'd started the fight, because he wasn't the chosen heir. I wanted something like that—like Romulus and Remus,

Claudius and the elder Hamlet, Michael and Fredo even. Instead I got Caligula and Drusilla—Drusilla!—with its sad, incestuous overtones. For a while I tried to spin it, pretending my birthmark was the poisoned shirt Deianeira gave Heracles, although if any trace of a female sibling endured in me it was more likely manifest through my sexuality than on my skin. And since the cause of my birthmark—or my sexual orientation for that matter—had no bearing on either its effects or its treatment, I'd mostly forgotten about the whole episode by the time I was twenty-three, when the possibility of multiple genetic populations attempting to obliterate each other like Serbs and Croats within the Yugoslavia of my body was refuted during the course of unrelated medical tests, and I was forced to accept that whatever mismatched attributes and impulses I harbored, they stemmed solely from me.)

All of that, however, was still years in the future. *Three by Stammers* wasn't shot until long after we moved to the Field; among other things, the three-person crew—cameraman, director, and producer, a hippie-haired Jewish woman who gave me a few puffs off a joint and then asked, "So is your dick purple too?"—could've never fit in the apartment above the bakery, let alone their lights and tripods, their dozen black nylon bags filled with cables, cords, wires, drugs. The High Street apartment barely had room for me and my mother, let alone her collections and toiletries and kilns and pots—at the time, ninety-two of them, minus the seven that'd broken and been ground to grog and the twelve she'd given away, including the three that served as cookie jars (peanut butter, oatmeal, ginger-molasses) atop the Browns' display case, which caught the eye of an art critic who'd been doing some research at the Academy and wanted something to "get the taste of quack" out of her mouth before heading to the airport. It was the morning crunch. The bakery was filled with "half-awake students and half-asleep professors in dowdy, dour gowns milling about in the black-and-white CCTV monitor like an antediluvian game of Pac-Man" (just one of many displays of arbitrary context-making that showed how little business the critic had at the Academy). Mr. Brown was a genius at knowing the exact moment when the mouth-watering effects of standing in a fragrant bakery crossed from impatience to hostility (whereas Mrs. Brown said it had taken 242 years before her ancestors won their freedom and she could give a flying fig how long anyone waited for a cup of coffee) and neither of them served the critic for several minutes, during which time she found her eye drawn again and again to the three cookie jars, which wobbled like Weebles every time Mr. Brown slammed the drawer of his old-fashioned cash register, but never fell down. At first she thought they were handmade, possibly old—possibly very old. It would be *just like* some hole-in-the-wall doughnut shop in Appalachia (really? why?) to have pre-Columbian artifacts stuffed with sweets on its front counter (oh, and: the Browns didn't sell doughnuts). But the Tyrian purple with which they'd been glazed was atypical to say the least, and the chromatic patterning ("like nevi whipped about by the current of an insatiable algorithm") was completely wrong. Then there was the fact that, although one of the vessels had a four-inch piece glued into it, they were otherwise incredibly similar in size, shape, and glazing, if not actually identical (she was right on the first two counts, wrong on the third, although it took a version of Interpol's fingerprint-recognition software, modified to work in three dimensions, to prove it), leading the critic to conclude that the pots must have been machine made. But even so, they were fascinating specimens—more compelling than anything she'd seen up the hill anyway—and when she finally reached the counter she asked Mr. Brown where he'd gotten them. Mr. Brown thought she meant the cookies, and he pointed to a sign over his head:

ALL BAKING DONE ON PR☺MISES

"No no," the critic clarified, "the urns. The vases? The jars?" *Sigh.* "Um, the *pots*?"

"What, these things?" Mr. Brown pinged one with his fingernail, and even though the pot was half an inch thick and half-filled with cookies besides, it rang with the crystalline tone you expect from wafer-thin bone china before fading to a nearly noiseless vibration whose sound on the glass counter I still remember every time I hear a muted cellphone. "Lady upstairs makes 'em. Probably has fifty more, a hundred, just like these."

PINGZZZ.

The sound, like everything else about Dixie Stammers's pots, unvarying from one to the next, or varying only in relation to what struck them and how hard: fingernail, teaspoon, the hollow horn of a ram (although in my case it sounds substantially different if I turn the left side of my face toward it as opposed to the right). You know it, even if you don't know you know it. Maybe you watched as the fifteenth Dalai Lama walked into Xizang Province, reversing the journey his predecessor took in the middle of the last century; that faint *pingzzz-pingzzz-pingzzz* in the background was the sound of a monk striking one of my mother's pots 108 times (one for each of the earthly temptations that keep a soul from achieving nirvana) with a gnarled length of root from the Bodhi tree beneath which Siddhartha Gautama found enlightenment. Or maybe you've listened to John Cage's "Farewell (to) Monotony," which features his nine-year-old grandson striking one of my mother's pots with a 128-Hz tuning fork at 2.3-second intervals (the time between each of the dying man's heartbeats), until, at the 1,024th tap, as Cage had predicted, the vibrations in the fork and the vitrified clay reached "critical synchronicity" and the pot shattered to dust (Cage himself lingered for another day and a half, his protracted death rattle forming the symphony's macabre second movement). And then Steve Jobs, on his third liver and second pancreas and only slightly more mobile than Stephen Hawking, forked out an "undisclosed but reportedly *enormous*" sum (a nondisclosure agreement prohibits me from telling you the figure, even though I never saw a penny of it) to use the sound as part of the "Same But Different" campaign introducing the PhoneBook, ultimately setting it as OSXtra's startup alert, which means that hundreds of millions of people all over the planet hear it at least once a day.

But again I'm getting ahead of things (forgive me, Master Renslow!): in the beginning there was just the one critic, the one article, and then, finally, the one phone call, each less ping than gong sounding the close of a childhood idyll—although the real culprit, if I'm being totally honest, was probably hormones. Well, hormones and genes: I was twelve when the critic discovered my mother. Her review came out six months later, and the following several years, as my mother became more and more famous, were roughly coincident with the ravages of puberty.

Adolescence was even more traumatic for me than it is for most kids because my birthmark grew at a slightly slower rate than did the rest of my skin, causing a variety of minor but annoying, embarrassing, and/or painful problems. My left ear rang constantly, my left eyelid drooped as though I had myasthenia gravis, and if I forgot myself and yelled or sang or opened my jaw too wide the left side of my mouth tore open like the skin of a blanched beet, and I would spend the next fifteen minutes with my hand cupped over my lips, my tongue furtively licking up blood (for years afterward whenever I got nervous I spoke with the left corner of my lips pressed together—that's right, dear reader, your narrator is adept at talking out of one side of his mouth). But heads don't grow too quickly or too much. The biggest problem was my rib cage. In order to lift my left arm higher than my shoulder I had to massage the side of my torso with cocoa butter (or shea butter, or olive oil, or even bacon grease, the various smells of which prompted Master Whitlock to say that I could drive a reformed cannibal to relapse). Monthly visits to the dermatologist in Wye became weekly; my treatment switched from flash-pumped dye lasers (which had done little to lighten the color of my birthmark) to Nd:YAG lasers (which stands for "neodymium-doped yttrium aluminum garnet" and was, for me, pretty much the most interesting part of the process). The treatments were meant to minimize scarring, hypertrophy, and other "disfigurements," which word, in this context, seems as richly ironic as the gift shop at Auschwitz. If you've ever had a tattoo removed—or a particularly flaky sunburn you tried to scrub off with sandpaper, or just doused yourself with gasoline and set yourself on fire—you have some idea what these sessions were like. Then, at fourteen, there was the indignity of a third (and final, although unknown to me at the time) operation to widen my anus, a part of the body that no teenaged boy, not even Antinous, likes to contemplate, let alone pad like a menstruating woman. It was during this period that I came to appreciate my cap and gown, which covered not only most of my skin but, now, the cuts and sores and blood-stained bandages that pointed up its deviance all the more vividly.

While all this was happening I was beset by the usual adolescent indignities—the acne, the strange growths of hair and uncontrollable vocal tics, the sudden desire to run, to kill, to rut, to cry—and, of course, by my mother, the budding superstar. Against everyone's advice she refused to place her pots with a dealer in Dallas or Atlanta or New York. If people wanted to buy her wares they would have to come to Marcuse and carry them away themselves. And come they did. The first went for a thousand, the second for two, the third for five, the fourth for ten. The price continued to jump by leaps and bounds until it stabilized at $150,000 around number 40, but then *Three by Stammers* came out and number 64 went for $325,000, and 66 (65 was missing and presumed broken) went for $600,000. But again, I'm skipping ahead. The only changes I noticed at first were my own: the little peanut that had been my testicles suddenly losing its firmness, its shape, until it bounced between my thighs like a mold-spotted leather pouch stuffed with two—unequal, alas—mounds of coin; the daily horror of shitting through an asshole ringed with scabs that split open when my sphincter dilated or were torn away wholesale by the outward flow of feces no amount of Metamucil and mineral oil could soften sufficiently; and of course the residue that I found in the fly of my pajamas most mornings, sometimes creamy as glaze made from mother-of-pearl, other times crusty as the slip that saturated my mother's smocks, and often as not tinged with the same colorful swirls as the organ from which it spurted.

On top of all that, there was the constant flood of people into and out of our apartment, who kept me busy straightening the piles they mussed, sweeping up their ashes, scrubbing their lipstick from wine glasses and coffee cups. (*"What?"* my mother gasped more times than I could count. "This piece of crap? Pottery Barn, $11.95—ha ha!") What these interlopers were doing didn't seem nearly as important as what my mother did, and often kept her from doing it besides—and, more to the point, kept me from what *I* wanted to do in my curtained-off sleeping nook, since my mother's callers often stayed from just after lunch until the wee hours of the following morning. My petty vengeance was to follow after them, running a rag over everything they touched or mopping their footprints away one step at a time or spraying Lysol directly into the clouds of smoke that spewed from their mouths. "Oh, don't mind Judas," my mother would say to her clients, laughing, as I glowered at some wattle-necked Swiss or big-hatted Texan, "He can't *stand* a mess. Yes, Mr. Beaumont, I said *Judas.*" Then, too, not a few of the men, on realizing my mother was single, were wont to play the suitor. She was "still young," as they said—as she herself said—although that *still* added a note of urgency, of years and beauty steadily eroded by the soaps and scrubs of her hourslong baths. But even though my mother did nothing to rebuff them—laughed at their jokes, accepted their gifts, welcomed them to her bed—they soon drifted away, because it was clear that even when she wasn't working with clay, when she was wearing a silk dress instead of a cotton smock, an open blouse that showed off the birthmark on her breast or a wrap skirt that revealed the taut line of her thigh, she was still thinking always and only about her pots, such that, minutes after licking the last creamy morsel of chocolate pudding from her spoon, she could flag down the maître d' and ask him if he had a bag of shells for her, which pungent bundle (tarragon, lemon, day-old mollusk) she would thrust into the hand of her startled date when he reached to help her from her chair. Wine and water were equally "refreshing," filet mignon and Hamburger Helper equally "delicious," suitors and buyers, men and women, strangers and, finally, her own son, equally "interesting":

"Mr. Hauser is quite an interesting man, Judas. You should get to know him."

"Ceci n'est pas une pipe told me something really interesting when—no, *Cecil*. Saint *Pepin*. Did you wash my smock today— or your ears for that matter?"

"Bobby says you wrote an interesting letter in response to that piece in the *Times-Picayune*. You should leave it out for me, I'd love to read it, it sounds very interesting."

The newspaper, folded open to the letter in question, had been sitting on my mother's bedside table for nearly three weeks when she made this remark. Every evening when I cleaned her room—or every evening when I could get in there anyway—I found that it had migrated to the bottom of a stack of cosmetic dermatological magazines and auction-house catalogs, and I moved it back to the top of the pile, only to find it buried again the next day, until finally she used it as part of the packing for number 62 when she sold it to a buyer representing some branch or other—oh, the irony!—of the Japanese royal family. *That's* what I blamed the critic for—not for making my mother so busy that she didn't pay attention to me, but for making me realize she'd never paid attention. For thirteen years we'd been so perfectly alone together that it never occurred to me our quarantine might not have been established for my benefit. Simply having my mother there, working her clay, her mortar and pestle, her brushes and glazes and kilns with metronomic regularity was all I needed. On the days I didn't have class or a doctor's appointment I waited in my sleeping alcove until she finished working—used cotton swabs to daub polish into the ornate crannies of the Stammers silver (the interlocked M/S that, in hindsight, I realize could've read S/M just as easily) or refolded the clothes Mrs. Brown had washed so they fit more neatly into overstuffed drawers or tore the pages from magazines and ripped the pages into pieces and sorted the pieces by color in preparation for a collage that I had no intention of making (although I had given it the rather grand title of "The Apparition of the Apotheosis in the Wine Stains Left on the Table After the Last Supper"), waiting always for the click of the bathroom door and the opening of the tub's faucets, the first sawing strings of Bach or Scarlatti or Purcell signaling that it was time for me to restore our world to order, to uncrack the egg, as it were, from which our life daily hatched. All of that was gone now. The routine that had defined our lives since I'd given up painting had been obliterated. In its place was an endless parade of visitors who tossed money around like confetti and renewed in me the sense of myself as a freak to be gawked at like a carnival sideshow or ignored like a carcass on the side of the road. Nocturnal emission might have alleviated adolescence's liquid accumulation but it did nothing to lessen the anxiety and anger building up in me like an air pocket in firing clay, excited molecules ricocheting against their cell walls until at last the bisque explodes, destroying itself and everything else in the kiln. I don't know what might have happened if, one day in early 1995, the phone hadn't rung.

You understand that the phone had rung before—had rung almost incessantly in the nine months since the *Art in America* review came out—but my mother never picked it up, just let the machine get it, and had me return the call, or not, as the mood struck her. But on this day she did answer. She'd just said to a prospective buyer, "He says it itches sometimes, and it's sensitive to temperature, and I think it's fucking up his hearing, but as far as I know it doesn't actually *hurt*," when the phone rang and she sighed almost gratefully and said, "Please excuse me a moment," and picked it up.

"This is she."

"Yes, I know who h-he is."

"Oh, I'm sorry to hear about that."

"Goodness, that was—please don't touch that, Mr. Ling—very generous."

"Just a moment, let me get a pen."

"Of course I'll relay the news. Thank you for calling."

In the time it took me to roll on my side—painfully, a three-inch blister along the outer left edge of my rib cage bursting like popped bubble wrap—the conversation was over. My mother held the corded handset a few inches from her ear as though it were the head of a poisonous snake, and the quizzical yet slightly wondrous smile on her lips filled me with a premonition in a way that none of the events of the previous fifteen months had that our lives were not just about to change, but to end. It wasn't the telephone that filled me with such dread. It was the fact that my mother was holding it. I myself used the phone regularly. But my mother never did. There was no explicit reason for her refusal. She never said, "I don't like telephones," or "Telephones are unclean," or anything like that. Rather, there was always a specific excuse not to answer when it rang ("Judas! My hands are covered in clay!" or "You get it, Jude, you're closer") or not to pick it up when she needed something ("It's such a beautiful day, let's walk down to the Lake to see if the strawberries are ready. We'll stop at the post office on the way back"). Certainly she wasn't a Luddite like the masters. She worked the halogen lamps that lit her table like Shiva's second set of arms, thought the sonic toothbrush one of the wonders of the modern world, replaced every one of her scratchy old Alton Ellis and Slim Smith 78s with CDs as soon as they were available and would've thought Spotify a latter-day Library of Alexandria. Nor was she particularly antisocial: at the age of thirty-one she'd taken up the old ladies' habit of folding a quilt over her bedroom windowsill and leaning out of an evening to chat with the novices making their way down High Street toward the Foundry, gowns open if the weather was warm or poking from overcoats like mourning crinolines if it was cold, and at least once a week—well, exactly once a week, every Thursday afternoon at 3, when Mrs. Brown retreated into the basement with the laundry and a portable television she "hid" in her sewing basket—she installed herself at one of the tables in the bakery and chatted with Mr. B. about obscure pastry facts (apparently the best water for parboiling bagels was drawn from the Dnieper River, but only upstream from the factories of Kiev, and only before the Communist Revolution in 1917), the latest piercing trends among the students at the public school in Wye (eyebrows giving way to lips, lips to nipples, nipples to navels, navels to "Oh, Miz Stammers, don't say it, I don't even wanna *think* about it"), whether the ice would crack on the Lake before or after the first daffodils bloomed on its north-facing banks (after being unusual, but for the same reason a harbinger of a cold spring that would translate to a late planting of the soybean crop and a bad yield come August), or if anyone could ever love someone with a face like a baboon's ass ("Kids is putting metal and tattoos and just about any old thing in, on, and around they faces now, so who knows—and no one likes a eavesdropper, young man, so whyn't you grab yourself a cookie and run on upstairs?"). But there she was, the phone hovering near her ear for one more moment, and then, starting, she returned it to its cradle. "Mr. Ling, *please*," she said, "sit down and *don't touch anything*," and then she walked toward my room. She paused on the threshold, her gaze aimed obliquely from the bed, as if I might be up to something, or as if someone had, for the first time since I was three or four, made her self-conscious about her son's appearance.

"Judas," she said, addressing the far wall. "I have some news to report. Your great-uncle has died."

I'd been looking at my mother expectantly, but now I too turned—turned the right side of my face toward her, the left side away—as if I'd been caught out, or caught a glimpse of some hideous stranger on the street and realized it was my own reflection.

"This was your f-father's uncle. Anthony. He lived in Texas, which is why you never met him."

I never met my great-uncle Anthony—never heard of him for that matter—because my mother had had nothing to do with any family member since she moved out of the President's House a decade and a half ago. I wished I had a book with me so I could turn a page, pretend to be reading, but the only thing on the bedside table was a bottle of Bigeloil, a horse rub that one of my dermatologists thought might make my birthmark more pliable by dilating the capillaries under the skin, and I grabbed the bottle and squeezed about half of it onto my left arm and began rubbing it in with my right hand.

"Apparently there was some money. Quite a—Judas, please don't do that, you're going to get stains all over the bed. Quite a bit of money. Apparently."

The truth is my mother had had nothing to do with any family member, hers or mine—by which I mean, she'd had nothing to do with my "f-father"—since the day, a few weeks before she fled the President's House, she discovered she was pregnant with me. I rubbed my arm harder. A side effect of the Bigeloil was that it deepened the color in my birthmark, and my left arm, normally more rosé than true port, now glowed unctuous burgundy.

"And, well, as next of—Judas. *Please.* That quilt was sewn by your great-great-great-great-grandmother. As next of kin, the money goes to you."

And. Well.

And well it seemed to me that my "f-father" was closer kin to his own uncle than I, but I thought that if I continued to rub my arm, which throbbed purple like a tourniqueted limb, sprayed oily froth all over the quilt (which had not, in fact, been sewn by my great-great-great-great-grandmother, but by one of her slaves), my mother would—f-finally—explain this too. And well I knew that anyone who couldn't see my left arm, could see only my right arm sliding back and forth, would think I was jerking off (and that I was hung like a stallion!), even though the action reminded *me* of my mother's hands as she rolled out her clay, and at the thought of that I rubbed even harder, and the bed-frame began to creak beneath my scabbed ass.

And. Well.

And, well, the next thing my mother said was, "You don't want that one, Mr. Ling, Judas pooped in it when he was five," and a moment later the apartment was filled with the sound of breaking ceramic. "Oh dear," my mother said as I ran for the safety of my broom. "That's really gonna cost you."

AFTER SHE BECAME famous my mother developed the habit of deflecting questions she didn't want to answer by claiming that "she only knew what she knew" (or, well, "I only know what I know," because, although Dixie Stammers had many eccentricities, referring to herself in the third person wasn't one of them). She knew, for example, that for thousands of years of early human development visual art approximated the role that writing later came to play (hence her love of ◑) and that some forms of writing developed out of visual, that is to say, mimetic representations of the world. But she also believed that both the numeral "1" and the letter "I" were stripped-down pictograms of stick-figure drawings of the self (which, just in case you're as suggestible as my mother, they're *not*). She maintained to her dying day that the colony of monk parakeets in the gardens behind Stammers Hall had come to these parts as the local version of the canary in a coal mine (to be fair to her, no one knows where the parakeets came from, but the canaries in Marcus Stammers's coal mine were in fact canaries) and though she reluctantly came to accept that Thomas Crapper didn't invent the flush toilet, she never fully relinquished her belief that the plumber's surname lent itself to the euphemism by which it is referred. Nor was she convinced that the "&" symbol wasn't invented by André-Marie Ampère ("Ampère's 'and'") or that bloomers weren't named for the temperance suffragette Amelia Jenks Bloomer. Yet another thing my mother apparently didn't know, and that I didn't know either, until that phone call from Texas, was that my father had had an uncle, a wealthy uncle apparently, named Anthony DeVine—oh, and that my father was dead. She didn't know that either. But she knew to answer the phone the day my uncle's lawyer called to say that he—he being my uncle, but also my father—had died.

She told me once that she didn't know his name, and then she told me that she did know but wasn't going to tell me. She told me he wasn't an Academy man and then told me he'd insisted she get an abortion, which the way she said it (it would be "wrong" to add "another consciousness" to a world overfilled with beings so "alienated from the real" that the only way they could cope with its destruction was by "diffusing it in spectacle") made him sound *exactly* like an Academy man. She told me she only knew what she knew, and that I really, really, *really* didn't want to know the few things she could tell me—and then, biting back a smirk, she said, who knows, I was a dirty little boy, maybe I *did* want to know. She told me he was the most beautiful boy she ever laid eyes on, and then she told me they only had sex one time—though for a long time before that, she told me, they did everything but ("B-U-one T but, Judas. Get your mind out of the sewer. Although speaking of: Have you moved your bowels today?"). The most beautiful until you, she said then. Until you. She told me there were 1013 cells in the human body, and that if you started with the two cells she and my father contributed it took a mere sixty-seven rounds of division to produce all the cells needed for a fully formed, fully functional future citizen of the republic, and that every time she made a pot she was trying to get back to the perfect kernel that had been the end of my father—the end of her—and the beginning of me. My mother's pots were the most important thing in her life. To be compared to one was her way of giving you a kiss—an open-mouthed, bare-breasted, bottomless kiss, her tongue snaking down your throat and her hand sneaking down to guide your penis inside her—which is to say that, yes, having my mother compare me to her pots felt like a violation of Oedipal magnitude, as if she'd not just propositioned me but actually climbed on top of me, hair pulled to her off shoulder like a porn star's so the camera wouldn't miss one gory detail. (In fact the two cells necessary for conception merge to create a single-celled zygote, so there was one more round of mitosis than she thought, one more backward step in the path she was trying to retrace at her potting table. But that was just one more thing my mother didn't know. No wonder she was never satisfied with me. Or, as she put it: "Stammerers have been marrying their cousins for five generations. No doubt that's the reason we're all the way we are.")

Which point, however jokingly she made it, ignored the obvious: like a purebred dog suffering from hip dysplasia or a designer strain of wheat that can no longer resist even the most common rusts and smuts, I was proof that conscious attempts to manipulate heredity tend to exacerbate hidden flaws that come to catastrophic fruition just when you think the lineage has been perfected. The most visible manifestations of this phenomenon are biological, obviously—those poor Habsburgs and their jaws!—but to the Academy way of thinking it's every bit as true of culture as it is of the bodies who produce it. The masters cite epochal moments in history to validate their position: the transformation of the Roman Republic into a proto-fascist monarchy at precisely the moment it believed itself to be at the peak of its creative power; or the wholesale slaughter, by Spanish conquistadors fresh from driving the Moors out of Iberia, of untold millions of Native Americans, and the squandering of the plundered riches of same on vainglorious wars against the Turk, which, far from unifying Europe behind the imaginary banners of race and religion or even geography, merely laid the groundwork for the First World War, an unimaginable conflagration that, in light of the rest of the 20th century, seems less aberration than inevitability. All of these arguments, however, were superfluous in our house, where my mother's efforts to atone for the mistake of making me resulted in the creation of a set of artifacts so monstrous that, in the words of one critic, "they violate every notion of what it means to be human," and that, far from saving me, or her, or us, or the Stammers name, destroyed us all, which process began in earnest not when my mother sold her first pot, nor even when she conceived me, but when I received my father's uncle's inheritance.

It was, in other words, all my fault.

The bequest came, after it was liquidated, and after lawyers' fees, brokers' fees, and taxes, to a little less than $400,000, which my mother spent months making sure I wouldn't have access to until I turned twenty-one, before turning around and asking what I *would* do with my windfall, if I could spend it right now. I was caught off guard by her question, but I knew the answer before she'd finished asking it, because even as she was speaking I was looking around our apartment and seeing just how futile my efforts had been—how organization creates its own disorder, cleaning its own decay. We'd lived above the Browns for almost fourteen years. During that time myriad objects had trickled steadily into the apartment but nothing had left—nothing besides vegetable rinds and empty bottles and $8 million worth of pottery. Now I saw the narrow trails winding their way through shapeless, unidentifiable mounds; saw the gaps where my scrub brush had dislodged dozens of filaments from the parquet; saw couches and chairs whose cushions were so abraded by the fabric brush of our ancient Electrolux that the dyed strands of the weft had been worn away, leaving only the coarse white strings of the warp; saw the archipelago of patches where I'd scoured paper and paint off the walls, in some places plaster too, exposing chalky lath like layers of shale; saw the wisps of dust that, like the fine coating of hair on early hominids, fringed the ninety-six rosewood saints lined up on a ridiculously high shelf I'd never been able to reach; saw my mother's smock hanging from its peg like toilet tissue from a tree the morning after Halloween, the fabric whiter than snow and almost as insubstantial, having been nearly disintegrated by its daily dousing in lye; saw, finally, the doorless sleeping cabinet that housed my bed, which couldn't conceal my desire, let alone contain it, and I said:

"I want the hell *out* of this dump."

Over the previous few years I'd developed the habit of turning my right ear toward people so I could hear them better. I didn't realize I was doing it at the time, and most people, I'm sure, thought I was simply shielding them from the mottled left side of my face, which infuriated me, especially since I could feel them take advantage of my averted gaze to stare. My mother was as guilty of this as any stranger. Now, when I jerked my face back toward her, her mouth dropped open in a gasp and she looked away, only to gasp again, one wrinkled hand, prematurely aged by her work and her penitent baths, flying to her mouth and trying vainly to stuff the breath back into her body. Her eyes darted about as mine had, though what they noticed is anyone's guess. Maybe she saw how the apartment, all things considered, had accommodated us so well for so long; but I think she saw how, in fact, it was *we* who had adjusted our movements to our cramped shoebox, by inches and degrees, by hunched shoulders and tunnel vision and a shuffling one-foot-in-front-of-the-other gait like the Cherokee trudging onto the Trail of Tears after they were forced from these parts in the 1830s. As her eyes took in the smallness of the setting and the vastness of the effect it had had on us, she finally realized that it was we who sheltered our home rather than it sheltering us, and a look of profound longing settled on her face, or perhaps was revealed there, as though something—a mask, a birthmark, or maybe just her porcelain skin—had been peeled away, revealing the skeleton of loss. You understand that the desideratum is not a condition one associated with Dixie Stammers, who had the uncanny ability to bring into existence exactly what she wanted, be it a lover or a fortune or a sixty-fifth or -sixth or -seventh perfect pot—anything but a son whose harlequin skin made him jester to her attempt to rebel against her heritage—and for a moment I thought she was going to refuse me, even cast me out. But she clapped her chapped hands together and said:

"I know just the place!"

And that's how acclaimed potter Dixie Stammers and her parti-colored, preposterously named, but otherwise unexceptional son, Judas, townies born and bred, with no more affinity for nature than pigeons or socialites, ended up living on 216 acres of scrub bisected by the serpentine shallows of the White Woman Creek, in a three-story brick building that purported to have started out as a lumber mill despite the fact that it stood half a mile from the streambed. It stood equally far from the Post Road, half hidden behind a sandy hill held together by a thicket of stunted sassafras and cedar, which lent more credence to the story that the building had in fact been a whorehouse, although the more probable truth is that it had simply been a warehouse, or maybe just a fancy barn.

There'd been money before my great-uncle died, of course—my mother had sold more than sixty pots by then. But to her way of thinking that money had been given to her under the delusion that her pots were somehow worth more than what they *were*, what they *could do*, which was hold a few dozen cookies or a couple liters of water or leave a nasty bruise if someone beaned you with one. Even if you filled them with silver or gold or beluga caviar they wouldn't be worth what people had paid for them, and I think that on some level she believed the money would disappear, would evaporate or be reclaimed when her buyers realized that, after all, her pots really were just pots. (She turned out to be right in one sense, although completely wrong in another.) And of course there'd been money before she started selling them. Marcus Stammers's fortune never quite reached the standards of the most famous nineteenth-century robber barons but, after personally chiseling a cool million in gold from the Magic

Mountain (as the peak later renamed the Palatine was then called), then exhausting the substantially more extensive copper deposits beneath the gold, an enormous seam of stone coal had revealed itself. The coal was buried deep in the mountains, under the gold, under the copper, and under hundreds of feet of particularly hard feldspathic sandstone, which is why it took so long to discover it, and it was the profits from this final enterprise that endowed both Lake Academy and the Magic Mountains Conservancy and left enough for Marcus's children and their families to live on, if not in splendor—he donated the grand stone mansion he'd built in the 1840s to the Academy, but he also built the plantation-style President's House so his descendants wouldn't end up on the street—then at least as local gentility. The Stammers heirs had none of their forefather's luck with money or reproducing, and one civil plus two world wars wiped out all of them save the great-great-great-grandson whose money and genes, both rather depleted, found their way to my mother, and then to me. Though most of the assets were tied up in various trusts, annuities, long-term T-bond hoody-hahs and various other complicated financial instruments made all the more byzantine by the passage of a century, the interest and dividends and whatnot were still enough to provide a reasonable living for a single mother and her only child, even if the one had a ridiculously profligate potting hobby and the other required shockingly expensive, screamingly painful dermatological treatments, most of which weren't covered by insurance because they were deemed "cosmetic." "Paper breeds paper," my mother told me more than once as she took a stack of checks the bank had mailed her back to the bank, where she deposited them so they could earn her still more interest. "Cash breeds cash and debt breeds debt. Whether it's dollar bills and stock certificates or credit cards and property liens it's all paper, and it reproduces like a virus."

If I said that, in hindsight, the move seemed inevitable— seemed, just months after we arrived, to have been what both me and my mother had been waiting for, if for very different reasons—I'd be violating one of the central tenets of Academy philosophy. History (or history as it's taught elsewhere than the Academy) accustoms us to the reassuring notion that our future makes the past inevitable, so much so that we forget life is lived in a blind present, in previous eras as in our own. Academy historians (and at the Academy all teachers are historians, whether their field is mathematics, political economy, or physical culture) continually remind their novices that nothing's inevitable until it's happened, which point is so crucial to the Academy world-view that complines conclude with a request for the sun's return the following day, or the serenity of spirit to accept it if it doesn't. To view the past as somehow intentionally producing this moment is to deny that our forebears possessed free will or were susceptible to the universal machinations of chance. In an alternate future my mother and I still live above the Browns' bakery in an apartment so filled with detritus that we have to burrow our way through like termites. In another she never left the Academy and neither did I; we still live in the four-pillared President's House on the top of the hill and I still hide my skin beneath flowing black robes and mortarboard. In yet another she heeded my father's advice and never had me, and in still another she was born a man, was steeped in Academy doctrine and took her—"his"—place as its fifth president rather than sneaking into the odd class and learning just enough to reject something she never really understood. Not one of these alternatives was obviated until a woman named Kennedy Albright stabbed my great-uncle Anthony DeVine in the throat with the stem of a wine glass (I know: *dramatic*); until a freelance critic and occasional contributor to *Art in America* decided she couldn't hold out for Dunkin' Donuts at the airport and stopped in at the Browns' bakery; until teenaged castaway Dixie Stammers ignored the pleadings of her lover and carried her baby to term; until, the year before that, Dixie, unexpectedly orphaned, decided to leave the Academy founded by her great-great-great-great-grandfather to its own fate; until a spermatozoon carrying Marcus Stammers's great-great-great-grandson's X chromosome, and bearing a mutation on the RASA1 gene (judging from the occasional nevus that shows up in family portraits, the mutation was most likely carried on the Stammers line), outswam its competitors and fertilized the ovum hanging out in Elisa DeVine Stammers's fallopian tube. Thus Dixie Stammers; thus the unlikely but incontrovertible origin of my abomination.

Of course, alternate futures are, in the Academy view, even more aberrant fantasies than precognitive pasts. The cat in the box is alive or the cat in the box is dead, and though we might never know which it is, *we know it's never both*. The significance of these fantasies isn't that they *might* exist on some other plane of being or in a parallel universe, it's that they *could have* existed in ours. That the lives we lead today, and tomorrow and tomorrow and tomorrow, aren't forged by us, but by the world, whose primacy we obscure when we substitute the words "chance" and "will." Every other child in America learns that his life is his to shape, but Academy boys are taught they can only observe it; that the things other people consider life—love, career, social status—are mere symptoms and shadows. *Real* life is nothing more or less than a body in four dimensions, a semi-stable set of atoms in constant collision with other sets; everything else is byproduct, distraction, ultimately irrelevant. In January or February, 1981, my mother had sex with a man bearing *the same genetic mutation Marcus Stammers had passed to her*—a one-hundred-million-to-one possibility, or about 300 times worse than the odds of dying in a plane crash. But odds or no odds, it happened: I'm the evidence, and I bear witness every day of my life.

But to claim that my birthmark or the chain of circumstances that produced it somehow makes me "more unique" than anyone else is to admit that human beings don't actually believe in our much-espoused individuality. That, in fact, we fear we're all the same, or, even more plaintively, *wish* we were the same. Follow this line of thinking to its logical terminus and you come to the inevitable conclusion that each person believes himself or herself to *be* the world: that space and time are nothing more than an extension of individual consciousness, a sight brought into existence by our eyes, a song unsung till our ears hear it, a lover whose flesh doesn't exist until we stroke it into being. Hence animism and anthropomorphism, hence organized religion, hence metaphor itself, whose one true function is to measure the gap between reality and what we wish it were. Academy teaching on art starts and ends with the premise that *art has no material form*—is nothing but a perceptual mode superimposed on an object or experience, i.e., a shared illusion, given false reality by meretricious metaphor, which, far from illuminating the phenomenon to which it is applied, is in actuality a deliberate statement of notness that takes the specific form of a replacement of one thing by another. "X is like Y" is really just another way of saying "X is not X," and since, qua nineteenth-century physics, X is—must be—X, then the assertion that X could ever be anything other than X must be false, and not useful in ascertaining what X is: namely, a system or collection of component parts whose delineation was the masters' holy grail. And I mean yeah, sure, that's pretty obvious to anyone who's paying attention. But isn't metaphor also an index of the human desire (human not as in *weak* but as in *living*) for something more than the material, the actual—something that's been lost or might still be gained? My mother's pots let people believe in the possibility of pure, perfect expression, a one-to-one correspondence between thought and deed, as if each pot wasn't a copy of its predecessor, nor even a clone, but was in fact *the same pot*, just as the world Hephaestus forged on Achilles's shield wasn't a copy of the one in which the war between Achaeans and Trojans had dragged on for a decade, but was in fact *the same world*. To describe the gods' acts of creation as Homer had described them was one thing; actually to manifest them was another, and for a mere mortal not just impossible but abominable. It was this impulse as much as the pots themselves that a second wave of critics came to denounce as inhuman, just as the first fans of my mother's work celebrated it as superhuman. But the truth is all it was *was* human. Not imperfect. Just incomplete. The sameness of the pots' emptiness manifested as difference by virtue of the thousand, the million, the billion different desires with which their viewers filled them, by which I mean that there was no way my mother's pots could resist becoming symbols. Not once they'd gone out into the world.

But disagreement over what they symbolized bitterly divided her audience. Did the pots in their identicality resemble human beings—not evolutionary *Homo sapiens*, but, rather, Adam shaped from clay by God's hand—distinguished only by their individual contents, their inner desires, which some commentators went so far as to identify with the soul? Or was the thing these people called the soul really just a projection, no more real, no more relevant than shapes seen in clouds, and, more to the point, preventing us from seeing the real cloud—the real pot, the real world, the real self?

To which my mother would only shrug and say, "All men are donkeys or men and donkeys are donkeys." I.e., meaning is often a question of emphasis: where you place the commas and conjunctions, which books you read and bring to bear on the proposition in question. Which is to say, again, that my mother didn't care what people thought her pots "did" in the world. But my mother's sophistic dismissal of questions about her work made me realize that she didn't care what *I* did either. That she cared only about the fact that she'd made me, and that I'd come out flawed. Years before the Gospel of Judas became available to a general audience, my mother was aware of the theologian Irenaeus's denunciation, in his *Adversus Haereses*, of the Gnostic belief that Judas Iscariot "accomplished the mystery of the betrayal" not only with Jesus's knowledge but at his direction. Enraptured by the idea of an act of treason that was actually a secret expression of loyalty, my mother christened her son Judas in the belief that his name would make clear that her apparent rejection of Academy doctrine was in fact the only way she could bring Grandpa Marcus's ideas to their fullest expression. "You shall be cursed for generations," Jesus tells the instrument of his apotheosis, "but you will exceed all of them, for you will sacrifice the man that clothes me." What she (apparently) didn't know was that even in the Gnostic version of things Judas is unable to bear the burden of his role, and dreams of being—longs to be—stoned to death by the other Apostles. More to the point, she also didn't realize that pretty much no one in Marcuse would know this story, let alone care about it, and often reacted to my name far more violently than they did to my face.

So, Judas Stammers, the flowering of: I was made in secret in the lowest parts of the earth. Plant poisoned seeds in cursed soil and its fruit shall bleed royal tears; yea, verily, you shall reap what you sow. *Nasciturus pro iam nato habetur, quotiens de commodis eius agitur*: the unborn is deemed to have been born to the extent that his own inheritance is concerned. *Sola fide, ecce homo, noli me tangere. Vae, puto deus fio!*

So:

My birthmark cups the left side of my face like a fat, flattened, four-fingered hand. One finger pressed down so tightly on the edge of my lips when I was born that I couldn't open my mouth wide enough to feed and had to have surgery when I was three days old to slice it apart, although after it healed I refused to take the breast, or a bottle for that matter, and my mother had to force, first, an eye dropper and, later, a turkey baster between my clenched lips, until I was eighteen months old. (But you knew that already, didn't you? Not the exact shape maybe, but just as a person in a darkened room can recognize a peach—by smell, by touch, by taste—you knew exactly what you'd see if the lights snapped on and my face emerged into view like an Easter egg laid sideways in purple dye.) The second finger presses on the bridge of my nose and across my left eyelid and, aside from a tendency to stiffen and droop that requires periodic laser treatments to soften it, has never given me much trouble, while the third finger covers most of my left ear, reaching deeply into the canal and coating the drum like a wax seal that gradually stiffened, causing me to lose a little more of my hearing each year until, by the time I was sixteen, I'd gone pretty much deaf on that side. (Does this help? Does knowing the specifics contain the situation like a wax seal, or does it in fact free your mind to go elsewhere, to abandon the actual for the emblematic, the real for the unreal, the unreal for the ur-real: not birthmark but "birthmark," not Judas but "Judas"?) The fourth finger curves under the ear and extends into the hairline on the back of my head. The hair that grows there is—no one knows why— hypopigmented, i.e., as colorless as an albino's (the rest of my hair is, vulgarly speaking, brown) and looks, more than one person has noted, exactly like Somalia, although people have also said Peru (reversed) and Vietnam (united), a flamingo's beak, a sabretooth, an arrowhead, a Roman nose, and just about anything else if I let them stutter on long enough. But no one ever says that the birthmark itself looks like anything other than a hand, even though it only has four fingers, and even though it looks more like a wrinkled glove than a hand. No one ever says, simply, that it's ugly—at least not to my face. (Still, I understand why it was necessary for me to say it straight: no matter how many clues I dropped, no matter how sure you were that you understood what I was saying, you'd have found a way to deny me if I hadn't let you touch my flesh, to save yourself the pain of contemplating what it must be like to be me.) The wrist of the hand stretches down the left side of my neck and spills around my arm all the way to my knuckles. Its path down my torso is as torturous as the White Woman's, curling in wide thick loops that island nine distinct patches of pale skin; it's fairly solid on the outside of the ribs but as it approaches the midline it striates into darker and lighter patches like a brindle-coated thylacine. (And perhaps I shouldn't be so hard on you. Thomas didn't believe either, not till he'd put his finger in the holes in Jesus's hands, and look where he ended up. Oh, that's right: he ended up martyred in India, his Eastern-inflected gospel excluded from the canon, his name—which was Judas actually, "thomas" being an Aramaic word meaning "twin," though who or what this particular Judas was twin to is a subject of much contention—forever associated with the refusal to accept the evidence of things not seen. Is it any wonder he was the de facto saint of the Academy?) In front it reaches to the base of my penis, and though only a few dribbles extend down the shaft these lines are particularly thick and, even today, prone to tearing at the most inopportune moments. It's more aggressive in back, coiling around the bottom of my left buttock before slipping into the cleft and lidding my anus the same way it once gagged me. The blockage was so severe that I had to have three surgeries to correct it, the first when my mouth was fixed, and then again when I was three, and a final one when I was fourteen, about six months after we moved to the house my mother insisted on christening Potter's Field. ("Know what is in front of your face, and what is hidden from you will be disclosed": that's what Jesus said to Thomas Judas, and that's why, now, I've given in, lowered the mirrored window between us and shown you your true reflection, "for there is nothing hidden that will not be revealed.") Yes indeedy, every last gory detail's coming out now. To wit: I was on stool softeners for most of my early childhood and then again for a good part of my adolescence; until I was six years old, I moved my bowels in one of my mother's pots so she could check for unacceptable amounts of blood. At that point they had yet to become artifacts so sacred that even the idea of using one as a gazunder was a desecration (c.f. poor Mr. Ling), but still—why'd she make me *shit in a pot*? Why did my mother, who wouldn't drink champagne out of anything but a flute and owned the same style of T-strap Birkenstocks (the Gizeh, if names are important to you) in no fewer than twelve different colors; who at the height of her fame thought nothing of smashing one of her pots with a hammer (well, no, not a hammer, that wouldn't be Dixie Stammers's style, but a bobble-capped length of *lignum vitae* that was said to have been a clapper in a bell in the second Coptic cathedral of St. Mark in Alexandria) and spreading the pieces on the bottom of a $40 cedar windowbox to ensure proper drainage for her geraniums; who during the filming of *Three by Stammers* tossed a hundred-thousand-dollar *objet d'art* like a basketball in order to show the director (who caught it, then started weeping hysterically) exactly what they were worth to her who could make a new one as easily as a mint makes money—why did this woman refuse to buy me a potty training seat or let me go directly into the toilet and check for blood there, instead of requiring me to squat on a nine-and-a-half-inch *ceramic ball* that, however well-balanced, wasn't meant to accommodate a confused toddler (an ashamed preschooler, a mortified first-former who made the mistake of bringing a class-mate over for a playdate) as he tried to center his anus over a hole less than four inches wide? Why, after I had fallen over for the eighth or ninth or twentieth time in the act of voiding my bowels and broken a jagged piece out of the top of the pot, did she replace it with another, unbroken one rather than let me take advantage of the larger opening? ("We'll just give this one to the Browns, okay?") The only mercy in the whole ordeal is the fact that my sphincter itself wasn't damaged, and I don't suffer from incontinence, which more than one doctor had predicted (although skinny-dicked men *do* have a tendency to bang against the sides of my rectum like a spoon stirring a pot of pudding, a ball clapper summoning the faithful in Egypt, or at least those who don't respond to the azan). By which I mean that yes, I'm as guilty as you. I want my birthmark to acquire the meaning only narrative and exegesis can impart: not "a birthmark" but "The Birthmark," not Judas Stammers but Nathaniel Hawthorne, not a kooky neo-Parmenidean Academy but the Sanborn School, where the children of Hawthorne, Emerson, Henry James Sr., and John Brown were educated in the spiritual democracy of American Transcendentalism. But like Thomas, I doubt, and cannot believe until I've poked holes in my own story. And though there are any number of reasons why I loathe my body, having an accommodating asshole isn't one of them.

2

The last portrait of Marcus Stammers, painted two years before his death in 1896 at the age of ninety-eight, shows an ascetically thin man, a transparent fog of colorless hair combed back from a deeply rutted forehead, a wispy beard falling down his chest like a waterfall more mist than liquid. Open jacket, string tie, the affectation of an anthracite-capped copper stud in his third buttonhole. The painter dutifully recorded the stains the stud left on his starched dickey (black from the coal, green from the copper), but omitted what was generally considered Marcus's most striking feature: the two gnarled ironwood staves (one was a staff, two were staves, and they were never, *ever* called canes) he'd been forced to use since a rearing horse fell back on him when he was forty-seven, crushing his pelvis. The fractures set poorly, which is another way of saying Marcus was lucky to survive—although he was quick to point out that the horse had had to be destroyed, whereas all *he* suffered was a lifetime of excruciating agony. At any rate he was never again able to stand unaided, and even with his pair of five-foot-tall sticks (sorry, Grandpa, "staves" just sounds corny in the twenty-first century, as I suspect it did in the nineteenth) he tipped precariously forward when he walked, back curled like a fishhook, hipbones splayed from his ruined pelvis like a nag's withered croup. His grandson Chester's fiancée made the mistake of comparing him to Rocinante, for which impiety the engagement was broken off.

From the birth of his first great-grandchild in 1888, Elizabeth (not Chester's child—he died of consumption before finding another suitable marriage candidate—but the daughter of Marcus's oldest son, Henry's, middle child, Viola), he was referred to by the family as Great Grandpa Marcus, the hyphen that would have delimited "Great"'s genealogical significance omitted because it was clear by then that Marcus Stammers's magnificence was unbounded by any notion of ancestry, let alone mere gonadal accomplishment. Grandpa Marcus was great not because of the children he'd made but because of the world he'd built: the business, the town, and, later, the school, and school of thought. His was the kind of great usually preceded by a "the": the Great Zambini, the Great Pretender, the Great Communicator; and the fact that all of these associations contravened the third and most lasting of his accomplishments was just one of many instances of exceptionalism in the Stammerses' relationship to their own traditions (another example, one to which I am beholden and of which I'm also a victim, would seem to be the having of children). Well: the greatest lawmen often turn out to be the most notorious criminals, political liberators are almost always flagrantly dictatorial, and the most venerated prophets often doubt their own message, if they don't just make it up. Marcus Stammers was a bit of each of these things, and if his canvas was proportionally insignificant in comparison to those of J. Edgar Hoover, Mohandas Gandhi, and Joseph Smith, his dominance over his homeplace was that much more total. Although his own existence—and, through guilt by association, his family's—flew in the face of virtually every principle he came to be associated with, neither his own nor his descendants' actions were ever questioned by his subjects. Beyond the borders of Marcuse and Wye it's a different story, but it's also someone else's story, to live and to tell—and to be fair to Marcus, he didn't come up with the Academy until very late in a very, very long life.

Families tend to characterize themselves as either "normal" or "exceptional," the first term a euphemism not so much for poverty, be it mental or fiscal, as for a perceived sequestration, sometimes voluntary, sometimes forced, from the kinds of sociopolitical phenomena that schoolbooks like to designate "history"; whereas the second connotes a role, accidental or intentional, in those same events. Stammerers, obviously, place themselves in the latter category, but when I compare our dynastic drama to those of other families it seems to me that the majority of genealogical narratives are no less steeped in history than ours is—it's just less apparent, because they don't sync up with the national myth in the very visible ways the Stammerses' did. To wit: in 1841 (c.f., the Indian Removal Act of 1830, the Treaty of New Echota of 1835, the Cherokee departure for the Trail of Tears in 1838), a Scottish immigrant named Marcus Stammers, forty-three years old and flush with cash from his copper mine, negotiated a deal to purchase 32,000 acres of former Cherokee land at the ridiculously low price of $3.89 per, including the entirety of Mt. Inverna, the southernmost and second largest of a range of eight small mountains the Cherokee called "Tsistuyi," a word I've seen translated as "antlers of the deer," "spearheads of the war party," "saliva-covered teeth of the bear," and "glaucous." Three hundred- and 400-foot-tall splinters of bare graywacke (which turns dark—very dark, almost Prussian—blue after it rains; hence its more common name of bluestone) alternated with tenacious stands of rock oak and longleaf and loblolly pine (as well as, presumably, Sonderegger pine, a naturally occurring cross between the two) and dozens of slivered cataracts that froze each winter into tubes of ice that looked to one European observer like "so many empty intestinal casings waiting to be stuffed with sausage." The deal's terms stipulated that Marcus had to remove the shanty-town that had sprung up on Inverna's north slope, a fairly simple feat, since the encampment was largely populated by miners who worked at Magic Mountain Copper, as well as their families and the sizable colony of tradesmen and whores who serviced them. The workers had originally settled at the western foot of the then-unnamed peak immediately south of the Magic Mountain (the one now known as the Viminal), but Marcus, who didn't yet own that land, threatened to fire anyone who failed to relocate immediately, because he suspected (incorrectly, as it turned out) that the copper buried in the Magic Mountain was also present in its neighbors, and he wanted to make sure there were no claims against his eventual exploration and acquisition of the mineral rights. The workers were moved eight miles to the south, to the only large patch of unowned, unoccupied, and, it must be said, undesirable land in the vicinity, which sat on Inverna's damp north-facing slope above a four-square-mile patch of bogland where the muddy waters of the White Woman Creek debouched across the flat terrain like a spilled cup of coffee spreading over a carpet. They'd lived there for just over three years, had built something like an actual town when Marcus chased them away a second time, but on this occasion he promised to give them nicer homes to return to. This he surely did, razing their shacks and regrading the entire north slope of the mountain and building upon its terraced surface the village of Marcuse—not the name he claimed to have chosen, which was variously given as Arcadia, Elysium, Novus Tsistuyi, and New Auchterarder, but the one his workers "insisted" upon "to honor him" (or perhaps just to save themselves the headache of learning to spell, or say for that matter, "Tsistuyi" or "Auchterarder"). The manufactured town's gently sloped lanes angle off arrow-straight High Street like barbs from a feather's rachis; Marcus, who claimed to have emigrated from Glasgow as an eight-year-old (although some accounts give his age as eleven, sixteen, twenty-two, cite his actual birthplace as Newcastle-upon-Tyne or Greenwich, Connecticut), referred to his (possibly) native city as a "Shite-Hole" and chose to model High Street after Edinburgh's Royal Mile instead—modeled after in the sense that the Royal Mile is understood to be a route between Edinburgh Castle, the city's ancient keep, and Holyroodhouse, the residence of the monarchs of Great Britain when they're in town. Thus the bottom of High Street (before the Foundry was built anyway) was a plaza at the southern edge of the Lake, on the far side of which the Magic Mountains, which were in many ways Marcus's castle, Marcus's keep, stretched for more than ten miles, while at the other end of the hill, 5,294 feet due south and 916 feet further above sea level, sat Stammers Hall. The street is graded to guarantee that the top of the mountain is never occluded. Even the trees have to cooperate, so High Street is lined with more than three hundred ginkgos, whose crowns tend to grow up rather than out. Marcus considered Lombardy poplars and Mediterranean cypresses and English oaks, all more genuinely fastigiate trees, but opted for the ginkgos because of their fall foliage, which every October cloaks the path to Stammers Hall in a pair of lemon-yellow curtains seventy feet high and a mile long, behind which winter waits like the second installment of a Greek trilogy. Marcus knew about the ginkgos' brilliant fall foliage but, like my mother, he also only knew what he knew, which is to say that he didn't know that the fruit of the ginkgo is filled with butanoic acid, which smells pretty much exactly like shit. He knew that the seed of the ginkgo is edible, knew too that ginkgo seeds are associated with improved memory and sharpness of wit, and so ordered nine females for every male (on the assumption, I suppose, that a few male trees would help the females bear fruit in the same way that the presence of a rooster is supposed to encourage hens to lay), but he didn't know you had to tear through the disgusting pulp to get to the seeds. My mother used to tell me to say that the fruit smells like rancid butter or rotten eggs rather than shit, but I told her that the idea of associating the ginkgos' foul odor with something edible was even more disgusting than associating it with excrement, i.e., something that *had* been eaten, and she must have agreed because she stopped correcting me (although she did try to get me to say "poop" or "doo-doo" in the company of strangers; I suspect that by this point in our narrative you won't be surprised to learn that I refused).

The side streets, in which Marcus originally erected 243 terraced houses (there are about 600 now, most of which were added in a second wave of construction in the 1850s), were graded with similar care to ensure that all of his workers, whose rent was deducted from their wages (which were, at any rate, paid in scrip), knew to whom they owed the luxury of a home with *four* rooms on *two* floors, plus space for a kitchen garden in back, just by looking outside—or, for that matter, at the shadow that the colossal edifice atop the hill cast on their south-facing windows. Stammers Hall eschews the Greek Revival aesthetic of the era for a cooler Georgian style reminiscent of Edinburgh's New Town. The sheer size of the building renders it less elegant than monumental: three stories of local bluestone polished to a high sheen and crowned by a massive hipped roof of slate diamonds beneath which lived the three families of slaves who saw to the mansion's upkeep, including the ancestors of the bakers Brown. With the exception of the rusticated quoins of the first and second floors and the fluted pilasters that segment the north and south faces into five equal bays, the alternating peaked and arched lintels over the building's 120 windows and French doors (forty-five in front and back, fifteen more on each side), the three-foot-long conch-shaped corbels supporting the soapstone gutters hidden in the copper cornice and, finally, the scrim, also copper, and worked in a tight Greek key, that screens the attic windows (although to the attic's occupants, who were responsible for making sure the railing was tinted by not even a fleck of verdigris, the scrim must have looked rather more like what it was, namely, the bars of a cage), the building's facade is unadorned save for four friezes in the pediments of the massive faux gables that were tacked onto each of the house's exposures almost a decade after the original structure was completed: allegories of mining, commerce, education, and service each carved in situ from fifteen tons of anthracite. The masters regularly denounce the friezes as sentimental claptrap and refuse to clear the ravens' nests from them, not to mention the raven shit, so it looks as though the various miners, misers, masters, and slaves are all scarecrows losing their stuffing, and suffering from acute cases of vitiligo to boot.

But the mansion was, in many ways, the least impressive aspect of Marcus's estate. Behind it, on Inverna's southern slope, more than four hundred acres of sculptured gardens cascade down the mountainside like a courtesan's hooped panniers. Combining the older French formalism of André Le Nôtre with Gertrude Jekyll's Victorian mania for "nature, perfected," the gardens are almost always referred to in the plural (even in the Dog Latin name preferred by the novices, the Botanica Balbi). The upper levels are a patchwork of the kind of overwrought horticultural brocades associated with Versailles or Kensington: cherry, peach, olive, and myrtle parterres; boxing ring–sized mandalas woven from pleached roses; a yew labyrinth the size of a football field at whose center lies a second maze, itself the size of a squash court, cultivated from lavender and rosemary, whose lines mirror those of the outer maze, though the open and closed passages are reversed. Everything reeks of an overeager, almost hysterical quality, not just to make an impression but to *impress*: from the eleven fountains, each adorned with a statue originally executed in the classical mold but which, because they were carved from anthracite, gradually eroded to, first, an amorphous Henry Moore–like bulbousness and thence to Giacomettiesque emaciation, to the massive gravel field dotted with 512 eighteen-inch boxwood balls planted in quincunx pattern. Even the lawns, greens, and parks feel overdetermined, starting with the fact that some are called lawns, others greens, and still others parks, depending upon the type of grass they're made of, how short it's cut and whether it's meant for tennis, croquet, bowls, or simply taking in a well-planned vista. But the *pièce de résistance* is undoubtedly the Parrot Pagoda. Named *ex post facto* for the colony of monk parakeets that settled in its upper reaches sometime between the first and second world wars (which is to say, Mom, about fifty years after the mines closed and the last canary was set free), the eight-sided, eight-story tapering tower, eighty feet wide at it base and eighteen at its apex, is fashioned entirely from flowering or fruiting trees, shrubs, and vines, a fugacious floral arrangement that's as much Vegas casino as it is Zen temple. The foliage tends to peak in late April or early May, so you can just imagine the number of brides-to-be who've asked to be married within it (including, according to my mother, *her* mother). But unless you're familiar with the Academy, you'd probably be surprised at the malicious glee with which the masters turn down every single request.

The lower two-thirds of the mountain—more than two thousand acres—is swathed in garlands of forest and streams that empty into little lily- and lotus-covered ponds. The massive limbs of spiny-leaved live oaks writhe from their boles like kraken erupting from the brine; stands of white birch poke from bracken-covered soil like the fingers of giants buried alive at the close of the age of Titans; honey locusts brandish clusters of spikes as long and red as bloody knitting needles, through which hummingbird moths flit as cavalierly as clownfish in a coral reef. There are more than a dozen beech trees each as big as a barn, their bowered trunks etched with Theban dyads reaching back a century and a half, a dozen more magnolias the size of circus tents, their purple-tipped petals blowing across the lawns every spring like frothy wine spraying from a shook bottle, while every fall bands of aspen and sorrel and coffeewood and tupelo gird the lower third of the mountain in ribbons of russet and pink and pale yellow and bright red like a Monet landscape brought to life. More exotic specimens include blue gum eucalyptus from Tasmania, kadota fig from Turkey, and umbrella thorn acacia rarely seen outside the Serengeti. The most noticeable trees, though, are undoubtedly the two giant sequoias—the first to be planted east of the Continental Divide—which, at 224 and 198 feet respectively, are easily the tallest trees in the Atlantic states, more than twice as tall as their nearest competition, and dwarfing the alder, aquilaria, ash, banyan, baobab, beech, birch, box elder, buckeye, cedar, chestnut, cocobolo, coffeetree, cuipo, cypress, ebony, elm, fir, goldenrain, hawthorn, hazel, hemlock, hickory, horn- and hophornbeam, jacaranda, jujube, kapok, laburnum, larch, linden, locust, magnolia, mahogany, mangrove—mangrove!—maple, mimosa, oak, pagoda, persimmon, pine, plane, quebracho, redbud, rosewood, rowan, sassafras, schotia, spruce, sugi, sumac, sweetgum, sycamore, tulip, walnut, and zelkova trees like the Petronas Towers shadowing the shorter skyscrapers of Kuala Lumpur. And yes, I know, that list was excessive, but imagine how much worse it could have been: if I'd listed the trees' species, *Lebanese* cedar and *African* baobab and *Japanese* zelkova and *Kentucky* coffeetree and *London* plane, yellow pine and copper beech and silver birch and red and black and white and pin and live and willow and cork and water oak; if I'd demarcated the specific cultivars, *Styphnolobium japonicum* "pendula," the weeping scholar, *Schotia brachypetala*, the weeping boerbean, *Cupressus sempervirens* "pendula," the weeping Mediterranean cypress, and of course *Salix alba* "Chrysoma," the famous offspring of *S. alba*

"Vitellina-Tristis" and *S. babylonica* "Babylon," better known to
Patsy Cline fans as the weeping willow, and—and, well, I'm sure
you get the picture: there're a lot of different trees (a lot of which
like to cry), and which require not just distinct but conflicting
environments in which to grow, which in turn requires an
extraordinary degree of horticultural micromanagement.

But perhaps the lower gardens' greatest triumph—and greatest transgression—is that, though they appear the very picture of
primeval harmony, they are in fact far more artificial than the
mansion they surround, or the picture-postcard village of Marcuse or, for that matter, the megalopolis that's grown over the
Atlantic seaboard like kudzu. Because however tall its buildings
grow, however wide it sprawls and however many people it
houses, however great its manipulations of and impact on its
local environment, the Northeastern megacity still arrived at its
form by a process of evolution, of trial and error and accretion
and erosion that stemmed from its citizens' habits and, however inadequately, reacts to their needs, and isn't merely the sui
generis expression of the will of a single man. It's one thing to
come upon a stand of swamp cypress, liveoak, loblolly pine,
and *Ficus aurea* all bearded in Spanish moss and growing in and
around the edges of a pond covered in duckweed. It's altogether
another to get a desert-growing baobab to thrive in the shadow
of a dawn redwood plucked from China's Hubei Province a
stone's throw from a pneumatophoric banyan from tropical
India and a clump of Patagonian cypresses from the Andes. It
involves managing the flow of water from both the ground *and*
the sky, manipulating the composition of the soil and even the
rays of the sun, and it was only with the help of 384 resident—
that is to say, captive—gardeners that the Academy managed to

pull it off for a century. The average Academy novice could have told you more about inosculation or lime nail gall or the habits of the fig wasp (imported before there were restrictions on this kind of thing, to make sure the kadotas bear fruit) than about the progeny of the Roman emperors; you might have stared in confusion at black-robed teenagers angling silver-painted sheets of glass at the under-canopies of baobab trees to warm them in winter, while they'd have wondered why you knew so much about the peccadilloes of horny priests—and even while they were working could reel off a complete list of the names and dates of all 261 popes through the turn of the 20th century (including the five antipopes but not the original Stephen II, who died after his election but before he was consecrated), as well as every leader of the western empire from Julius all the way through Honorius and Rome's sack, since those are two of the Academy's three required mnemonic tests, the third being a list (no points if you saw this coming) of the tree species represented in the lower gardens (first, second, and third formers are allowed to give their common names, but fourth, fifth, and sixth formers have to supply the Latin as well). But despite all the drama in the back of the house—and God knows there's *a lot*—my favorite trees are actually in front, on the lower terrace, which is bordered by a simple colonnade of sycamores whose eczemic bark is stubbled by an infestation of *Trichaptum biforme*. The fungus protrudes from the trees like pancakes hurled into them by gale-force winds. They're pancake-colored on top but on the bottom striated purple like a clamshell, like my face, and eventually they'll kill the trees from which they grow: half the trunks were half hollow the last time I saw them, and braced with rusty steel trellises to keep them upright for a few more years.

As an exercise in vanity Stammers Hall and its gardens isn't quite Biltmore or Hearst Castle, nor is Marcuse nearly as big as Pullman, Illinois, or McDonald, Ohio (the former owned by the Pullman Company, the latter by—no, not McDonald's, you history buff you—but Carnegie Steel). Then again, none of these entities existed to be outdone in Marcus's youth, and Cornelius Vanderbilt's private correspondence indicates that Stammers Hall was one of his inspirations—"a bit of Frippery that shall look like a Hindoo Bungaloe beside My Creation." But it was a folly nevertheless, and Marcus's coffers, which were never as deep as his mines, were emptied out by the endeavor. Marcus broke ground on the estate in the forties, remember, before the coal that truly made his fortune had been discovered. In fact, the original plans weren't nearly as grand as what was ultimately built. The mansion was brick rather than stone, the workers' houses clapboard rather than brick, High Street paved with macadam rather than its famous bluestone "Cubed Cubits." But in the years after his accident Marcus became obsessed with building a monument whose durability would stand in permanent contrast to the physical form that had failed him so painfully. For the first two years of his convalescence he was carried by four slaves on a palanquin up and down the mountain, hopped up on laudanum and deliriously overseeing the construction of his mansion one minute, the dredging of the swamp the next. To distract himself from his pain he had full-size models of his workers' houses built in various colors of brick of various sizes and densities and textures, ultimately settling on Norman bricks in a porous pockmarked pale yellow. He ordered two acres planted with twenty different types of grass to decide which variety best complemented the bricks (which would turn black a few years later from the soot that spewed from the razed mountain range to the north, as would, for that matter, the blue grama he planted in their yards). He even went so far as to order a twenty-foot-tall scaffold be erected so that he would know what future generations of Stammers boys (by which he meant not his sons but his slaves) would see when they swung from the wych elm he planted as the town's hanging tree. He removed somewhere between sixty and seventy million cubic yards of earth from the bog to create the body of water that, despite Marcus's best efforts ("Tsistuyi Bay," "Loch Auchterarder," etc.) has never been known by any other name than the Lake. Part of the reason he moved so much dirt was to use the fecund soil for his mountainscaping, but it was also because his engineers were unable to find the place where the White Woman entered whatever underground conduit carried its waters to wherever it carried them, and which Marcus had hoped to plug so he could divert the stream's nutrient-rich silt to his farms south of Mt. Inverna. The bog was large, but the volume of water that flowed in the creek would've made a swamp a hundred times larger than the one that existed if there hadn't been some sort of natural qanat draining it. But though the central basin was dug to a depth of 150 feet, Marcus's men never found anything besides an increasingly treacherous soup of mud, and after excavating a twelve-acre lightning bolt–shaped cavity and stocking it with smallmouth bass, walleye, pike, alligator gar, and, just for fun (and because that's how he rolled), giant catfish from the Mekong River and even bigger sturgeon from the Caspian Sea, Marcus called it a day.

The only thing he didn't pay attention to during this period was his mine, by which I mean that he ignored his geologists' increasingly panicked reports that the Magic Mountain's reserves of copper weren't nearly as extensive as had been previously thought, and that beneath them lay nothing but more of the feldspathic sandstone (a.k.a. graywacke, a.k.a. bluestone) that made up most of the range. The hardest sandstone is still softer than granite as well as more durable than limestone, which makes it nice for building but still difficult to bore through in a mining operation, particularly hundreds of feet underground. Oblivious, impervious, or perhaps just imperious, Marcus ordered the stone be cut in blocks and used to face the mansion atop the hill. When his engineers told him he could build a thousand mansions from the stone they were excavating, he doubled the footprint of the house (that's why the pilasters were added—to cover the seams where the extensions were tacked on), threw in a third story, then an attic, drew up plans for stables on one flank of the mansion and, solely for the sake of visual harmony, a "cottage" on the other, which today house, respectively, the Academy's gymnasium (including Olympic-sized swimming pool) and rectory, whose gabled main dining room can seat all 444 novices and masters. He directed, first, that the entire length of High Street be paved in cobblestones of the aforementioned cubed cubits, for which measurement he supplied his own forearm and hand (this from a man who, even after his accident, boasted that he would have to kneel down to look President Lincoln in the eye), later extending the decree to all its arteries—nearly sixteen miles of roadway paved with blocks of stone that weigh more than four hundred pounds *each* (which is why Marcuse's rain gutters, like medieval European cities', lie above ground, and its houses are connected to septic tanks buried beneath their kitchen gardens rather than a municipal sewage system: those blocks aren't going *anywhere*).

Things continued in this manner until the day Marcus woke to a silence so deafening that the only sound he could hear was the pain of his lower back shrieking like an electrical charge in his inner ear. He fumbled for the laudanum he kept on his bed-side table only to find that he'd depleted his supply during the night, or during whatever period of time had passed since his last moment of lucidity. All that remained were a half-dozen empty phials, a spotted syringe and a dozen blunt, bent needles, a bloodied tourniquet of India rubber. He rang the bell but no one came. The house servants had been sold the year before, replaced with (under-) paid employees who were motivated by neither the discipline of Old World domestics nor the fear of slaves—and who had, at any rate, cleared out several weeks ear-lier—so he struggled to his feet on sticks newly arrived from the Bahamas and staggered out of his bedroom with his peculiar tentpole walk, eventually making his way to the massive paved patio (only later, after he added the even larger lower level, would it come to be called the upper terrace) in front of his half-finished mansion. The entire north side of Inverna was visible below him. High Street, half made, half mud, flowed down to the half-filled lake as though he, Marcus Stammers, laird of the manor, were the source of its waters, not the sinuous stream that hung off its far end like the vestigial tail of an homunculus. The yellow-brick houses, many still skirted in scaffolding, lined the streets like bars of gold, and hundreds of ginkgo saplings in burlap-wrapped balls of soil leaned and lay in the plaza at the bottom of the street like so many Continental irregulars, but somehow it looked less like a new town than an old one, an Uruk or Pompeii being pulled from the encrustations of time, because no matter where Marcus looked—and he'd situated his house so he could see *everything*—he couldn't spy a single living soul. His crews had abandoned him. They hadn't been paid in three months, which fact Marcus was aware of but disregarded, because it never occurred to him that his men might not believe in his vision with the same fervor he did.

It was 1848 by then. Of the two hundred or so houses Marcus had built, more than three-quarters stood empty. Undaunted, he told his remaining miners to dig deeper, and he ordered truly terrifying amounts of dynamite to blast through millions of tons of rock. His workforce was down to fewer than fifty men by the early months of 1849, and he'd been forced to sell his cotton and tobacco farms to keep his creditors at bay; at one point the entire family sheltered in (rather ornate, it must be said) Bedouin tents in the ballroom of a half-completed Stammers Hall. The charge that was planted at a depth of 3,116 feet on March 15, 1849, wasn't exactly "Marcus's last stick of dynamite" as one local (but not Academy) historian put it, but it was pretty damn close. Nor is it true that Marcus's miners didn't recognize the shiny black rock they unearthed until one of their slag heaps caught fire—by that point Marcus's geologists were analyzing virtually every pebble that came out of the ground. But neither of these caveats takes away from the magnitude of the discovery. At its peak Stammers Coal produced nearly half a million tons of bituminous coal per year, and estimates of the total amount of recoverable ore in the Magic Mountains Seam range from 800 million to over two billion tons. STAMMERS COAL MAKES THE NATION BURN was the rather ill-thought-out slogan painted on the side of the three hundred coal cars that ran on six hundred miles of private rail line before connecting with the Baltimore and Ohio at Pittsburgh (an avowed anti-abolitionist, Marcus also thought secession was a doomed, not to mention foolhardy, endeavor, although that didn't prevent six of his sons and grandsons from enlisting in the Confederate Army). The depth of the ore made the mines less profitable than they would have been had the coal lain near the surface (hence the adage about the depth of his pockets versus the depth of his mines), which is one of the reasons why Marcus took the unusual step of replacing most of his white laborers with slaves in 1853. Contrary to later reports, Marcus did not himself own "more than 3,000 slaves," as 90 percent of his workforce was leased from local farmers (many of whom also sought work in the mines after pepper-colored clouds of coal dust rendered their land as barren as if it had been salted). As a consequence, he wasn't legally culpable for the deaths of more than 1,109 black men between 1853 and 1865, since by law the slaves' owners were responsible for the health of their property. These distinctions meant more to Marcus's lawyers than they did to Marcus himself, who referred to all the black men who worked in his mines, whether they were his slaves or someone else's, as "Stammers boys." Nevertheless, he was fond of pointing out that he treated his own property with more "care for his investment" than did most of the people from whom he leased his work force, which is to say that a "mere" seventeen of his own slaves died in the same twelve-year span, and of them only eight from black lung; five of the others died in accidents, and one was hung after his fourth attempt at escape. The latter was the only person ever strung up from the wych elm in the plaza (or the only one who's acknowledged anyway), but though his body was left on the rope for three days as a lesson to any other slave who might harbor fantasies of freedom, his name has been completely expunged from the official record. At any rate it's unclear how effective a deterrent his rotting body could have been, since only a few dozen slaves, domestics in Stammers Hall or the homes of Marcus's top managers, were allowed to set foot in Marcuse; all the rest lived on their owners' property, or in the purpose-built shanties of Wye, which was sited on the same sooty slopes from which Marcus had chased his white employees just eight years earlier. Though many accounts refer to this reversal as "ironic," I'm pretty sure it's just sad.

After the failure of the rebellion, of course, things changed. Marcus made a point of hiring any former slave who'd worked in the mines (and who didn't set off for parts north as soon as the war ended). He paid some of the best wages available to black workers in the South (although still three times less than what white miners were receiving), and he cut down the wych elm and replaced it with a state-of-the-art hospital for his employees in the building that now houses the Foundlings Nursery. After the explosion in '81 he tried to make the hospital seem like a philanthropic rather than practical gesture, but a letter of 1878, in which he argued that "High Street needs an Anchor lest Stammers Hall drift away like a Chinaman's Box-Kite" didn't do much to bolster his credibility, nor the fact that the hospital's front facade was built of the same bluestone as the mansion up the hill (though rusticated, so as not to compete with the house's polished magnificence) even as the other three sides of the building were made of bricks left over from the workers' houses—the white workers' houses, I should say, since black workers still weren't allowed to live in town: hence Wye, which less than a decade after its founding had five times as many residents as Marcuse, though not one brick or stone building, not a single ginkgo or strand of bluegrass or cubed cubit—no paved streets at all, in fact, save for the one that led to and from the mine, because Marcus didn't want his workers "inconvenienced" by a muddy road in the spring. Then, too, there was the fact that employees' visits to the hospital were mandatory, and like their rent and the cost of the food, clothing, and tools they purchased at the commissary, paid for through an "insurance" program whose premiums were deducted from their pay. All things considered, however, it was as close to honest labor as was available to black men during Reconstruction, and much was made of the fact that 66 percent of Marcus's four thousand employees had sons who also worked in the mines, and 28 percent had grandsons as well.

But none of this was able to stave off the two disasters that ultimately brought down Stammers Coal: the explosion beneath the Quirinal in 1881 that killed 239 workers, and the lawsuit brought by "a Pack of Northern Wolves" that shuttered the company permanently in 1883. No one's exactly sure what caused the explosion (it was a Sunday, and though the mines ran two twelve-hour shifts seven days a week, no blasting was done on the Sabbath), nor why it was so large. The most persuasive theory is that thirty years of mining had filled an undiscovered cavern with large quantities of fire damp, a.k.a., methane, which was ignited by a spark from the pickaxe of some unsung John Henry breaking through a wall, resulting in an explosion estimated at about eight kilotons—the shockwave blew out the front *and* back windows in Stammers Hall, fourteen miles away. Judging from remains recovered from the mine, fewer than a dozen people were killed outright by the explosion, but more than four hundred others were trapped underground, and, over the course of the next three months, 216 bodies were recovered, with twenty-three more people missing and presumed buried or obliterated. Most of the victims appeared to have succumbed fairly quickly to injury or toxic gas, but twenty-eight of them lingered for somewhere between thirty-one and thirty-five days in one of the mine's waystations (the hatchmarks on the timber trusses offered confusing evidence, not least because no one was sure how the miners, not one of whom was in possession of a watch, had determined the passing of days). The chamber's water barrels were still half full when the bodies were discovered forty-eight days after the explosion, but three of the bodies had been partially cannibalized, and one of these (a white foreman, as it happened) had been strangled.

But the event that damned Great Grandpa Marcus to permanent ignominy was nothing so macabre—although it was, in its own way, more shocking. The explosion occurred on May 6, 1881, and Marcus didn't show up at the mine until the morning of May 9. Even then his visit had nothing to do with the three hundred workers still unaccounted for. No, he had seen something "Truely Tragic and Unbearable" from his study window (in which the glass broken by the explosion had already been replaced, the watered-silk curtains repaired and rehung) in the now-completed mansion at the top of the hill: the White Woman Creek and the lightning-bolt lake he had excavated at its terminus had disappeared overnight, leaving behind nothing but a slug's winding trail and a damp brown gash that looked like a massive uncovered latrine in which the shimmering ten-foot-long balloons of his exotic catfish and sturgeon twitched in the mud like shat-out intestinal parasites. Marcus looked down on the world he'd made and saw that it was not good. "Like Xerxes Bridgeing the Hellespont, my Hubris has Offended the Gods," he wrote in his diary. "I am Ashamed. I am Undone. I am— Eclips'd." Though he hadn't been on horseback in more than three decades, he commanded that a mount be prepared and rode to the scene of the disaster as swiftly as his inosculated pelvis would allow, where he demanded that his engineers find out what had dammed the White Woman's waters and correct it immediately. When his men protested that they were needed for the rescue effort—that there was every reason to believe hundreds of miners were still alive beneath the rubble—Marcus thundered his now-infamous epithet, which very nearly became his epitaph: "Let the Coal have 'Em!" Unfortunately for him, journalists from the *New York Tribune* and *Sun* and *Herald* were on the scene by that time. There were journalists from the Atlanta papers as well, from Memphis, Louisville, Columbia, Charlotte, Mobile, and St. Louis, but it was the New York journalists that did Marcus in: the journalists, and the sketch artists, and what they showed the world.

The conventional method of extracting coal at the extreme depth of the Magic Mountain Seam—blasting, pickaxing, and chiseling through billions of tons of rock and carting it out one mule-drawn trolleyload at a time—was, to employ anachronistic corporate jargon, cost-ineffective, and even if there had been some notion of environmental consciousness a decade before *The Origin of Species* it's doubtful a man who saw the world the way Marcus saw it—as, if I can use a pointed metaphor, malleable clay upon which to impress his will—would have paid any heed. Instead he blew the top off the renamed Palatine and four successive mountains, filling in the spaces between them with rubble so that, by the time of the explosion, the variform Tsistuyi of the Cherokee had been reduced to a twelve-mile-long cairn of blackened stone and soot. In contrast to the voluptuous sculpted gardens on the sunny side of Inverna, no tree, no shrub, no flower or blade of grass grew for an area of almost ten square miles, and a shivering cloud of coal dust three times that size (by comparison, the island of Manhattan is only about twenty-two square miles) darkened everything animal, vegetable or mineral that had the misfortune to fall within it. "The land is blasted black as far as the eye can see," one of the newspaper accounts ran, "which is not very far, because the air is black too—the black of coal, of smoke, of Negroes both living and dead. But the blackest thing of all is the conscience of the grand personage who believes he owns them all, man as well as mineral, landscape as well as land." The black-and-white drawings that appeared in the weeks and months following the explosion are as stark as Dürer woodblocks, their monochromatic palette uncannily suited to a landscape as completely colorless as any that ever existed on this planet—even Marcus's horse, said to have been a cremello stallion, was depicted in almost every drawing as an ash-colored gelding, and in the most famous of the drawings, by Thomas Nast, Great Grandpa Marcus's staves have multiplied from two to four and migrated from his hands to his back so that he appeared an eight-legged black spider, the lone pale spot on his body an hourglass-shaped patch that glowed on his gaunt abdomen like a lantern, and cemented in the national conscious-ness his transformation to black widow (apparently, like Marcus and like my mother, journalists of the era only knew what they knew, or their editors were content to bank on their readers' ignorance of *Iatrodectus*'s more deadly sex, despite the species' rather pointed common name).

But the newspapers were less content to allow other facts to fall by the wayside. Nineteen years earlier, they reminded readers, Abraham Lincoln had written, "If there be those who would not save the Union, unless they could at the same time *save* slavery, I do not agree with them. If there be those who would not save the Union unless they could at the same time *destroy* slavery, I do not agree with them." Lincoln wrote these words to Horace Greeley, whose *New York Tribune* led the call for the Stammers family to be stripped of the possessions of which its members had shown themselves unworthy. Greeley had been dead for almost a decade by the time Stammers Coal exploded, the *Tribune* had begun its long slide into the yellow journalism of its competitors, but its editors were still conscientious enough—which is to say cynical enough, or racist enough—to remind its readers why President Lincoln had led the country into the bloodiest war of its history: "My paramount object in this struggle *is* to save the Union, and is *not* either to save or to destroy slavery. If I could save the Union without freeing *any* slave I would do it, and if I could save it by freeing *all* the slaves I would do it; and if I could save it by freeing some and leaving others alone I would also do that. What I do about slavery, and the colored race, I do because I believe it helps to save the Union." Stammers family lore claims that the word "moonscape" was used in one of the descriptions of the mines to describe a terrestrial environment for the first time, and it's the inventiveness of the term that finally gives away the target of the articles' outrage, and their authors' and editors': not 239 dead men "who, though they be largely Negroes, do deserve better than this rude treatment," but, rather, the despoiling of a land that 150,000 soldiers had given their lives to ensure remained within the borders of a single Union. It wasn't the *land* the newspapers cared about, in other words, let alone the men who lived on its fruited plains or died beneath them: it was the myth of the New World pastoral, this second Eden God had provided for a new race of men, and it was the violation of this most American of compacts that prompted one writer to declare: "If the moon were black it could not be any more barren than Marcus Stammers's soul."

3

My mother was twelve or thirteen when she saw the house on the eastern bank of the White Woman for the first—and, until I bought it, only—time. But though she never spoke of it, I realized later that she often spoke *from* it. That part of her imagination had resided there for almost twenty years, and part of everything she made was formed with the view from its windows in mind. Her father had taken Guy on a tour of the conservancy to familiarize him with the scope of his future responsibilities. The public school in Wye was on break ("Easter?" my mother said, the word dropping from her lips with the same lack of comprehension that one of her classmates might've said "Eid?") and she was allowed to tag along because she'd recently manifested a rebellious streak that got her into "mischief and mayhem" when she was left alone. The old mill, or bawdy house, or whatever it was, wasn't actually on Stammers's land. It sat almost directly opposite the Capitoline, more or less in the middle of the range, and after conducting the twins on a tour of all seven hills—standing over the two-hundred-foot-deep well from which the pellucid, polluted waters of the White

Woman rose in speckled turmoil; walking them into 150-year-old adits still glittering with exposed sheets of coal; even leading them down a pair of shafts to convey the torturous conditions under which the family fortune had been amassed—my grandfather shooed his children back in the car and drove them to the east side of the creek in order to show them just how big 33,000 acres was.

Had them driven, I should write, by the chauffeur that came with the car that came with the stipend that came with the hereditary positions of president of Lake Academy and director of the Magic Mountains Conservancy. My grandfather, who died before I was born, wasn't so much stuffy or pompous as intellectually inflexible ("I never heard the man use a contraction in his life," my mother said once; "when he found out I'd been going to classes dressed as Guy he made a remark about my stealing 'the robe belonging to your brother' instead of 'your brother's robe'") and she paid scant attention to his lecture. (When I pointed out that "your brother's robe" was a possessive, not a contraction, she rolled her eyes. "You know what I mean.") She'd heard it a million times before—from him, from her grandparents and the servants, from the masters and the residents of Marcuse and Wye, who still stood aside when a Stammers passed on the sidewalk, still said "Morning, Mr. Stammers" or "Afternoon, Miz Stammers" and no doubt still would have doffed their hats if the custom for men to keep their heads covered in public had continued in force. But she perked up when they crossed to the east side of the creek and she saw the seven perfect domes of the Magic Mountains stretched along the horizon like the spine of a sleeping dragon. By that point she'd been sneaking into Academy classes for years, but she'd

only recently begun to question what was taught in them, and as
a consequence was also taking painting lessons in secret with a
man in Wye who, in the finest tradition of Bob Ross, taught his
young pupil that no more meet subject existed for a budding
"paintress" (I'm guessing she made that up) than the glorious
sunset, sunsets qua sunsettiness being universally glorious fans
of light illuminating mother rabbits or deer, or tender, toothless
wolves sitting watchfully while kits or fawns or cubs gamboled
about on dark green grass. After less than a month she'd grown
bored of the man's watercolored, watered-down sentimentality.
But this—this was a sunset! It streamed from the hilltops in a
wind-whipped cloak of the intensest oranges, reds, and purples
she'd ever seen. There wasn't enough color in her teacher's
paintbox—in the sunny catalog from which he ordered his pigments—to capture a tenth of its gradations, its depth, its weight.
It was, my mother said, the most arresting thing she'd ever seen,
not just because it was what it was, but because it *wasn't* what
she'd been taught it was. It wasn't "beautiful." It wasn't "awe-
some" or "sublime." Or if it was these things, they were just
by-products of radiance and refraction. In this she sensed a
troubling correspondence to things she'd heard in the Academy
classes she'd trespassed, but before she could parse the thought
it was eclipsed by something even more dramatic.

Between the onlookers and the hills lay a strip of reedy land,
so perfectly flat that the White Woman ribboned across it in
loopy meanders more than a mile wide—if pulled straight, her
father told them (redundantly: did he think his children couldn't
read the "Fun Facts" on the placard commemorating the victims
of the 1881 explosion?) the creek would measure nearly forty-
eight miles from the spring on the north side of the Esquiline to

the mouth of the Lake, despite the fact that only seventeen miles separated the White Woman's source from its tail. But then her father abruptly stopped talking as, simultaneously with his children, he saw the sharp-edged shadow of the Capitoline push out from its base and glide toward the flood plain like an avalanche peeling off the side of the range. The mountain's shadow didn't so much push the light forward as shim it from the ground, slipping under it "like crème de cassis into a pousse-café" (my mother wasn't prone to metaphor, but when she did use one she went for it). It was as if the day, as if the universe itself was being wedged open, the clockwork motoring the planet around the sun about to be exposed. All three onlookers waited speechlessly for the revelation, barely breathing as the darkness surged toward them across the vast expanse of reeds and water and then—oh, and then!—washing over them, the shadow so solid that my mother half expected to be lifted up and knocked to the ground.

The temperature fell ten degrees in the space of a heartbeat. The barometric pressure dropped so rapidly your ears rang. If you opened your mouth your tongue felt like it would fly out like a cuckoo from a clock. Her father, Academy empiricist, turned nonchalantly to watch the shadow continue to bulldoze the day away. Gaius, his traitor's heart at the mercy of a sycophant's limbs, turned also. But my mother couldn't tear her eyes from the darkness deepening like the fog of memory between her and the hills. She tried to ascertain if the colors she was seeing, the phragmites's green, the bright yellow of the goldenrod that poked up here and there among the reeds, the bruised purple loosestrife that fringed them, were based on information her retinas were actually receiving, or if her visual cortex was in fact supplying the palette from stored data. She wondered if the phragmites Great Grandpa Marcus's scientists had planted to clean up the creek was the native *P. australis americanus* or the invasive *P. australis australis*. She asked herself if the oceanic feeling that had surged through her body a moment ago had been nothing but wishful thinking, no more miracle than the burning bush that lured Moses out of Egypt, the delusions of grandeur that condemned Jesus of Nazareth, the schizophrenic echo that spoke to Mohammed in his cave. And then, for the third time in as many minutes, nature paid good.

A herd of deer, thirty of them maybe, maybe forty, maybe fity or more—a host of deer stood up from the reeds on the far side of the stream where they'd been sleeping the day away and, moving as a single entity, hopped westward toward the more palatable ryegrass that grew at the base of the Capitoline. The deer were barely visible in the twilight, and distance and the sound of the stream were enough to swallow whatever noise they made. But there was nothing to suggest that my mother's eyes were playing tricks on her, and her gaze flitted ecstatically from one white rump to another, the white tails flickering in the gloaming, as if morsing out a private message while her father and brother's backs were turned.

"Dixie," her father called. "Mrs. Brown will be keeping supper."

"Just a min—"

"No."

The deer were all but gone by the time this brief exchange was over, banished by her father's voice or swallowed up by the shadows at the base of the hills. Sighing theatrically (maybe I'm making that part up, but my mother's been a champion sigher—and gasper and groaner—for as long as I can remember), she turned, and this time it wasn't nature that surprised her, but something made by human hands.

When they first drove up the chauffeur had parked next to what she'd taken to be an abandoned house. She hadn't paid the building much attention because her gaze had been glued to the polychrome horizon. Now she realized it probably wasn't a house. It was too big, too plain, the brown bricks laid in the most basic Flemish bond. ("What do you mean, how do I know? The brickmaker's the potter's next of kin, that's how I know.") The only relief from the sameness was a large patch on the northwest corner built of bricks that were paler, pinker, smaller than those that composed the rest of the building. If it *had* been a mill, that explained where the waterwheel'd been, though not why it stood so far from the nearest loop of creek. Three tiers of five tall narrow windows stretched down the west side of the building, all fifteen aflame with the light of the setting sun. The glowing windows weren't as grand as the sunset, as the shadow-wave or the deer, but they weren't supposed to be: the building had been placed there, my mother understood suddenly, not to compete with the view, nor become part of it, but to take it in. It was a novel concept to her thirteen-year-old mind: that you might make something not so it could be appreciated in itself, but so it could help you appreciate something else. It was, she said once, why no one understood her pots: people were too busy oohing and aahing to hear what the clay might have to say about *them*.

It didn't occur to her, not then—not consciously anyway—that she could live there. No Stammers had lived elsewhere than the President's House for a century, and she didn't get the idea to leave campus until five and a half years after her brother disappeared. But still, the image stayed with her, the semicircular patch of pale bricks (*"Store-bought,"* she sighed when I questioned her fascination with this detail; "the original structure was built from bricks baked from the land it sat on, but when they tore off the waterwheel they patched the hole with bricks from a goddamned *Home Depot"*), the fifteen windows ("Let me tell you, Judas, it says something—about the house, about the people who live in Marcuse and Wye, I don't know which—that no one ever broke *one single pane* of those windows in the thirty or forty years that building sat empty"), the sunset they looked out on, the hills' shadow, and, finally, the deer, who every night would rise like ghosts to forage on the aquamarine grass of the place Marcus Stammers had, at the end of his life, taken to calling his own Megiddo. She never mentioned what she'd seen to her father, nor even to her brother, who, though he said he thought the exclusion of Dixie from the Academy and the Stammers inheritance was "ridiculously archaic," not to mention "like, totally sexist," never made any noise about refusing it either, or sharing it with her once it was his. Well: the land might all be Gaius's one day, the Academy too, but this vision, Dixie decided, would be hers alone.

For the first time I had a palpable sense of the Northern Passage of patriarchy my mother had had to navigate as she grew up, the monumental act of will it must have taken to pursue a path of her own, an art, a child. For a moment I thought we were about to get our life back on track. She would go back to her clay and I would go back to my brushes—scrub, not paint—and things would go back to normal. But, alas, she kept talking:

"He was gone within the month."

My mother said these words with a strange tone in her voice. Not plaintive, not wistful, not defiant or self-pitying. It almost sounded like she was angry, and, warily, I said,

"Your . . . father?"

"My *brother*. He left a note saying he had to find his own path, and he disappeared."

Again I didn't understand.

"He was . . . giving it to you?"

She shook her head vehemently.

"He *pushed* it on me," she said to me on the day we decided to move out of the apartment above the Browns' bakery, and even though it wasn't the last day we lived there, it *was* the last day our imaginations were contained by its walls. Though it took another four months to purchase the land and make the building habitable, from that day forward we took no more notice of the apartment than we would of a train station or an airport. Let the dust collect until it was a solid body, until it grew limbs, digits, and cranium and required only a scroll pushed down its throat to make it motile: the apartment had finally been revealed for what it was: someone else's responsibility, someone else's problem, and, most importantly, someone else's home.

"Guy forced me to shoulder a burden he didn't want to carry himself," my mother told me later that day, when we were back in the apartment—the apartment that she officially inherited five years after her twin disappeared, just as she inherited the couple whose family had rented it ever since Abolition liberated them from Great Grandpa Marcus's attic, and who continued to cook and clean up after us (you didn't really believe she entrusted the task to a *five-year-old*, did you?) after she forced them to move into what had, until then, been *their* attic. "Browns have lived on

Stammers property for 160 years," she said by way of justifying this displacement, and although American history would suggest that the situation was slightly more complicated, my mother shrugged and said, "I only know what I know," and then, picking up a pheasant's banded tailfeather and staring at it as though it were a syringe on a park bench, she said:

"You were supposed to be my revenge."

"Against the Browns?" I said, even though I knew what she thought she was saying.

"Oh, Judas!" my mother giggled, and she reached out and pushed her fingers through my hair and pulled it over my mottled left cheek. "Against the Stammerers!" she said, even though she knew that I knew what she thought she had said, and when she dropped the feather on my clean floor it was all I could do not to smack her in the face.

SHE SAID HE was the prettier of the two. Not feminine—"not like poo"—but finer of feature, delicate even. ("And you know damn well I said 'not like you,' not 'not like poo.'") A harrow-shaped face arbored by ringlets of dirty blond hair, limbs kept lithe by swimming and rock climbing and what my mother was pretty sure was an eating disorder. "Orthorexia *avant la lettre*," she said, and though I thought I'd misheard she repeated the same bizarre combination of syllables three more times. "We were almost indistinguishable but even so, Guy was twice as pretty as I could ever hope to be." Said wistfully, and the fact that her longing was directed at herself, at the beauty she felt she hadn't been blessed with rather than the twin brother who disappeared when they were thirteen, almost made me feel worse for her. "When he was here I didn't need a mirror. I looked at him and saw a version of myself a mirror could never match. And despite my doubts about my appearance I believed I did the same for him. I don't know, maybe I was deluding myself. Maybe that's why he ran."

Until the year before he left, she said, she outweighed him, could beat him at arm wrestling and outrun him too. But it was a question of ounces, not pounds, strength of will rather than limb; for all intents and purposes they were identical. Half the time they were mistaken for twin girls, not infrequently for twin boys. It was the rare person who saw one boy and one girl upon first meeting them, and every once in a while someone got even that backwards. So it should come as no surprise that my mother was able to sneak into her brother's classes in the Academy, even though there were rarely more than fifteen novices in a room. Maybe it was the fact that my uncle was the only white person in the school by that point, or maybe it was just because he was a Stammers, but Gaius was treated as a kind of privileged observer by the masters; they almost never called on him, and when they did it was usually a softball, the kinds of questions that even my mother, with her scattershot knowledge, could answer, and when she couldn't she would simply stare off into space. Once or twice, my mother said, she got a double take from one of his friends, but apparently none of the masters had a clue—"or just didn't give a fuck, the old pederasts." She went so far as to sit for his second- and third-form portraits. Since these are paintings rather than photographs, it's hard to challenge her assertion, but when I compare the eight- and ten-year-old faces with the twelve-year-old in the fourth-form picture for 1975 (which according to my mother Gaius *did* sit for) I see a difference, not so much in feature as in expression. My uncle's twelve-year-old face is taciturn, shy or bored or peeved or put upon, I couldn't tell you, but he refuses to look at the painter directly, just stares off to the right—not *at* anything, you can tell, just not at the painter, whose impotent "Look this way"s are almost audible on the canvas. My ten-year-old mother, by contrast, confronts the painter with a mocking, defiant expression, as if daring him to guess her true identity or reveal it in his portrait. Her shoulders are square, her hands rest on her thighs, whereas Guy slouches, arms plaited across his stomach, hands invisible inside the muffed sleeves of his robe. My mother, in other words, looks for all the world like a cocky, privileged boy, coddled merely for possessing a penis, rewarded simply for being a father's son, which is remarkable not only because she was able to pull it off but because it was so far from her brother's experience, which his own body reflected more clearly: the burden of expectation as palpable as his robes, as if his flesh were a garment propped up by Academy philosophy and he wanted nothing so much as to strip it off.

Which is exactly what he did. He didn't just run away; he disappeared, hiding himself so well that the estate had no choice but to declare him dead *in absentia* shortly after he (would have) turned eighteen, which action was forced on the trustees by my grandfather's unexpected death at the age of forty-three. Great Grandpa Marcus had placed "a perpetual stipulation of cognatic primogeniture" in his will, which meant that after the extinction of every single male heir my mother was awarded (I would say begrudgingly, but there was no one left to begrudge it) sole control over the various Stammers family concerns—male genes, all else being equal, trumping female, but a daughter of the Stammers line being more capable, or at any rate more tolerable, than a son from any other family. Despite its name, the Magic Mountains Conservancy and Trust was a private corporation over which Marcus's heirs had absolute authority; as the only surviving Stammers, my mother was spared the internecine feuds that rent brothers and sisters and sons and daughters through most of the twentieth century. As chairman of the Board of Trustees of Lake Academy she held not quite as much sway—Academy by-laws forbade not just female students but female faculty and administrators, including, of course, in the office of the President—but even though she had access to a quarter of a million dollars per year in discretionary funds, as well as "such Slaves as are required to maintain the proper Office and Estate of a Gentleman" (bear in mind that this stipulation was written in 1891, in Marcus's own hand), let the record show that my mother claimed not one penny of Academy or conservancy funds or personnel for herself. "*I* paid the Browns," she insisted when I prodded her. "I *paid* them."

In fact, though she claimed to disagree violently with the principles of both institutions, the one and only aspect of Marcus's bequest she changed was the stipulation that they remain under family control. When she discovered that she was pregnant—when she made up her mind that she was going to keep me—she altered the terms of the two entities to *prohibit* any Stammers from having a hand in their day-to-day management— a largely nominal gesture, given that she retained ownership of both the conservancy and the Academy, and as such directed less at herself than at any male progeny to whom she might give birth. From 1981 until the end of time, her sons and grandsons would have only two options available to them: live off the interest derived from the conservancy's endowment while watching the principal trickle steadily away, or sell the whole kit and caboodle for once and all—school, land, investment fund, even Marcuse itself, which remained a (money-losing) Stammers asset right until the very end.

The day we moved into the Field she took me into the yard to watch the sunset stream over the Magic Mountains in miles-long bars of gold and red light. The shadow that she'd seen twenty years earlier didn't make an appearance, but even so the view was beautiful in the way that sunsets, surprisingly, still are, and after a long pause during which I assume she was waiting for the return of her beloved deer, she sighed proudly and said, "That's what I saved you from, Judas."

It seemed absurd to me that my mother insisted that people regard her pots as nothing more than cookie jars even as she projected the most wildly symbolic psychological significance onto the natural world. Of course the Magic Mountains were hardly pure manifestations of nature—were, like Mayan pyramids, mostly riprap cosmetically concealed by Stammers's labor and circumscribed by their imagination. But manmade or not, they were still *mountains*, or, well, good-sized hills, and the only way my mother could have saved me from them was if they were falling and she pushed me out of the way.

But we were moving forward after the disruptions of the past year and a half, and I was determined to meet her halfway. And so I turned and gazed dutifully across the stream-bisected bog. There are prettier mountain ranges, more dramatic or bucolic, but none that possesses the Magic Mountains' eerie uniformity, as if nature had made them for the sole purpose of gracing Kodachrome postcards captioned "Wish You Were Here!" in rainbow bubble font. But nature didn't make them: Marcus

Stammers did. In 1882 he preemptively shut down the mine and had the entire mountain range placed under the auspices of the newly formed Magic Mountains Conservancy, whose ostensible goal was the "rehabilitation" of the land the mine had destroyed but whose actual purpose was preventing the fortune it had made the Stammerses from "dribbling into the Purses & Pockets" of the families of the 239 victims of the 1881 explosion, not to mention the "Accurs'd Attorneys" who represented them. The seven original peaks, which had stood between 1800 and 2200 feet, had by then been razed to a single mound of debris, coal-black and barren, ten miles long, three miles wide, 900 feet high. I doubt that the muckrakers and carpetbaggers who went after Marcus expected him to do anything more than cover this mass of broken boulders with a layer of dirt (if even that) and let Zephyrus blow in what seeds he would. But Marcus took to his new status as the land's steward with the same zeal with which he'd raped it, electing not simply to rehabilitate the mountains but to restore them to an idealized condition. The crews of miners who'd torn them down—the ones who were still alive anyway—built them back up into seven identically perfect inselbergs, each as smoothly domed as a bell jar and possessing a similar air of imminence, as if a hand might at any moment reach down from heaven and pluck them away, revealing whatever pickled corpses sheltered beneath. There are those who say that the Magic Mountains Convervancy was the work of someone who saw nature as man's canvas, and to decorate it was not just his right but his duty. But I don't think Marcus had a concept of nature, or, at any rate, a concept of nature that separated it from the things of men. It's not that man was a natural entity. To the contrary: there was no such thing as nature. The world was a mere extension of man's psyche. Hence the mansion, the gardens, the town of Marcuse; hence the Magic Mountains, which in Marcus's vision had nothing to do with the Tsistuyi that had stood there before save that they occupied the same coordinates of longitude and latitude. The Tsistuyi were Cherokee hills; the Magic Mountains were Marcus's, and would stand until someone with an even stronger will came along, and replaced them with whatever he saw fit.

Or maybe the explanation's simpler than all that. Marcus had millions of dollars at his disposal, after all, and in the wake of his settlement this money could be spent on nothing but the conservancy, and, what's more, *had* to be spent, or would disappear in fines, levies, taxes, damages. Marcus's *horror vacui* had manifested itself long before he was forced to close his mines, as had his beavery mania: if he didn't chew on *something* his teeth would grow through his skull, and I couldn't help but wonder if that's really what my mother thought she was saving me from. Not the Stammers hubris but the Stammers compulsion: for sameness, for repetition, the illusion of mastery over the world. Seven identical mountains, 174 identical pots, generation after generation of black-robed acolytes chorusing their "From nothing, take nothing, make nothing" mantra. But all I saw were seven round hills covered in second-growth pine, and all I said was:

"How'm I supposed to get to classes?"

My mother cocked her head like a crow catching the sound of a mole digging a few inches below the surface. She waved a hand at the creek. "You want a boat? A jetski? An inner tube or basket of reeds?"

"I'm *serious*."

"Hey, these are the same reeds that carried Moses down the Nile. If they were good enough for the savior of the Jews—"

"*Bul*rushes."

"Hum?"

"Moses's basket was made of *bulrushes*." My voice grated in the bucolic setting. I liked the way it sounded, and made it even more harsh. "How am I going to get to *school*?"

My mother didn't acknowledge me immediately. Sighing—I know it's uncharitable of me, but I'm pretty sure her sigh was for the deer who refused to appear rather than her increasingly truculent son—she turned away from the hills.

"You know, we're on the Wye bus route. If you wanted, you could start high school there. What would you be, a freshman, sophomore?"

"What I'd *be* is better educated than most of the *teachers*."

My mother shrugged. Her eyes strayed back toward the hills. "I just thought you might want to see the world from another perspective."

There was a question in her voice, as if she wasn't saying what she wanted but was trying to find out what I did, and I waved my hands like a drowning sailor.

"Hello? Look at me, Mom. I've always seen the world from 'another perspective.'"

My mother grimaced. "Good," she said, and after a moment, "Good" again. She turned her whole body now, not so much toward me as away from the sunset, away from memory, from expectation and disappointment, only to be confronted anew with the failure of her child's face. Still, she nodded as though we'd negotiated some important settlement. "I'd prefer it if you continued at the Academy through high school," she said, even though this clearly contradicted her earlier suggestion.

My mother knew very well that the Academy didn't have high school, it had fifth and sixth forms, but all I said was, "Um, *because* . . . ?"

Another wince, followed by a smile that I think she meant to be tender but came off as condescending. "Because you can't reject something until you understand it."

"It didn't stop *you*. And what makes you think I'm going to reject it? Not that I could actually accept it if I wanted to. Not since you"—I waved an arm at the horizon, which a century and a half of history said should have belonged to me, no matter what color my skin was—"*saved* me from it."

"Because you're not just a Stammerer," my mother said immediately, as if she'd known what I was going to say—as if, almost, she'd wanted me to say it. "You're also my son. As your misplaced hostility makes all too clear."

I'd like to claim I didn't understand what she meant, or that she wasn't right. I'd like to tell you that I really *was* mad at her and not at something else. But I did understand her and she *was* right, and if I was pretending to be mad at her it was only because the thing I was actually mad at needed, like the thousand apparitions of Vishnu, a material form to make it comprehensible to human senses.

"Whatever," I said, and started for the building that, whatever it had been, was now our house. "I want a Triumph," I tossed over my shoulder.

"A triumph?" my mother called. "Like, elephants and acrobats and, um, *sacrifices*?"

"Don't forget the captured slaves and tribute from

conquered kings." And then: "A *motorcycle*," I added quickly, because part of me was afraid she might respond credulously to my demand—to her perception of my demand—and when I slammed the door behind me three of her unbroken panes jumped from their mullions and shattered on the stoop. *Oh yeah*, I remember thinking as the clatter filled my ears. *Point to Judas.*

THE HOUSE HAD three floors, as I've said, and without any discussion the first became my mother's and the third mine, the second being reserved for everything that had been in the apartment above the Browns' bakery (everything that didn't belong to the Browns, that is, which turned out to be more than I would have guessed—the shrunken heads, for example, a relic of Mr. Brown's service in the Pacific in the Second World War, along with the diving helmets, and Mrs. Brown laid claim to a bentwood rocker that materialized from beneath what had been nothing more than a shapeless mound of quilts for as long as I could remember). We should "start fresh," my mother said, and offered me "free rein" to pick out whatever I wanted in the way of "paint and doorknobs and switchplates." I will admit to having had very little in common with most teenaged boys, but I was never so far gone that I gave a shit about switchplates. All I did was order the most basic objects from IKEA, which choices my mother, not surprisingly, vetoed out of hand, by which I mean that when they arrived she didn't let me take them out of the boxes or even return them, but piled everything in the yard, doused it with gasoline (we kept a can at the house for my Vespa, which is what she gave me instead of a Triumph), and set it alight.

Then she disappeared.

She was gone the better part of three months, from sometime in February, when we moved into the Field, to early May. Only gradually did I realize she was combing every antiques store in a parallelogram roughly bound by Galveston, Louisville, Richmond, and Savannah (which coordinates I base on the return addresses on the packages that began arriving a week or so after she left and continued to show up for months after she was back). She didn't tell me she was going, just left me with two treasure-chest ice boxes filled with TV dinners and frozen pizzas, as well as a standing order with the IGA for perishables and a strongbox containing $23,362 in "pin money." She came home every eight or nine or ten days, less to check on me than to deliver something small and inordinately expensive or fragile. Just before she set out for the third time I asked her how she knew I'd be there when she got back. My mother knew her son well enough to understand that this was less threat than declaration of loneliness, though not maternal enough to try to make me feel better. "Oh, good God, Judas, *run*. You're not exactly the hardest person in the world to *find*."

She addressed the packages to herself or to me depending on which floor they were intended for, and it was because of both of these things—because she was gone, and because they were addressed to me—that I ended up with my father's books. Before we moved in my mother had Potter's Field gutted to its bricks and beams, leaving only the floorboards intact. Each story was thirty-two feet wide by forty-seven feet long, narrow staircase tucked into one corner, stingy bathroom in the opposite. I pushed the furniture (Paul McCobb, Heywood-Wakefield, an array of bent, blond plywood by Aalto, Saarinen, the Eameses) against the south wall, separating out only those items that came in boxes, which, rather than unpack, I stacked into a low-walled room-within-a-room where, for the first time in my life, I masturbated with utter abandon. I'd masturbated before, of course, despite the lack of privacy in the apartment—had occasionally managed to squeeze one out in the tub while the faucet was running, and sometimes I raised my hand in class (my left hand, of course, so that the sleeve of my gown fell down and exposed my purple arm) and asked to be allowed to go to the bathroom, where I beat my meat with a tight grip so that my hand didn't slide up and down the shaft of my penis but rather moved the skin back and forth over the engorged corpora cavernosa, which was hardly the most pleasurable way to take care of business (more than once I ended up with blisters) but was the quietest. No doubt most adolescents learn to pleasure themselves in some measure of silence and secrecy—yes, and shame too—and no doubt there are horny teenagers who can't wait till they get home to get off, who hide in toilet stalls with their feet on the doorframe thinking no one knows they're there, unaware that behind the sound of the blood pumping in their ears the stall is rattling in time with their suppressed—compressed— orgasm. But they at least have the *option* of waiting until they're behind the locked door of their bedroom, parents and siblings safely asleep, uncloistered imaginations free to roam the contours of their phantasmal partners instead of listening for the sound of approaching footsteps, an opening door, a maternal giggle: "Don't worry, Judas sleeps like a cock. Yes, *Dick*, I said '*Judas*.'" I had none of that—not until we moved into the Field and my mother went off on her shopping spree, leaving me alone in an empty house, the nearest neighbor a mile away. I jerked off on every floor, in every position, at every hour of the day or night, but after a certain number of boxes addressed to me (by which I mean seventy-nine) had arrived, and after my mother came home unexpectedly one night and nearly caught me on her bed, and then again on her potting table, I more or less confined myself to the cardboard-walled stall I built for myself on the third floor. I played out a host of captive fantasies on its bonded brown surface: bricked up in a crypt like Fortunato or locked in a garret like Ugolino and his sons and grandsons (I was always one of the latter, my climax invariably coming when I felt my grandfather's toothless mouth start to gnaw at my penis) and once I was Rapunzel in her tower, my hair purple rather than gold and, rather than the instrument of my liberation, the method of my restraint, its long coils binding me at wrists and ankles while a shadowy figure, half witch, half prince, daubed my body with viole(n)t enchantments that left me scaled within a seamless, sexless integument, no penis or vagina, no anus or mouth, no eyes, ears, or any other opening, no fingers and toes and eventually no arms or legs: just a cocoon of pure purple flesh inside which my desire writhed like an unborn emperor butterfly or undead mummy.

The fact that my sexual imagination was so steeped in twice-told tales made it that much more shameful to me. Not only were my fantasies grotesque deviations from what was normal, they weren't even *mine*. They weren't even *me*. I was a stranger to myself, a character in someone else's story; my life, by which I mean not just my appearance but my name, last and first, my position in the Academy as laird among tenants, so patently denied me any status as an object of sexual desire that I could only be aroused either by replacing my body with an unmarked— unmarred—substitute, or else by amplifying my defect and imbuing it with totemic power, which power was invariably used to imprison me. The Academy had separated the sexual act from reproduction for a hundred years. Far from condemning homosexuality, the masters viewed it as a socially enlightened form of sexual activity, since it was guaranteed not to produce offspring (this, along with the robes and prohibition against "making," led to repeated charges that the school was a pederastic cult, despite the fact that sexual relationships between novices and masters were only permitted if initiated by the novice and he was, in accordance with the local age of consent, at least sixteen years old). But as in all else, the Academy taught that sex was an encounter between material beings. To cloak these beings' flesh in fantasy, in narrative—in, God forbid, *history*—was a denigration of the individuals involved. Don't misunderstand me. The Academy didn't teach that all beings are perfect as they are— one-legged, cross-eyed, fat as a boar. Perfection implied imperfection, and the Academy rejected both categories. Rather, it taught that all things merely are what they are. Regardless of what they had been or might become, nothing can negate or supersede their form at any given moment—and if the thing in question is a person, then the key to right living (happiness and sadness being two more states the Academy regards as illusions) is to acknowledge what you are—not your psychological *nature*, but your material *being*. I was a freak. I should accept that, and get on with life.

I was in the middle of violating this most fundamental of Academy tenets—for the third time that day—when the books arrived. My mother's shopping spree was into its second month. She'd been gone for five or six days on this particular occasion, and I hadn't showered in at least that long. God only knows what I smelled like. Well, no, pretty much anyone can guess what I smelled like: I smelled like dried sweat and dried semen, and a lot of both. It was spring in the South and I was fourteen and shoveling more loads a day than an earth mover at Ground Zero (9/11 was six years in the future, but the metaphor's just too good to pass up). The only reason I got dressed and came downstairs at all was because our regular UPS man carried a package in his brown shorts more interesting than anything he could have pulled out of his truck. But the heavy tire tread I'd heard on the driveway gravel wasn't UPS after all, but a big rig with a three-man crew, two boys two or three years older than me and a man in his thirties. The boys had already opened the truck's back panel by the time I got downstairs, already started rolling a set of identical boxes down one of those ramps composed of a series of metal-wheeled axles, which rattled so loudly as the boxes slid down them that the older man had to shout to be heard:

"Delibery for You—" He squinted. "Delibery for Yudas Stammers?"

Like almost everyone who meets me for the first time, the man did his best to stare directly into my right eye, and when I closed it he swayed a little as if he'd stepped off a merry-go-round.

"Please pardon our appearance while we renovate!"

The man tried to put his pen in my right hand but I reached for it with my left because, even though I'm right-handed, I'm also an asshole.

"Third floor. All the way in back, please. Breathe through your nose!" I called after him, then secreted myself in the first-floor bathroom to finish what I'd started.

But I was done before they were, and even after I'd showered, and jerked off again in the shower (my mother had a mentholated something or other that made it feel like I'd plunged my penis in an ice bath, inspiring a fantasy about a Neanderthal recovered from a glacier thawed by global warming, a low-browed hairy halfman whose penis curved like a mammoth's tusk, and, well, you can probably see where this is going), they were still at it when I came out, wrapped only in a towel because I could've sworn I heard my underwear *crack* when I tossed them on the floor, and even I couldn't bring myself to step back into them.

"Motorboat and titty fuck." It was a phrase I'd heard come out of a passing car a few days earlier, and though I wasn't entirely sure what it meant I'd been dying for an excuse to use it. "How many boxes *are* there?"

"Fifty," one of the boys said, doing his best not to stare at my chest, which looked as though I'd slipped one arm into a tattered flamenco blouse but left the other bare. "Five seventy, uh, five seven hunturd." He shrugged. "*Cinco ciento setenta y siete,*" he said, and carried his load up the stairs.

"What the hell is *in* them?" I asked the next boy, but he just shook his head.

"*No inglés.*"

"I don' know wha's in them," the older man said, coming in behind the boys, "but is sure as shit *heavy.*"

The return address on the shipping manifest was in Kansas (a state from which I'm pretty sure nothing good has ever emerged) and for the first time it occurred to me that the boxes might not have come from my mother. They were covered with a thick oily layer of dust, the kind of grimy sediment that takes years to build up, some all the way across the top but most just along one or two edges, as if the boxes had been crookedly stacked atop each other in one of those forgotten places that removes its contents not just from sight but from memory. I ripped one open, saw that it contained books. So did the next, and the next, and the next. I looked at the wall of boxes, which already covered most of the back wall of the third floor in a three-deep stack, and because that's how my mind works, I had to stop and count all the books in all the open boxes, which averaged twenty-eight per. I did the math. Someone had sent me something like fifteen *thousand* books. "*Muchacho,*" the second boy came up the stairs just then, "*su toalla, por favor,*" and I looked down and saw that it had fallen off.

It took the three men three more hours to unload the rest of the boxes, after which I tipped them a thousand dollars (each); it took me two weeks to unpack them, by the end of which I was convinced they'd belonged to my father. My mother had been home twice during that period, but I didn't ask her about the books and she didn't venture onto the third floor ("Sorry, I haven't had my shots") and it was only after I'd unpacked all the books, divided them by language and genre and alphabetized them, that I confronted her. She gasped when she saw them stacked around the perimeter of the room—the entire perimeter of the room, 314 stacks each almost seven feet tall, although even now I can't tell you the exact number because I came up with a different figure all four times I counted them, and there's a limit even to my OCDishness. Fifteen thousand plus or minus a hernia, that's all I can say. My mother tried to convince me that the books must have belonged to my great-uncle, but I pointed out that, in addition to the fact that there'd been no mention of even a single book in the inventory of his possessions, there was no record of an Anthony DeVine in the Academy's rolls. "You looked?" my mother said quickly, and even as I nodded she tried to backpedal. "How do you know they belonged to someone who went to the Academy? These are trade editions."

My mother was right: the books had been printed by commercial publishers, by which she meant that they hadn't been printed on the Academy's press like standard Academy texts. Even so, the collection sported a full complement of Greek, Latin, and Arabic classics in the original languages as well as in Academy-approved translation, along with highlights from Egyptian, Indian, and Chinese literature and an exhaustive survey of the world's religions—sacred texts, apocrypha, and commentary—along with an extensive catalog of European literature. The catalog ended conspicuously in 1896, and all the editions had been printed before 1981, the year I was born. The fact that the books had been purchased rather than made suggested that after the man in question had left Marcuse he'd replaced virtually every book that he'd abandoned along with my mother and their unborn child. But this was hardly a typical reading list. The breadth of the texts went far beyond the standard purview of an Academy education, and well into the Academy's version of advanced training. I.e.:

"He was studying to be a master."

"Who was studying to be a master," my mother said, not even trying to make it a question.

"My *father* was studying to be a master. Although I know he didn't make it, since there hasn't been a white master in at least fifty years."

"Sixty-nine," my mother said absently, picking up a copy of the *Metamorphoses* and thumbing through it even though she didn't have Latin. "I really don't know," she said then, putting the book back on the stack, and from her tone I could tell that she meant yes, but also that she didn't know.

"Jesus fuck. Is he"—I knew the answer but had to ask anyway—"still *alive?*"

"No," my mother said so quickly that it was tempting to think she was lying. "He really is dead," she said furiously, "but I guess that doesn't mean he's done fucking with me," and she turned for the stairs.

"I'm keeping them," I called after her, because even though that might seem obvious, one had either to claim things or reject them in the Stammerses' world, lest they be stolen from or thrust on you against your will.

My mother paused on the first stair below the landing, and when she turned back to me she had to look up because the difference in our height had become a matter of attitude rather than inches. She smiled one of those wistful half smiles that parents assume before they communicate a truth they know won't be believed until their children have suffered through an experience for themselves.

"You don't keep books like these. They keep you."

From another mother it would have been a sentimental comment, a platitude even: *Literature! The gift that keeps on giving!* But I could hear the warning in her voice, the trace of contempt, and even as she tried to scare me away from Academy pedagogy I wonder if she realized how much she sounded like a master.

What I am saying? This was Dixie Stammers. *Of course* she realized how much she sounded like a master.

SHE OFFERED TO buy me shelves, but I turned her down. I didn't want my father's books to read them. I wanted only to possess them, to build them into a bulwark against my mother and her designs for my life, whatever they had been, whatever they were still. That didn't mean I wanted to yield to my father. I didn't want to be an Academy believer, let alone a master. I only wanted to know what it meant to live circumscribed by such a particular cultural tradition and its even more esoteric application. I suppose reading his books was the most obvious way to arrive at that understanding, but it also exposed me to five thousand years of cultural drift, and despite my snottiness about Wye's high school faculty, I didn't think I possessed the mental equipment to resist that kind of mass, let alone make sense of it. So I opted for a more literal method of surrounding myself with my father's books:

I surrounded myself with my father's books.

I tore down the cardboard cell and replaced it with a twenty-five-foot-wide vortex composed of four spiraled wedges that came together near the middle of the room, so that four of the eight openings led to dead-ends (which caused my mother no end of consternation over the next three and a half years) while the other four led to my bed, which was just a mound of blankets and pillows and clothes at the spiral's hollow center. Can you visualize that? If not, here's a picture:

I experimented with different bond patterns before settling on the same stolid but solid Flemish bond in which the walls of the house had been laid, which, for those who are kin to neither brickmaker nor potter, consists of two rows of bricks (in my case books) laid next to each other and alternating spine out–base out–spine out–base out (or, in masonry terms, stretcher-header-stretcher-header), which seems only slightly clearer than the description of my book spiral, and makes me wonder if the editors of ◗ weren't right after all. At any rate, here's another picture:

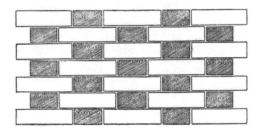

The headers, laid perpendicular to and across both rows of stretchers, join the two rows together, making them substantially more stable then a single wythe laid in running bond (think Legos), which has a tendency to fall over after it grows beyond five or six feet. The walls of my spiral reached all the way to the rafters, and at its center my semen-steeped nidus filled a ragged chamber about eight feet in diameter. At least four double rows of books stood between me and the rest of the room, and although the books didn't fit together as tightly as bricks—they weren't all the same size, after all—they were still more than thick enough to protect me against spying eyes and ears (though every once in a while something pounded the floor beneath me; I assume it was my mother, but couldn't be bothered to go downstairs and find out).

She'd settled into the first floor by then, although packages continued to arrive from as far afield as New York, London, Istanbul, complicating my original estimation of her perigrinations (or, you know, not: Dixie Stammers could work a catalog as well as any other well-heeled woman with a black card). The arrival of something as simple as a floor lamp or a Dresden doll necessitated a complete reassessment of the first floor's feng shui, and when I wasn't masturbating and I wasn't at school or the doctor's office I could hear the faint squeaks of couches and bureaus scratching up the heart-of-pine floorboards two stories below, and I don't know, maybe I was too busy jerking off or maybe I'm just a jerk, but it wasn't until spring was almost over that it finally dawned on me:

My mother wasn't making pots.

Hadn't, now that I thought about it, made a single pot since the *Art in America* article came out well over a year earlier.

There'd been gaps before, a month here, a month there, but she was never not working in one way or another, mixing glazes or seasoning clay or just playing with it, rolling out one eighteen-inch-long coil after another and braiding and unbraiding the coils with the fingers of one hand while the other completed sudoku puzzles at the rate of eight or ten per hour (lest you think she was truly a freak: she got all the puzzles wrong, and based on the way she filled in the boxes I'm pretty sure she had no idea how the game worked). But of the hundreds of boxes that arrived after we bought the Field, not one contained clay. Her smock hung on a peg beneath a shirt and a windbreaker and a jump rope and straw hat, the only evidence of its existence being the crumbs that cracked off its wrinkled surface whenever something new was hung over it. Her pots were harder to ignore.

Custom shelves stretched down one wall, each pot nestled in its own backlit cube like a skull in a reliquary. No matter where you were you could see them, or, rather, they could see you, *fui quod es, eris quod sum.* The only place to escape their *memento mori* admonition was outside. And at Potter's Field, outside meant for all intents and purposes the White Woman.

I said that the house sat about a half mile from the creek. But this isn't quite true, or, rather, isn't always true. For ten months of the year, yes, house and creek were separated by several hundred yards of rich black earth sloping almost imperceptibly toward one of the White Woman's many U-shaped turnarounds. But each March, when the spring melt came, and the spring rains, the stream widened dramatically, from the fifteen-foot-wide core meander to a glassy sheet more than a mile across, though rarely more than a foot or two deep. I was well aware of this, of course, but the full impact of the transformation never really impressed itself on me until the day I watched the stream double in size in less than four hours—then double again, and again, and again, and again, and again. And *again*, until a week or ten days after it started to swell the creek was licking at the foundation of the house (a neat line of moss, reaching nearly a foot up the fieldstone, suggested that in some years it did more than lick). The sheet of water lay on the land for five or six weeks, reflecting so vast a swath of sky that, staring into it from one of the third-floor windows, you could get disoriented and think you were tumbling into Heaven's opened vault. By the time my mother returned from her shopping spree the water had begun to retreat. Hummocked trails of twigs and leaves stretched across the mud in Art Nouveau ogees, and mosquito larvae and transparent tadpoles raced the sun's rays in the hundreds of puddles that dotted the flood plain like coins scattered from a giant's hand. My mother wandered the wrack, in rubbers first, then rain boots, then fisherman's waders, and often came home so covered in muck that she resembled a golem, the only white on her body the sheepish, wondrous smile she couldn't keep off her face.

For the life of me I couldn't understand her fascination. I mean, it was just weeds and water as far as the eye could see. Or, rather, reeds and water. When the White Woman resumed its flow in 1883, its return as mysterious as its disappearance, its waters were suffused with coal dust, and after several strike-outs Marcus's scientists finally hit on the then-novel solution of planting the entire course of the stream with phragmites, which left the flood plain a virtual monoculture: reeds and water, as I said, stretching from the foot of the mountains all the way to the Marcuse-Wye Road (which only Stammerses still call the Post Road), the glass-smooth surface broken only by the thin, whitened trunks of lodgepole pines poking up here and there like tapers on an emerald tablecloth.

But my mother was a Stammers and, God bless her, she gave the phragmites the Stammers due. She stripped its leaves and wove them together, into doilies first, then fans, then curtains and tablecloths and tents; then baskets whose first iterations were simply structured yoni that quickly evolved into two-handled amphorae so tightly woven they could hold water. She ordered a dozen Shaker chairs and ripped off their seats and recaned them herself, then hung the chairs on pegs and made new ones entirely from reeds, long-necked sacks that hung from the rafters as though a colony of orioles had moved in with her. She bored holes into harder reeds to make flutes, bound them together into mouth-organs, hung the organs outside (on ropes woven from reeds, natch) so that the wind blew through them with a sound like a slide-whistle orchestra. She even ground the shoots of young plants into a paste that she toasted and smeared on bread. She said it tasted like marshmallow but I refused to try it.

All this ended as quickly as it began when, one day in early June, ringing a cow bell like a leper, she braved the stairs to the third floor bearing a few stalks of a plant I didn't recognize, but clearly wasn't phragmites. The small, wispy stalks looked familiar though, pale green, with nascent umbels and threadlike, rubbery leaves—like fennel, though the roots showed no sign of a bulb. She held it to my nose. She hadn't bothered to shake the dirt off and that was what I smelled first, a solid odor, wet, feculent. Then a lighter tinge floated in, tart yet cool, almost mentholated, and my mouth watered with a remembered taste of potato salad, borscht, salmon, pickles. Lots and lots of pickles.

"Is it . . . dill?"

My mother smiled so brightly I might've won the county spelling bee.

"It's all over the back of the house. There must be a quarter acre. Strawberries too, though there aren't any ripe ones yet." She walked me to a window, pointed to the ground directly behind the house.

"Look."

I shrugged; looked; saw: green. Green and brown and . . . green and brown, all the way down to the stream, all the way across to the mountains.

My mother noticed my wandering eye and put her hand on

my cheek, angled my face down. "Here," she said, again indicating the land just behind the house.

She let her hand sit on my cheek, her finger tracing the outline of the purple finger that pressed against the corner of my mouth. The odor of dill and dirt filled my nostrils. It took an effort to focus, but when I did I still saw nothing besides green stalks, brown smudges, green leaves, brown smears. Green. Brown. Then a breeze swept across the flood plain and something flickered at the edges of my vision. An outline. A circle, the dark vegetation of my mother's dill and strawberries set off against the paler phragmites shoots that surrounded them. Once I'd seen it the border was as sharp as the moon's penumbra at full eclipse. I swallowed my gasp because I didn't want to give my mother the satisfaction. But she could tell I'd seen.

"I think it's the pit," she said in a hushed voice, as if describing an archaeological find. "Where they dug the clay for the bricks? It must've silted up during the floods and they turned it into the kitchen garden."

"Holy Nile River Delta, Batman!" I said so loudly that my mother took a step back and her hand finally left my cheek.

But now that she'd pointed it out it was all I could see. The circle was maybe twice as big as an above-ground swimming pool, nowhere near the quarter acre my mother had suggested, but even after the passage of a century and more—a hundred floods, a hundred summers and winters and who knows how many shortcakes and pies and creams and potato soups and salads—its edge was still clear, the delicate dark dill and strawberry already dwarfed by the new growth of phragmites surrounding it, yet remarkably inviolate, as if protected by a witch's chalk circle against the invading reeds.

I sniffed the dill in my mother's hand again, resisted the urge to bite it.

"Dill and strawberries?"

When she didn't answer I turned to face her. She was staring at the long curved tiers of books that spiraled in toward their hidden center.

"Flemish bond," she said, proudly but skeptically. Then: "You know I despise masonry? The idea of taking solid earth and puffing it up around empty space, making it hollow, dead . . ." She shuddered, as though the horror were self-evident. "And the sameness. The repetition. How do they live with it?" She laughed. "I know what you're thinking. You're thinking, Isn't that what *you* do? But it's the utility that terrifies me. To do the same mechanical task over and over because *you have to.*" And then, without any transition, in the same faint, proud voice with which she'd said "Flemish bond," as if I'd learned a lesson or earned a reward: "I suppose it's in your blood. You were conceived in a room lined with books, after all."

I waited for her to say that I was conceived in a room lined with *these* books, by which I mean that I waited for her to say my father's name. Because that's how she'd do it. Off the cuff. By-the-by. There's dill growing in the backyard. Your father's name was Master Moustache. There are also strawberries. But all she did was look down at the green stalk in her hand and start, as if she'd forgotten she was holding it.

"Dill was the most popular herb in the nineteenth century," she said as if she'd only just remembered, "and strawberries give fruit all season long. Great staples for an inn or roadhouse or—"

"Whorehouse," I said, though I was looking at my father's books when I said it. (Also: there really was a Master Moustache.

He was the Egyptian and Near East scholar for more than forty years.)

"One that served its pussy with a side of pie." She shrugged. "I'm sure there were other things. Potatoes. Corn. Beans. Tomatoes."

"Dick."

My mother didn't blink. "I'm guessing that was the masters' innovation."

"You'd think. But if there's a single unreconstructed pedophile among the whole lot, I haven't been able to sniff him out. Unlike you," I threw in, and waved a hand at the books to make sure she got it.

I expected another stone-faced reaction, perhaps an eye roll, maybe even a gasp. What I got was laughter. "Oh God, Judas, promise me you won't!" A green-pennanted wave at my spiral as she headed for the stairs. "A master! It'd be like sleeping with your own father!"

I woke the next morning to music floating up from the back of the house. A single track on repeat, my mother's agnostic falsetto warbling atop Clyde Orange's Pentecostal rasp:

"She's a brick. *House.* She's mighty mighty. She's letting it all hang out."

I endured three revolutions before I shuffled out of my maze and threw open a window, but when I looked down at my mother's magic circle my shout died in my throat. Where yesterday had been a delicate dark green disc, there was now a half moon of bare, black soil waxing rapidly toward the creek. A mound of greenery as big as a muskrat lodge lay to one side—all the dill and strawberries my mother'd been so excited about eighteen hours ago. She stood at the outer edge of the plot, pitchfork in hand, ankle deep in muck and covered by a straw hat, so that she couldn't have looked more like a human flower if she'd tried (from this angle especially, which made me wonder if I was the one she'd dressed for). She worked the pitchfork methodically, used weight rather than muscle to push the tines into the soil, then lift them out again. The exposed earth was dark as chocolate, as charcoal, so primordially black that it cried out for the scattering of seeds—the serpent's teeth from which Cadmus grew his Spartoi rather than the potatoes, corn, beans, and tomatoes my mother sowed over the course of the next few days in homage to the garden that might or might not have existed a century ago.

The whole enterprise was typically, ridiculously Stammers: my mother saw a plot of dill and strawberries she professed to love, and she dug it up. Of course she didn't see it that way. She wasn't "digging anything up." She was "gardening." But she wasn't just gardening: she was asserting her control over the land. Finding out not what it could do, but what she could make it do. By which I mean that the plump, ripe vegetables she produced interested her only in so far as they were proof of her mastery. Though I sometimes saw her pick a bean or peapod and munch on it as she wandered down to the creek, it seemed never to occur to her to bring her crops indoors, to cook them or serve them in a salad or sell them from a stand by the side of the road. (God knows she never offered me anything.) If her failure to harvest her crops wasn't proof enough that her motivation for working the earth had nothing to do with food, then the slabs of soil she began cutting from the ground before her first plantings flowered gave away the game. The cubes were a foot and a half on a side, probably weighed fifty pounds each, but she pulled them intact from the ground and slotted them into a wooden milk crate that she hauled into the house on a Radio Flyer. The wagon's plaintive squeaks echoed my confusion until she upended the crate on her potting table and wiggled its damp contents free in a chorus of farts, and I saw that it wasn't actually dirt she was harvesting, or just dirt: it was—drum roll, please!—clay. Clay mixed with a lot of stones and sticks and other organic matter, but clay nonetheless, darker than the kaolin she'd worked with all my life, and not nearly as dense, at least when she first harvested it, but still: clay.

A few days later I realized I'd made another mistake: it wasn't a milk crate she packed her harvest in, but a box she'd built based on the dimensions of Marcus's cubed cubits. I wondered if she was going to make bricks from them, like the people who'd built our house a hundred years ago, and she did indeed dry the blocks she dug up, only to dissolve them in water and run the slurry through a screen, repeating the process two or three times until half a cubic yard of black earth had been transformed into a golden-brown slab that looked less like a brick than a bar of jaggery: dozens of bars, which she stacked in the storage kiln in crisscrossed layers like ingots in a vault. ("It has to set, Jude, not sit. *Set.* I will give you ten thousand dollars to shave that skidmark off your lip.") The purer product lay farther down, and her holes grew five, six, seven feet deep, until they resembled (no doubt intentionally, c.f., "Potter's Field") a set of open graves. There were three pits by the end of that first summer, scattered inside the garden's circular border at right angles to each other, so that the plot had the look of a Kandinsky or Miró, red- and orange-dotted washes of green fenestrated by aggressive dark rectangles of negative space. The holes stole glimpses of the sky through the garden's foliage all summer and fall, then gaped starkly when winter came and the annuals died and the frozen moisture in the holes' walls glittered like icy asphalt until the spring flood swallowed everything the following March. When the water retreated in April the holes were filled with a soupy quicksand too soft to support a human step, and even after it dried the fill was too fine to be mined, but that much more fertile. My mother planted her vegetables in the new soil and shifted her spade a few feet over to harvest a fresh crop of clay, dissolved it and dried it and packed away the amber ingots in the broken kiln until, two years and four months after she'd last made a pot, she sat down at her slab of porphyry, switched on her halogen lamps, and, before the raptured, stoned gaze of the *Three by Stammers* crew, rolled out three pots in three days, numbers 124 through 126, each of which, when dried, fired, and glazed, was as perfect as, and perfectly identical to, the 123 that had preceded them. *Three by Stammers* had its premiere at Sundance, and even before the festival was over an anonymous benefactor had purchased the set for $5 million and bequeathed them to the Metropolitan Museum of Art, where they were displayed beside the 1200-year-old funerary casket that had inspired my mother to become a potter almost a quarter century earlier, and where, not quite three years later, a little over a month after she died and ten months before an outfit calling itself Clean Energy Solutions reopened the Magic Mountain Coalfield, all three pots—and all forty-five she made after them—disintegrated into dust.

4

A black cloud hung over the ruined remains of the Magic Mountains nearly two years after the last stick of dynamite had been
planted beneath the range. Depending on the wind, it sometimes
stretched for twenty-five or even thirty miles along the horizon,
yet there remained something ethereal about it, unreal, as if its
ombré tatters of soot and shadow were nothing more than a
dirty curtain that would at any moment blow aside, revealing
Appalachia's unsullied—unsulliable—vales and scarps and leas.
It was the cloud the muckrakers wrote about and the cartoonists
drew, the cloud and the tumulus of rubble it shrouded, and to
the degree that the Stammers family exists in the American
romance it was the cloud and the rubble that closed the mines,
and not the hundreds of black bodies that had died beneath
them. Marcus Stammers had defied God and defiled nature; had
been rebuked and reduced; had reformed and atoned. Everything after was coda, from the conservancy and the Academy to
Dixie and her pots and progeny.

But the truth is Marcus had been looking out on this ruin for
thirty years, and it was all but invisible to him. Though May 6,

1881—the day of the explosion—is almost always recorded as the date Stammers Coal ceased operations, in fact Marcus reopened the mines three weeks later and kept them going seven more months, until it became clear that shutting them down was the only way to keep the family fortune from falling into non-Stammers hands (and if that fortune was reckoned only in the millions earned during the second half of 1881, we would still have ranked as one of the wealthiest families in nineteenth-century America). No, what held Marcus's eye was something that *wasn't* there, namely, the White Woman and its vanished waters. The creek had always fascinated Marcus. In years gone by he had tried to find its source and failed; had tried to dam and divert its course and failed at that as well; had settled for excavating the Lake and stocking it like a private pond only to see that project, too, evaporate with the morning dew. Like a spurned but enlightened Lothario, he'd come to regard the White Woman with a grudging respect, and it struck him to the core to have it vanish "in such Preternatural Fashion," which enigmatic phrase might refer to the mystery of the creek's disappearance, or simply to the fact that it had stopped flowing without his permission.

Every morning during the second half of 1881 and all through 1882 he crabwalked onto the upper terrace, an eighty-three- and eighty-four-year-old emaciated opium eater leaning into the splayed crutches that had recently replaced his sticks. For two or three hours or the entire day he would stare down at the sperm-tailed muddy basin at the end of High Street, as if, like a lookout in the crow's nest of an ocean-going whaler, his peeled eyes must at last be rewarded with a geyser of spume. But all he saw, hour after hour, day after day, was the frayed coils of the waterless streambed shredding the coal-blackened flood plain like the welts of a cat-o'-nine-tails on a slave's back. A dense growth of moss and sedge had dulled the streambed's scar by the end of that first summer, though you could still make it out in the same way you could make out the circle of dill and strawberries behind the Field (or could until my mother dug them up anyway). To Marcus, it seemed as if nature was erasing the White Woman not just from the landscape but from memory and, half panicked and even more furious, he hired a small army of hydrologists, geologists, and engineers to find out what had caused the blockage. Decades after his death this team was ret-conned as the first step in some grand ecological/pedagogical master plan, but in fact it was another year before he began to restore the mountains themselves, another eight before he made any mention of the Academy. At the time he seems only to have wanted to assert his continued mastery, not just of his present domain, but past and future as well.

But nature continued to toy with him. For two years Marcus's scientists searched vainly for the source of the blockage, only to have the creek surreptitiously resume its flow beneath the spring melt of 1883. But now a new problem presented itself. The resurgent water flowed as powerfully as it had before its disappearance, but it returned suffused with an anthracitic particulate finer than truffle flakes. The flecks sparkled prettily as they bubbled out of the ground, but within a couple of miles the creek ran black as gunpowder tea. After ten it was sludgy as tar, and by the time it oozed into the lake was prone to combust. Filtering the sediment from its subterranean source was out of the question. At twelve cubic feet per second the White Woman barely qualifies as a second magnitude spring, but the discharge was still strong enough to prevent a diver from making it any-where close to the bottom of the well shaft. Nor could Marcus's team risk entry underground, lest the water burst into the mine and emerge from who knew which adit or air shaft. No, if the water was going to be cleaned, it had to happen on or near the surface. The narrowness of the well offered a logical focal point for their efforts, but every filtration system the scientists designed was overwhelmed by the sheer volume of solute and water. The sieves and screens and strainers gummed up within hours, and before they could be cleaned or changed were hurled from the shaft by the hydraulic force behind them. It took nearly four years for Marcus's men to hit on the idea of phragmites as a natural filter (if in fact they hit on anything: by all accounts the reeds sprang up of their own accord, and all Marcus's team did was notice that the water apppeared cleaner after it passed through them). In the inter-val—in the background, as it were, apparently as a kind of busywork—Marcus's workers had rebuilt all seven mountains to a uniform height of 1,900 feet, a gargantuan undertaking that seems only to have been done in a kind of nervous anticipation, to provide a more suitable backdrop for a body of water that was not yet, and might never be, clear enough to reflect it. Indeed, even after the phragmites had cleaned the water that rose from the spring, so much coal dust poured off the recreated moun-tains every time it rained that the reeds' benefit was rendered moot, and as far as I can tell this is the only thing that prompted Marcus to cover the camelbacked slag of the rebuilt range with five feet of soil dredged from the lake bed. The fertile mud was sown with a combination of deep-rooted bunchgrass and spreading grama to hold it in place, and, since trees would have sprung up anyway, Marcus took charge of them as well, ordering more than a quarter million saplings planted over the course of the next four years—a combination of longleaf, loblolly, and Sonderegger pine, mirroring what had been there before, though Marcus's choice seemed to have less to do with fidelity than convenience, since longleaf and loblolly and their Sonderegger offspring are among the most common trees in the region.

And so, by fits and starts and trial and error, the curtain of dust lifted and the moat-girded Magic Mountains materialized in its place, millions of years of geological activity compressed into a single decade of frenetic and, as far as I can tell, wholly orological unpremeditated activity. The pines were no taller than a teenaged boy in 1891, no thicker than that boy's wrist or ankle. From a distance—from Stammers Hall, presumably, or maybe a little lower down on High Street—they scored the hillsides like the individual hairs of a teenager's stubble. Or at least that's what they look like in three watercolors by Jorge Castell Davis, the Catalan-Canadian dendrologist who oversaw the reforesta tion project, as well as in about half a dozen cruder sketches in Marcus's diaries. Marcus was ninety-three by then. He had no expectation of seeing the trees achieve anything like their full growth, but he'd lived too long to feel any anxiety about this. Perhaps he was simply too impressed by what he'd pulled off. The size of the project was unimaginable, its cost incalculable. In fact, from an engineering standpoint it was pretty mundane. It was basically seven big piles of rock and dirt, differing little from the monuments constructed by North American mound builders five thousand years ago. It was only scale that made them unique. Imagine razing the whole of Manhattan island and restoring every one of its lost hills and streams and forests. Now:

double that. At its peak Marcus had more than six thousand men working on the project—50 percent more than he'd employed in the mines—and was estimated to have spent nearly $50 million on the job (in 1880s currency, mind you, or a cool billion in 2001 dollars), which amounted to about 95 percent of his fortune. If the final product was a little cartoonish, like early computer graphics—an indication of real things rather than a depiction of them—it still had the gasp-inducing flourish of a magician's trick. A flash, a puff of smoke, *et voilà*: the rabbit appears! Except in this case the flash was an explosion that killed 239 people and the rabbit was seventeen miles long and covered in 33,000 acres of wrinkled baize lanugo, which half-formed creature Marcus blithely handed off to his assistant while he turned his attention to his next trick.

That assistant was of course the Academy, whose paired mission statements—to "Perfect and Preserve Nature's Beauty" and "Brighten the Lot of the Darker Races"—reek of tongue-in-cheek hypocrisy. Even at this late date there's little evidence of enlightenment in Marcus's actions, let alone altruism. In 1891, when he had the school's articles of incorporation drawn up, he actually named it Mountebank Academy. He scratched the first word out later, scribbled "Lake" in its place, but didn't bother to order a clean draft of the document, which seems like a pretty good measure of his investment in the project. Though his "personal dispatches" (think of them as 19th-century analogues to the tweet, which he dashed off to whatever newspaper had earned his ire or admiration that day) made much of the fact that "23 or 24" of the first "noviciates" were the orphaned sons of the victims of the 1881 explosion, he failed to mention that all 307 members of the school's inaugural "corpus discipulus" had been his employees for years or even decades, a group of glorified field hands ranging from their teens to their fifties whose (halved) salaries were now called stipends, and whose six-day, sixty-hour work weeks had been extended by fifteen hours of "maieutic rehearsal," in which one can only assume that the call-and-response of the work song stood in for the traditional question-and-answer of the Socratic dialogue.

Even four years later, as the Academy's first class was "graduating" (read: getting fired), Marcus was still referring to the school as "gangue." A particularly charged word from a miner. He could have called it "binder," which refers to impurities within a seam, or "rider," a thin, often unprofitable layer of coal that runs above the primary deposit. But he chose "gangue," which refers to the commercially worthless material in which ore is found (although sometimes he used "goaf," which is basically gangue after the minerals have been extracted). The terms were dismissive, of course, but also conferred a kind of distinction, gave the extraneous matter a mental heft neither pickaxe nor TNT could destroy. If the gold wasn't present, the copper, the coal, the diamonds or bauxite or aluminum or mica, we wouldn't notice the earth and stone that surround it. But by its proximity to a desirable commodity gangue acquires, not utility, but meaning, just as goaf's negative aura adds another layer of significance to the orcs freed from its grasp, which in addition to being coal or copper or gold become also not-earth, not-stone; not-gangue, not-goaf.

Which only now makes me wonder if, instead of the hills and creek sparking Marcus's deathbed conversion, it might not have been the chance use of a pair of words—words that had been in his lexicon for more than three-quarters of a century, but had taken that long to impress their significance on his mind. Marcus had pulled millions of tons of coal from the earth, yet this was just a fraction of what he'd had to sift through to procure his wares. How absurd to think the rest merely incidental! He'd spent millions restoring the mountains, but had he done right in attempting to return them to their previous state? Their natural state? *Had* he returned them to a natural state, or had he unintentionally built a different kind of mine, one whose ore lacked the fungibility of coal, but whose potential energy was infinitely greater? And as he sat stiffly in the "wheel'd-chair" he had, at ninety-eight, finally surrendered to and contemplated his "jerry-rigg'd Megiddo" and its reflection in the stream he had (at least in his own version of things) pulled out of the earth like a thread of saffron from a crocus blossom, he found himself wondering not *if* this strange monument he'd made would endure after he was gone, but *what it meant* that it endured—*after he was gone.* And if we're to believe the evidence—which consists almost entirely of his own words, recorded in his diaries or in a pair of newspaper interviews he gave in the last nine weeks of his life— it was only then that he began to wonder if he'd made a mistake. Wondered if he'd treated nature as the gangue from which he extracted the ore of his experience—of his consciousness, of his self—when the truth is *nature mines us.* That, far from being perfectible, nature is by definition (*by nature*, duh) unchangeable, while civilization—culture itself—rather than humanity's greatest achievement, is, in nature's absence, so much deracinated goaf. The things we do in an effort to change the world *only change us.* But because we are an aspect of that same world, we, too, remain unchanged and unchangeable.

As satori goes, Great Grandpa Marcus's was unheralded and

as such (from the historian's point of view anyway, the biographer's, the novelist's), unsatisfying. Indeed, unbelievable, save for the fact that the evidence is recorded in a page-and-a-half diary entry dated "March 32, 1896" (April 1 obviously, as several outside sources confirmed, although no one knows if Marcus's error was intentional or accidental), in preternaturally lucid handwriting that *looks* like Marcus's, but like a perfected version of it. I mention this only because in recent years the majority of his diary entries had become unreadable, by which I mean not just not legible but *not writing*, the unconscious squorls and whirlihoops of a man whose opiated mind dances with word pictures that have no more connection to language than the helium in a balloon has to the child's finger around which the balloon's string is tied. We know from his valet's ledger that Marcus awoke that morning in a rave; that he took three times his usual dose of laudanum and chased it with two fingers of (Scotch, not American) whiskey; that he swept his glass from his lap table, bid pen, ink, and paper set in its place, then commanded his servant to "Fetch the Pyramid Builders," as he referred to the Academy's faculty. Except that morning he didn't call them "Builders." He called them "the Priesthood," and by the time they arrived he'd finished his epistle. Who knows, maybe someone transcribed Marcus's dictation as Zayd transcribed Mohammed's; maybe all Marcus did was repeat a revelation conveyed to him by his own Jibril. But whatever the source, whoever the scribe, the words that made it onto paper are undeniably his. The grammar and cadences are of a piece with fifty years of previous entries, not to mention the esoteric spelling (apostrophe-d instead of "-ed," "shun" for "tion," &c., &c.), and even if the *sense* of the sentences is utterly at odds with everything he ever said, the *sentience* behind them remains pure Marcus. A working-class dithyramb peppered with tautologies and *sesquipedalia verba* and the bloviated self-confidence that what he's saying is true *because he's the one saying it*. So inexorable was the connection between Marcus's desire and its appearance in the world that he'd come to regard his thoughts as tantamount to physical phenomena, which makes his final recursion that much more paradoxical. Because even as his last words repudiated everything he'd ever done, they were uttered with the pharaonic conviction that they would be enacted with the same slavish (sorry, but there's no other word for it) obedience that had rolled the Magic Mountains across the land like pastry dough, then puffed them back up like a clutch of dinner rolls.

The entry begins banally enough: "The only Constant is Change, yet Change is but Illusion." It's a measure of the (lack of) profundity of Marcus's thought that he seemed to have no idea he was riffing on someone else's idea, let alone whose. It closes, notoriously:

FROM — NOTHING

TAKE — NOTHING

MAKE — NOTHING

Marcus's valet records the hoarse rasp of the master chanting these words in his bedroom, alone at first, then gradually joined by his Ansar "til the chamber door fairly shook with the Quire" (which, as siccable statements go, is kind of brilliant). A century later 444 voices were still chanting those words every day at matins and complines—in Latin, natch, so they didn't sound quite so creepy. What they do sound like is Parmenides's "*nihil fit ex nihilo*," and while it's possible Marcus knew the phrase (he pulled "maieutic" out of his ass, after all, though he also got "noviciate" wrong), it's hard to imagine it was any more significant to him than those quaint Shakespearean idioms ("what the dickens?" "dead as a doornail," "in a pickle") that most people think originated with their country aunt or funny uncle. But how Marcus had arrived at these particular words and what he meant by them were never revealed. After his faculty left he passed the rest of the day "in speechless reverie, chuckling at unheard trifles, [and] plucking invisible moths from the air." On the morning of the 29th his valet was unable to awaken him, and after lying unmoving for four days, his face "as serene as St. Sebastian's," he sighed once, "like Heracles at the conclusion of his Twelfth Labor" (the observations are those of his eldest grandson, Hugh, who hadn't been invited to the "Unveiling," although he had been granted the title of second president of Lake Academy), and then, as all men do, even great ones, even devils, he died.

WELL. MOST PEOPLE think of childhood as a continual present, unfettered by complex memories, unconcerned with a nonexistent future, when it's more accurate to say that kids live in a continual past. I mean the immediate past, of course, not the "weight of heritage" or whatever you want to call the things I've been writing about here, but in my case the two were indistinguishable. From my first word to my first poo to my first day at school, every milestone occurred in an atmosphere steeped in Marcus's legacy and shadowed by my mother's genius, so that learning how to be a person was, for all intents and purposes, learning how to be a Stammers. But children don't learn like adults. They absorb information in a fugue state in which knowledge isn't so much memorized as embodied in words and actions repeated over and over. It would be a mistake, however, to think of these repetitions as recreations of the instantiating experience. They are instead *the same experience*, time dragged forward with no regard for clocks or calendars. And unlike adults, whose more developed memories resignify even the most routine activity (usually by getting bored), children suffer no diminution of return. The thousandth game of fort-da is as pleasurable as the first, but *only if the re-enactment is perfect*. A single deviation provokes a temper tantrum; too many and the game loses its appeal. Certainly cleaning worked that way for me. I behaved as if I were following a script I'd written, but the truth is *the script wrote me*, guided me like the rails carrying a roller coaster, which, however thrilling the ride, is always the same ride. Which is why, when new elements were introduced—the flood of visitors who invaded our home, and the pots carried out like arks to a hidden altar—the apartment no longer felt, not clean, but *cleanable*.

No doubt if it hadn't been my mother's career it would've been something else. Puberty probably, or some more random event: a car accident or tornado, a tender word from one of the other novices or pornographic configuration that called into question everything I thought I'd figured out about human connection, physical or otherwise. Which is to say: at a certain point history exhausts itself and you find yourself in the present. You find yourself *in the world*, and have to start living your life. *You find yourself*—a Stammers, a boy, a freak, abandoned—and have to make a life out of what you've got. What you are. Though I made a few desultory attempts to keep house after my mother returned from her shopping spree, I knew I was playing a waiting game—in part because I didn't know what else to do, but mostly because it's what I thought she was doing. But however rigidly precise Dixie Stammers's potting technique was, it wasn't, like cleaning was for me, a ritual. It wasn't magic. The pots had to be unvarying, but the process of making them did not. If the initial method lost its charm, its challenge, she had only to find a new way to work. And this she surely did. But two years after we moved to Potter's Field I could no longer pretend that the change it represented had ever been anything other than wishful thinking on my part, or cynical manipulation on my mother's. Yes, she was making pots as she had during my early childhood, and yes, the number of visitors to our home slowed as their price skyrocketed. But her process was if anything more insular and time-consuming than it had been before, her clients infinitely more demanding. They showed up only once every month or two, but they came with retinues now, of assistants, lovers, art buyers, gawkers, expected dinner or at least drinks, and often spent the night (or several nights), often on the second floor, in a row of rusted wrought-iron beds that stretched down one wall like a noir vision of a syphilis ward, but just as often on the first, which is to say, in my mother's bed (which, unlike her bedroom on High Street, was cordoned off from the rest of the house by neither door nor wall nor curtain). But it was only when she sat for *Three by Stammers* and dredged up her new pots like a Scheherazadean goldpanner that I understood: she could keep this up forever, and I would never be anything more than spectator. I would have to find something besides cleaning to while away the time. Something, dare I say, dirty.

In keeping with family tradition, I tried the creek first. I dug a machete from one of the boxes on the second floor (because of course Dixie Stammers owned a machete, owned—*of course*—four), hacked my way through the reeds to the creek's central channel, tottered over the water on one of the fallen pines, fell into the water and nearly cut my ear off (no, really: there was blood), crawled out of the water on the far side, and hacked my way to the mountain beyond. Up close the Capitoline's brown-needled carpet was all dimples and bubbles, with ferns clotting the hollows and blue-green moss clinging to the sides of exposed rock. From across the flood plain the pine trees seemed to crowd each other like a concert audience, but in fact they stood at arm's length one from the next, and here and there the rock had fallen away as the fill settled, leaving tangled networks of roots crookedly tented over jagged voids. (Think those walking trees in Tolkien, or Louise Bourgeois's spiders, though what they reminded *me* of was Great Grandpa Marcus: of his staves and swayback and Thomas Nast's caricature of him; of his hubris and folly.) No doubt ten- or eleven-year-old me would've been enraptured by the mangafied surreality of the environment, but fifteen-year-old me knew that whatever I was looking for, it wasn't there. I devoted approximately sixty seconds to contemplating the crowning achievement of my great-great-great-great-great-grand-father's life, whizzed on a longleaf (I dunno, maybe it was a Sonderegger), then turned around and made my way back to the Field, then hopped on my Vespa and took off. I mean, we lived on a *highway*, for Pete's sake. An abandoned highway maybe—the Post Road, which floods out at least once a decade, was superseded in the late seventies by the interstate on the north side of the conservancy—but as it turned out the dearth of traffic was advantage rather than impediment. Sex rarely seeks out bright lights, after all, except maybe in porn.

State Comfort Station NE-28 had been built in the 1910s, when "motoring" was still considered more of an edifying novelty than a means of practical transportation. Its six acres had been as landscaped as a city park, including a pond fed by a canal off the White Woman and a lawn big enough for badminton and croquet. The lawn had long since been overrun by hackberry and sumac and the pond had silted up, though you could still tell where it had been by the stand of silver-barked poplars that grew amid the elms; while up front the rose of Sharon hedge that shielded the rest stop from (now largely nonexistent) traffic had turned into a kudzu-draped wall that completely blocked any view of the facilities from the road. The original building, with its service station and convenience store and cafe, had been torn down in the early '60s. Its more modest replacement housed nothing besides a pair of restrooms fronted by a narrow vestibule, but the structure itself was one of those happy marriages of vernacular architecture and midcentury forms. Its end walls were built of local graywacke fashioned into a pair of dry-stone buttresses, between which hung a steeply angled roof whose front pitch soared nearly twenty feet over a forward-leaning glass checkerboard that offered up a picture-perfect view of Marcuse and Inverna and the shining black roof of Stammers Hall at its apex—or would have, if half the panels hadn't been replaced by plywood at some point in the distant past (one sported a Perot-Stockdale sticker). What glass remained was streaked with spraypaint and countless t.p. bombs splatted and dried into fist-sized meringues. The vandalism reminded me of my mother's comment about the unbroken windows at Potter's Field, which is to say that somehow I knew the damage hadn't been done by locals—that the people who came here came from somewhere else, for something they couldn't get where they lived. But what really drew me in was the smell: a stockyard bouquet of ammonia and sulfur made all the more palpable by a perpetual fog of Lysol. My mother's cleaning fetish didn't extend to her environs, but she *hated* bad odors—said they got into the clay, rendering vitrification unstable—and the first time I set foot in that rank cave my eyes watered and my penis twitched, because I knew I'd found a place that excluded her as surely as Potter's Field excluded me.

Swallows darted in and out of a gap between a rotting panel and the frame into which it had been wedged. Dozens of mud nests clung to the exposed beams of the canted roof, splattered shit and feathers and the occasional corpse dotted the floor. Grimy swirls on the cracked terrazzo testified that someone was assigned the task of maintaining the facility (a Tuesday-Friday detail, I learned later) but it was clear that no one checked the cleaner's work. Even so, there were links to the outside world: a condom dispenser in the men's room, a tampon dispenser in the women's, both offering a variety of brands promising safety, comfort, and, ironically given the context, hygiene. A vending machine offered soda and water, both locally bottled. A pair of rickety wire racks displayed pamphlets advertising nearby attractions: my great-great-great-great-great-grandfather's mines, my great-great-great-great-great-grandfather's school, an otherwise nondescript house that had been a stop on the Underground Railroad and three more that had housed this or that Confederate "hero." Despite all this it was clear the rest stop had slipped from local consciousness. The heavy air breathed of the forgotten, the abandoned, and, inevitably, the illicit. Later I would learn that what I'd thought was Lysol was really stale poppers, but at the time all I knew was that the twitch in my stiffening penis was back, and more insistent this time.

Nervously, and chastising myself for being nervous—it was a public facility, after all—I ventured into the men's room. The stench was worse in there (although not as bad as in the women's room, which was regularly fouled to drive them away) and I was drawn in as if on a wire. Three crookedly hung urinals lined one wall, two at adult height, one set closer to the floor. Three stalls stood opposite, their metal frames and doors so dented they looked as though they'd weathered an earthquake or stampede. Graffiti had accreted on these bent canvases in layers from the forlorn to the satiric to the disgusted and faux-disgusted, the ignorant and confused and illiterate. It clung to the crooked fractals in a palimpsest of lust that could be rendered in standard English only at the expense of a hieroglyphic anxiety vested with at least as much significance as the words themselves. I AM THE ONLY ONE someone had scratched into the paint with the point of a pin, over which someone had written FUCK YOU FAGGOT!!! twenty-seven times with black marker, only to have someone else come along and cross out each and every YOU and replace it with ME in blue ballpoint. This same person, or another person with another blue ballpoint, had altered the original I AM THE ONLY ONE to read I AM THE LONLY ONE, to which someone else had drawn an arrowed note that read ITS LONELY COCKSUCKER, prompting someone else to write IT'S "IT'S," IDIOT. And this was just one of scores of impastoed narratives, all of them testifying to the mixture of lust and hatred that permeated the room as palpably as the smell of the toilets,

a shit-spiked perfume so insistent and isolating—insulating—
that before I'd finished untangling that first missive my penis
was fully erect, and as soon as I saw HOT 15 YR OLD BOI WILL
SUK YOUR DIK 564-2319 it was out of my pants. My first time at
the rest stop I jerked off to

HERE EVERY WEDS 6 PM LATIN HOT MOUTH TIGHT
HOLE USE ME
    LOOKIN FOR A FAGGOT TO EAT MY HOLE—"BIG" JIM
    TIME ME UP RAPE ME PISS ON ME BEAT SHIT OUT OF
ME DUMP ME IN THE CREEK I WANT TO BE A STATISTIC
    WHERE R ALL THE HORNY TRUCKERS THIS WKEND?
(11/4/92)
    STEVEY—TAKES IT UP THE BUTT, ALWAYS CLEAN
    WHO GAVE ME AIDS? I WANNA TO RETURN THE FAVOR

There was no editing this porn story, which was even more
random than those chains of fetishistically linked homepages
we used to navigate in the nineties, in which three or four
clicks could take you from a surfer-looking twink whose rep tie
had been pulled backwards like a dog's leash to an actual dog
fucking an actual man who was actually enjoying it. No way to
transcribe it or represent it either. Even if you surrounded
yourself with lifesize pictures of all four walls you'd still miss
the squeak of shoes over sticky tiles, the clammy breath of toilet water a few inches below your balls, and of course the
smells: of sweat, of cum, of piss, but especially of shit, which
had seeped into the drywall like an old coffee pot whose glass
has gone irremediably brown. Nor were the messages limited
to homosexual expressions of desire or contempt. There were

a few half-hearted, almost defensive heterosexual posts (IF YOU EVER GET TIRED OF SHIT ON YOUR DICK CALL MONICA), many of which had been tagged with comments like UR NOT FOOLING ANYONE and I TAKE CARE OF DICK BETTER THAN ANY WOMAN EVER COULD. A lot of stuff about "niggers" too, most of it so theatrically vitriolic that I wondered if something about our helplessness before the biomechanics of urination, defecation, and copulation brought out the hatred in people, or the comedian. NIGGER WIMMIN TAKE IT UP THE ARSE someone had written, to which someone had appended SO DO NIGGER MEN, YOU (LIMEY?) FAGGOT. But it was Jews who, if not as heavily represented, came in for the most inspired epithets, or at any rate the most elaborate. STOP THE WORLDWIDE JEWISH CON-SPIRICY someone had written, and Q: WHEN CAN A CATHOLIC FUCK A JEW? A: ONLY ON ASH WEDNESDAY. There were a few HEIL HITLERs scattered around and a lot more 88s, so many swastikas that that they spun like pinwheels before my slitted eyes. Some energetic liberal had written ANTISEMITIC and drawn lines to a dozen different comments about Jews, Israel, the Holocaust, Nazism, and one lone FREE PALESTINE! graffito, the tentacles reaching out in all directions like a genetically enhanced octopus, snaking around this expression of gut-deep contempt or that paean to thwarted love, and as it shimmied before my watering eyes I suddenly remembered that octopi reproduce only once: the female secludes herself in a crevice, lays her eggs, and dies, whereupon the hatching babies eat first each other and then their mother before the victorious canni-bals finally venture out into the world. EAT ME flashed on one wall, EAT ME on another, EAT ME EAT ME EAT ME, and then, with a jagged wheeze—I think I'd actually forgotten I was masturbating—I came, ropes of semen splatting just to the right of a vertical graffito that read

I

LOVE

DICK

before sliding down to reveal

I

LOVE **EMILY**

DICKINSON

the right-hand letters written in heavier ink than those on the left—which is to say, added by someone I just *knew* was a novice at the Academy—and it wasn't until I finished laughing that I heard labored breathing coming from the stall next to mine.

I jerked toward the sound, only to be greeted by the purple smear of my distorted face in the bulbous chrome cover of the toilet paper dispenser. A set of scrapes traced a rusty rainbow on the wall, as if the dispenser had been rotated up and back a thousand times, and even as one part of my brain assumed that this was how the dispenser was refilled another part was sending a hand out to—

—but when my right hand came into view I saw that it was as burgundy-blotched as my left. My eyes dropped to my crotch, which was still uncovered, by cloth anyway, but my penis, which was normally only pinstriped by three thick purple lines, was now sheathed in a dark film of blood, and just looking at it brought to mind the pain from the places where the skin had torn along the edges of my birthmark from too-vigorous tugging. But even as I winced at the remembered pain, I remembered also ignoring the pain while I masturbated, remembered maybe even enjoying it in the same way I enjoyed the cesspool stink, because it expanded the corporeal reality of what I was reading, let me feel as if the words darting around my head issued from the mouth of a man in the stall with me, a real man whose real teeth chewed at my penis until it bled, and of course it didn't make sense, how could even the most gifted cocksucker spew all this bigoted claptrap if my dick was in his mouth, but that was where my—

—and then the door of the right-hand stall creaked open and I shoved the toilet paper dispenser up on its axle to reveal a hole about as big around as a coffee cup through which I glimpsed the gaudily embroidered back pocket of a pair of jeans slipping out of the stall, followed by the sound of footsteps squelching on the tiles as their wearer hustled out of the restroom.

I let him go. I mean, I probably couldn't have stopped him, but it didn't occur to me to try. I'd never heard of a glory hole before, but some things you recognize instinctively. The edge of the hole looked jagged, but when I ran a finger over the folded metal the bumps were as smooth as keloids, and even though it was obvious they'd been filed down with some kind of rasp I let myself imagine that the metal had been abraded—eroded, as if the softening had occurred over a geological span—by the back-and-forth motion of countless cocks. When I looked to my left I saw a second hole on the opposite wall, its far side covered by a metal patch that was presumably the back of the next stall's dispenser. My left hand reached out, and then each arm was hanging off a socketed wall, I was still sitting down but it felt as though I dangled between a pair of buildings like an avatar in a video game, which is to say I knew there was something perilous about my position, something that bespoke mortal danger, but the threat felt contingent, as if, if I fell to my death, all I'd have to do is boot up my next life and who knows, maybe it would work out better.

Later on I imagined the suspension differently, not as a kid hanging from monkey bars but as a pig on a spit, run through from mouth to tail and revolving slowly as its flesh melted inside its skin. I never did manage the turn (though I tried, believe me, and somewhere there's a dude with a bruised dick who'll back me up) but I got speared more times than I can count, sometimes one end, sometimes the other, sometimes both, and when that happened I found that if I jammed my mouth and ass against opposite walls and braced the muscles of my neck and back and tightened my abs until my spine extended an extra half inch I was able to lift one foot off the ground and hook the knee over an elbow, then lift the other foot up and hook it over *its* elbow, and then, lips glued to one wall, ass sealed to the other, I was less pig on a spit than an extension of the stall itself, of the building, of the mountains from which its stones had been mined, and as I writhed between the pistons driving into me fore and aft I imagined them plunging deeper and deeper, John Henry diving in from one end, the steam engine boring from the other, until in an apotheosis of penetration they opened a tunnel all the way through my body, a mineshaft maybe (I was a Stammers, after all), or maybe a road, but I liked to imagine it as a qanat, a hundred-mile-long tube following the rise and fall of intestine and esophagus until the liquids coursing through me reached equilibrium and filled my gullet like the cistern of some ancient city.

Because even as they cored me they were rebuilding me. ("Shaft": it's its own antonym, a hollow tube, a solid rod, and "cleave" too, slicing open and sealing together.) The naive boy these men excavated was replaced with a worldly adolescent who, from the outside, still looked the same—still lurked in the back of classrooms, not because he was hiding, but because he wanted to make a quick getaway; still averted his gaze when he caught people staring, but smugly, rather than shamefully. (I almost wrote "shamefacedly" but that seems too on the nose, even for me.) I was being remade from the inside out, and if the gawkers didn't register my metamorphosis it was only because they were too distracted by "the man that clothes me," as Jesus told Judas, to see through to the godhead beneath. But at the rest stop I had only to lean toward the hole on the right side of the stall and present that side of my face to whomever was looking, and whether I was as beautiful as my mother liked to say didn't matter: I was fifteen, sixteen, seventeen years old, and any man who tells you he doesn't want to fuck a teenager is a straight-up liar. I wore a hoodie to obscure my face and long-tailed shirts to cover the stains on my lower back, kept my ass centered over the hole on the left side of the stall, buttocks pulled open so that the purple smear of my birthmark blended with pink stretched skin before disappearing into my anus, and I always kept myself lubed with the cocoa butter or bacon grease or Bigeloil I'd once rubbed into my birthmark, and also, after an hour or three, the jizz of the one or two men a day who were willing to stick their dicks through a hole in a wall into the ass of an otherwise unseen boy on the far side. Oh, I was invisible to them, no doubt, but I was also invisible to myself. I was nothing but mouth and asshole; and the fifteen square feet of skin that connected them, whether purple or pale, was nothing more than gangue, there to be ignored or plowed through, and afterwards discarded as goaf.

And over everything and through it, supporting it, infusing it, concealing and transforming and ultimately drowning it: the smell of shit, as thick as the humidity on a hundred-degree day. More than once as I waited in the center stall I heard footsteps enter the men's room, followed by a muttered "Lord Jesus give me strength!" and the feet hurrying back the way they'd come. And not just the smell. Shit was visible everywhere, from the floaters dissolving in tea-colored water to the tread marks on the cracked tile to the smears fingerpainted on the stall by someone who found himself without toilet paper or, who knows, just didn't want to use any. Someone who felt compelled to acknowledge the *sine qua non* of our love nest, maybe, or protest it—in there there wasn't much difference. I visited the rest stop almost every day for three years and the smell never once failed to take me by surprise. No matter how much I steeled myself for it, it brought the gorge to my throat and tears to my eyes. But I also took refuge in it, because I knew it was the miasma as much as the isolation that made the rest stop the haven it was. There were days when no one showed up and it would be me and an empty stall, and after a few futile hours the stink would overpower not just my senses but my consciousness, until I had to run home and scrub myself inside and out with a self-hating flagellation that would've made my mother proud. Other times it vanished from my awareness. When, say, I heard the tentative tread of prospective trade—the probing steps, as if the filthy tiles might collapse beneath his feet, the exploratory push at a stall door, the tight inhalation when he saw the open glory hole and understood that he was getting lucky today—or when my eyes were closed and a dick filled my mouth or my ass. But there were also times when I was caught up in a perfect double-ended in-out groove and would suddenly realize I was smelling shit. Not just smelling it but tasting it, savoring it, gulping it down with the cock in my mouth or kegeling it into my rectum with the dick that was plowing me, and even as part of me trembled with self-loathing another part glutted in the foulness, which stood as a negation of everything culture is supposed to do, to mean, and as such imbued me with a feeling of world-destroying power— the power of a Khan, a Napoleon, a Hitler. Because it was *my* mouth and *my* ass that held the men on either side of the walls. They were smelling what I was smelling and were as repulsed as I was, at it and at themselves, but they stayed anyway, because they couldn't get enough of *me*.

Which makes me wonder that it took so long before one of them made a serious effort to talk to me. Or, you know, not. By the late '90s cottaging had become an anachronism in the US. In the few places it persisted it was mostly a nostalgic act, its clandestine aspect recast not as necessity against homophobia but protest against heteronormativity. But the South's always lagged behind the rest of the country when it comes to questions of identity, not to mention liberation. If we have a greater tolerance for "eccentricity" than the puritanical, conformist North, that clemency's only granted if the weirdness comes across as über-mannish individuality or infantile weakness rather than learned, i.e., collective behavior. Isolated freaks are cool, in other words, but anything that smacks of tribalism has to be destroyed. My tricks were probably closet cases is what I'm saying. It wasn't that they didn't want to talk to me. They didn't want to be talked to—to be outed to themselves, let alone society, as faggots—and once they'd shot their loads shame and disgust hurried most of them from the rest stop with the same urgency with which lust had dragged them there. A few guys tried, of course. Would lean forward and smile at me through the glory hole, or, if I closed the dispenser on them, climb on the toilet and look down at me over the edge of the stall, but I'd just pull my hood further over my face and hunch over with my hands in my pockets until the smell drove them away. Sometimes all they wanted was for me to give them my dick as they'd given me theirs, but that was as impossible as showing them my face (although occasionally someone pressed his ass blindly against the opening and I got to fuck him). But one day, after who knows how many months and how many men, a voice floated through the hole without the intrusion of a face.

"Hey, Tuesday."

I jerked back, even though I could see nothing through the hole besides the far wall. It *was* Tuesday. I always went to the rest stop Tuesday after classes, which let out late, at four. The cleaner would have been there earlier in the day, and if someone wasn't already waiting I took a few minutes to piss on the floor and clog the johns with toilet paper and maybe even leave a mark of my own. But I also went to the rest stop every Wednesday, and Thursday, and Friday-Saturday-Sunday-Monday, and what my partner was really telling me was that *he* was the Tuesday regular. Which shouldn't have surprised me but did, and it was wonder as much as anything else that prompted my reply.

"Hey."

"It speaks!" the voice laughed. Just to spite him I didn't answer.

"You suck dick like no one I've ever met before. It's like you're trying to *merge* with it."

I swallowed a snort. "This isn't a play by Edward Albee. Say what you mean. Say what you want."

"Duh. I want you."

"Unless there's someone else in there, you just had me."

"Now who's talking like a play? I want all of you. Not just your mouth."

"You want the other end, go to the other stall. That's how it works."

"I know you got your rules. Your, whatever, system. I can even admire it in a way. But don't you ever want to lay down next to a whole man, feel more of him than just his dick?"

Mostly I wanted to correct his grammar, but even as he spoke my hand was fiddling with my penis, which was as sticky and limp as a shrimp pulled from the muck, but also twitching with faint signs of life. It's been decades since I was a teenager, but I still miss the recovery time.

"I ain't bad-looking. Everything's still where it's supposed to be. Mostly."

The man's pubic hair was as gray and threadbare as old bed sheets (as my bed sheets anyway), and when sometimes I pulled back for breath I caught glimpses of a stomach that was flat but soft—not soft really, but rippled, like a poorly hung tapestry that's begun to sag under its own weight. That didn't turn me off exactly, but I had no desire to see what it was connected to. The man-breasts drooping off the ribs like discarded coffee filters or the skinny legs with shiny sandbars at thigh and calf where the hair had been abraded away by pilling polyester. And of course if I was seeing the failings of *his* body, he was seeing mine, and somehow I knew that if even one person rejected me because of my birthmark, the illusion of my desirability would be shattered. The rest stop would become as useless to me as my brooms and mops and scrub brushes, and god only knew where I'd go from there.

"Yeah, you probably want someone your own age. I would too."

You *do* too, I thought, but that wasn't fair. For all I knew he'd fuck a sixty-year-old if that's what was waiting for him. Whereas I was terrified of fucking someone my age, couldn't begin to contemplate a sexual exchange based on parity, let alone mutual desire. But even so, my dick was fully erect again.

"You ever try the Academy?"

I'd love to tell you I came when he mentioned the Academy, but that's not exactly what happened. What happened was my vision narrowed, my ears rang, the toilet beneath my ass disappeared and I was four years old, sitting on the edge of one of my mother's pots and moving my bowels so she could check for blood, and out of nowhere I remembered that that's why she'd made her first pot all those years ago—so that she could take care of me—and then the pot opened up and swallowed me in a pool of my own excreta. *That's* when I came.

"The Academy's a school," I said when I could speak again.

"Holy crap. You just shot another load, didn't you? How young *are* you?"

"A boarding school. You prolly need ID to get into the dorms."

An ID card was no more welcome at the Academy than a branding iron and the Foundry's less dorm than harem, but I thought it was a pretty good improvisation under the circumstances. And that "prolly"? I should be on the stage.

"Don't need no ID card. Don't need to go to the dorm either. There's a spot in the library. Basement bathroom."

"There's no bathroom in the basement of the library."

"You sure you're not a student there? Whatever. All the way in back. Behind the stacks. No one ever goes there except to go there, if you know what I mean."

"Whatever, Edward Albee," I said, but I was trying to picture the basement of Stammers Hall, which I hadn't been down to in years. The family papers were down there somewhere, including the mining archives, which was probably why I never went. Or maybe it was because it was just a basement full of old books, and I already had all the books I'd ever need at the Field.

"If this was an Albee play," the man said, "we'd've been talking to each other through this glory hole for the past nine months. We'd've invented tortured pasts for each other, one violent, the other lonely, but both full of self-hatred, so that even though we made out like it was the world that had left us emotionally crippled, it would be obvious to anyone watching that we were really doing it to ourselves."

"And when we finally saw each other we would've been disappointed," I said, wondering if *he* was the Academy man. "Also, that sounds more like Genet, or maybe Manuel Puig."

"Hey, you ever think maybe people don't sound like plays? Plays sound like people?"

"Aaaaand scene."

"Whatever, kid. You tough, I get it. But you ever get tired of sitting on a shit pot when you suck dick, check out the bathroom in that library. At least they keep it clean."

And no, he didn't say "shit pot." I made that up. But it's what he meant, even if he didn't know it.

5

And time continued to pass. The present, once acknowledged, refuses to stick around, but rushes by like Heraclitus's river. The three and a half years my mother and I lived at the Field together are mostly a blur, of books and dicks, of pots and floods, and often when I try to zero in on one experience it dissolves into all the others, white penises on brown bodies, Gilgamesh popping up in *Song of Myself* to spout lovelorn rubaiyat, a succession of purple orbs bowling over a glassy stream before knocking down the mountains massed on the other side, which explode in a shower of dollar bills and copper coins.

More distinct are the things I *wasn't* obsessed with, the things I took for granted, like the flowers that showed up with each spring's flood: sunflowers one year; snapdragons the next, their orange blooms shimmering behind the wings of hummingbirds we'd also never seen before and never saw again; or a scattering of poppies that dotted the phragmites like the smears of blood from a coyote's meal (prompting my mother to look in the direction of Wye, six miles north, and say, "Someone's running an opium den out of their basement"). The flowers thrived for a season, only to be washed away by the following year's flood. Trees popped up too, at the edge of the phragmites, but most couldn't survive the acid in the soil and annual inundations, and even more were killed when the masters burned off the reeds every few years. The fate of the few that endured long enough to grow bark, to cast shade, to house a bird's nest or squirrel or possum or raccoon was evident in the whitened trunks that lay across the streambed—like sutures, my mother said once, sealing some ancient wound (never mind that in almost every other regard she spoke of the White Woman as progenitive, catalytic, nurturing), whereas I saw them less grandly as laces, of shoes or a corset or whatever else you tie up temporarily. Something utilitarian but also incidental, so that if they came unraveled (and every spring a few more washed away, ended up wedged in or across the streambed or lodged under the dock behind the Foundry) nothing terrible would happen, because their bond was never meant to be permanent. The creek had disappeared once, after all, and made no promises when it returned.

I remember the January afternoon in the winter of 1996 when Master Grissom deigned to acknowledge my request to begin the "Parable of the Man Lost in the Snow," the elenctic allegory which, though never actually discussed in class, still dominated both years of fifth form. I knew it was coming, of course. Most of lower fifth was already at it, for one thing, and, for another, my mother dated Gaius's disappearance to the parable's conclusion (which, if he did in fact claim that he had to "find his own path," gives his parting words nihilistic, if not simply suicidal, overtones). And as skeptical as I was of Academy pedagogy, I was still a little excited. I felt I was beginning a rite of passage, like a pork-loving, shiksa-dating Jewish teenager who nevertheless takes the time to memorize the Hebrew for his bar mitzvah—but whatever discoveries I might've made were forgone when, that evening, my mother saw me reading "To Build a Fire" and, sussing the sitch, gave away the parable's secret, which pissed me off but touched me too, a little, because I knew she'd played spoiler so I wouldn't run away like her brother.

I remember a January or February night the same year, when I snuck into the house in the wee hours and looked out my window to see no fewer than twenty-two deer feasting on corn stalks in my mother's garden—twenty-two deer and, towering over them like a giant among dwarfs, one enormous moose, who worked his way down the rows like a king greeting peasants, his cello-sized head reaching over the backs of does to cherry pick the ears at the tops of the stalks, his enormous rack, which looked in the moonlight like the whitened skeleton of some long-extinct cephalopod, sweeping a ten-pointed buck out of his way with the gentleness only the truly strong can muster. My mother burst that bubble too. "There isn't a moose for a thousand miles," she told me the following morning. "Not out of a zoo anyway. Tell me you're not doing drugs." And indeed, when I went out to the garden the only thing I found was a dead nutria, which had fallen into one of my mother's pits who knows how long ago, and starved or frozen before it could dig its way out.

And I remember an afternoon the following summer when my mother called me as I was hopping on my Vespa and dragged me out to what I'd always thought was nothing more than an overgrown bramble but turned out to be a tiny shed coccooned by a three-foot-thick wall of *Rosa multiflora*. My mother'd cleared a path to the door but couldn't open it. The door's boards had long since swollen into the frame, and in lieu of a knob there were only the friable fibers of what had apparently been a pull-rope, which powdered like dead vines when I pinched at them. The shed was barely wider than the doorframe and perhaps twice as long. I dismissed it as an outhouse (and not just because I wanted to get to the rest stop), but my mother insisted it was a gardener's shed, said maybe it held fifty- or hundred-year-old seeds and would I help her open it, it would be like planting the past? A couple blows of an axe would have done the trick but clearly she wanted a gentler approach. I fetched a small crowbar and, working with the patience of a philatelist, shimmed the door loose, which, after a half hour of ignoring my advances, sighed free from its frame and fell into my arms like an anorexic cheerleader. If there's any magic at all in this story, it was in that shed. Green-tinted light poured in through one tiny window, giving the room the look of an under-water cave. The first thing I saw was the crowbar I held in my hands (its twin, of course, and nothing magical about it, since this one had been in the house when we moved in). But the second crowbar was pristine, as was everything else in the shed. Not a film of dust or rust marred the trowels and edgers and shears and aerators and augers that hung from nails in the walls. No spider webs or wasps' nests, no mouse or rat holes, and the earthen pots of mustard and cucumber and tomato and celery and pumpkin seeds—yes, and dill and strawberry too—had been nibbled by not even an ant and remained untainted by the faintest speckle of mold or mildew. My mother and I stared into this aqueous, ageless chamber for perhaps seven or eight seconds, and then, with a sigh and a twist, like a little girl in a pinafore spinning down to the floor, the shed spiraled in on itself and collapsed to the ground, as if only its vacuum seal had held it up all these years. The rose bower held its shape though, and for the rest of that summer, and the summer after—the last of her life—my mother picnicked in its hollowed womb at least once a week. Indeed, it's standing still, even as the mountains cave in on themselves on the other side of the creekbed.

And a dozen other memories, little spots of color in an otherwise muddy swill of sex. But the most persistent of them all is less memory than feeling, a longing, one that's never left me, even to this day. If it seems strange that it took me nearly a year to talk to someone at the rest stop, it'll probably seem even stranger that, piebald hide or no, I never tried to hook up with one of my fellow novices. Don't get me wrong. I thought about it. *A lot.* Like every all-male institution from gay bar to monastery, the Academy was steeped in regimented, eroticized cruelty. My classmates recited Catullus 16 not as insult or manifesto but come-on, and I was pretty sure they were sucking each other off in the locker room and fucking each other in the Foundry and linking up in three- and six- and ten-person daisy chains on their hikes through the conservancy. I'm not saying they were all gay, or even more gay than the general population. I'm just saying they were 384 parentless boys who ate, studied, played, and slept together 24/7 for twelve years. They were *going* to fuck.

But though I floated in a river of boys, I couldn't get wet to save my life. Their hazing never escalated beyond anonymous notes or catcalls, the foot stuck out as I walked down the hall, the shoulder that "accidentally" smashed into mine, the soccer balls—and basketballs, footballs, baseballs—lobbed at me ("Oh shit, C., sorry 'bout that!") when my back just happened to be turned. ("C." was short for "Caesar," by the way, a reference to the color purple, and also, by the same logic, "Celie" [give it a moment, or google it]). But it was never said to my face. I was reviled for my birthmark, but only when the bulk of it was covered. When it was fully exposed all eyes turned away. In the locker room a dozen asses presented themselves for inspection, but they were closed to me, to my penis and tongue, to my fingers and anything I might wield with them, but above all to my imagination. God knows I tried. But though I reinvented myself in a thousand different guises in my fantasies, I couldn't do the same with my classmates. Even in reverie their bodies repelled me like the walls of Jericho or Troy or Constantinople, and I was never able to summon shofar or wooden horse or cannon to breach them.

And I write "bodies" but of course I mean "skin." Black skin. Brown skin. Skin whose gradations from one boy to the next attested to the nation's fraught racial history, yet was never other than smoothly blended in each iteration, unmottled, unblemished (except, of course, in my own). "Their skin repelled me" reads rather differently than the sentence I put down, but I'll own it. As a Stammers, I'd be disingenuous if I did anything else. ("Disingenuous," from the Latin "*ingenuus*," meaning "native" or "freeborn": by the time English speakers added the prefix "dis" in the 17th century, "ingenuous" had come to mean "innocent" or "lacking guile," and as such "disingenuous" never literally meant "slave," but the connotation seems apposite.) Although it was commonly assumed that the Academy's students were descended from Great Grandpa Marcus's slaves, or at least his employees, by the middle of the twentieth century virtually all the novices were recruited from orphanages across the country. Fewer than a dozen members of the student body were townies, allowed in on sufferance because of a clause in the Academy's charter that guaranteed admission to any descendant of the slaves and freedmen who'd toiled in Stammers Coal. But all of them, legacies and orphans alike, were aware of the provenance of the Academy's coffers, not to mention its philosophy, and to survive this affront to their psyches they united behind a collective identity that recast themselves not as victims of a tradition but usurpers of it, an army of Toussaint Louvertures liberating Haiti from colonial Saint-Domingue. (Indeed, in the masters' absence the novices called each other "maroon" the same way their hipper contemporaries used "nigga"; the term originated with 16th- and 17th-century slaves on the northeast coast of South America, who fled bondage to create independent communities beyond the colonial frontier, many of which endured for as long as the Academy did.) As the last descendant of the original master, I was allowed to remain on sufferance, but only so long as my presence, my identity as a Stammers, remained as oblique as my skin (which is why the maroon nickname they bestowed on me was Sinestro—dog Latin for Lefty—rather than the more obvious, well, Maroon). I could *be* a Stammers, in other words, I just couldn't *act* like one. This wasn't a condition I could protest, or, for that matter, one I found particularly unjust. Absurd maybe, but everything about the Academy was tinged with absurdity and contradiction: the 2,400 acres of garden and forest that novices spent thousands of hours maintaining over the course of twelve years; the incantatory feats of memorization required to pass between forms; the essays and drawings and models produced to ritualistic specification and destroyed with even more ceremonial fervor; but above all the second half of that mission statement—"to

Brighten the Lot of the Darker Races"—in which context the commandment to "make nothing" carried more than a hint of eugenic contempt. All things considered, I wouldn't have blamed my fellow novices if they'd lynched me. I just wished they'd fuck me first.

But if desire's a carrot, it can also be the stick. A hundred times over the next several months I found myself lingering in Stammers Hall, before classes, between classes, after they let out. The entrance to the basement was tucked behind the main staircase. All I had to do was feint toward the back door and hang a uey. No one would notice, and if they did they wouldn't think anything. It was a library, after all. In a school. People need books in schools. Especially students. But once the story made the rounds that Judas Stammers was trolling for dick the jig would be up. My pariah status would go from *de facto* to *de jure*, and neither hoodie nor robe would be enough to hide the marks of my caste.

But, you know. I also really wanted to have sex with one of my classmates . . .

FAMILY LEGEND HAD it that at some point Marcus planned to divert the White Woman to the top of Mt. Inverna so he could fill the basement of Stammers Hall like a Roman baths, an engineering feat that would have involved raising the stream a thousand feet above the water table, and heating it too. That seems excessive, even for him. (I did once see a diagram of a series of capstans and norias and Archimedes screws, but it looked more like a steampunk fantasy, Da Vinci by way of Rube Goldberg, than an actual hydraulic model.) Another story said that in keeping with his agrarian roots he wanted to sleep under the same roof as his animals, but that tale ignores both the massive stables erected at the same time as the house, as well as the fact that the only access to the basement lies beneath the mansion's main staircase. Though I have no problem envisioning Marcus parading mules and cattle and hogs over the brilliant mosaics that pave his entrance hall, not even he could have gotten them to walk down a flight of thirty steps. The basement was to have been the family crypt, the family dungeon, the family museum . . . all equally improbable, but equally likely as well, given the person; given his house.

In any event, the ceiling in the basement of Stammers Hall is twenty feet high, a good five feet taller than that of the piano nobile (which Marcus quaintly called the "parlor floor" till the end of his life). Stone pillars thicker than redwoods run the length of the space, dividing it into three parallel naves, groin-vaulted, ecclesiastic. Clerestory windows paned with forest glass line the ceilings, through which crepuscular rays beam with unabashed stereotypicality. The vaults immediately surrounding the central staircase contained the card catalog and a pair of library tables each as long as a bowling alley, but the flanks had been closed off piecemeal during the '20s and '30s to house the stacks. At some point the novices started calling them the crypts, and it was easy to see why. Sagging shelves wedged between the pillars had made a catacomb of the vast space, and the spindly scaffolding that provided access to the higher shelves only reinforced the warrenlike feeling. The scaffolding was floored with rough-sawn fir. I knew it was fir because they were the same planks my mother had used to make her work table—knew it, I should say, the moment I walked downstairs, though I'd never remarked it before. Nor had it consciously occurred to me

during previous visits that the shelves and scaffolding postdated
Marcus's tenure, though it seemed obvious now. If Marcus had
built them, the shelves would have been carved with reliefs of
the Muses and Furies and fronted with beveled glass. The balco-
nies would have been floored with limewood or walnut and
probably carpeted too, the staircases wrought-iron corkscrews
rather than rickety ladders as wobbly as the one in the back
porch of the High Street apartment. They still would've been
called crypts though. He'd've liked that.

Steel-meshed fans kept the air circulating and dehumidifiers
wheezed in every grotto, but even so the atmosphere was tinged
with the ticklish odor of book rot. Well, and it'd been the wettest
spring in decades. The White Woman's waters had risen almost
a foot higher than normal (remember that line of moss on the
Field's foundation?) and the house had been islanded by ankle-
deep water for more than two months. The Field had a high,
solid foundation and no basement, so the damage was negligible.
("People built *to* the land a hundred years ago," my mother said
nonchalantly when the waters engulfed us, "not against it," and
handed me a pair of wellies.) What did bother her was the
flood's duration. It was a month past the time she usually started
harvesting clay, and she'd long since used up her winter supply.
But when I suggested she dig a little further from the streambed
she rolled her eyes. "You don't think I didn't fry that? What?
No, I meant 'try.' Sorry, *I'm* a little fried." The clay behind the
house was different, she insisted. Maybe because the filled brick
bed was entirely silt, maybe because the plot had been tilled and
compacted for so many decades. She only knew what she knew:
that this clay was more viscid than any other she'd dug up, which
gave her more control when she built her pots. There was an

anxious note in her voice that I'd never heard when she spoke of her work. It seemed more than the inconvenience of the flood or the months since she'd last made a pot, but I didn't fully understand until after she died, when I found dozens of cracked or crumbled misshapen pots hidden in boxes on the second floor and realized she must have dug up and down the creek during the fallow period of 1995 and 1996, and only the clay behind the house had worked. At the time I thought she was just jonesing. "You could order some," I said, "like you used to." I was trying to be sympathetic, but the look she gave me was enough to shatter glass.

The top of Mt. Inverna wasn't subject to flood but the damp had still set in, and you could tell it had gotten into the books. The odor was nowhere near as heavy as the stink at the rest stop, but just as insistent, as if the smell were as much a component of the books' meaning as their words. It reminded me of my books, by which I mean my father's, which, though they'd been sealed inside cardboard and packing tape for who knows how many years, still gave off the same nose-wrinkling whiff of dust and mold. If you put your face right in them you could imagine the smell intensifying as time passed, as the books aged, as the damp crept in, and the spores, as pages melted together and words congealed until the books came to be what they resembled: bricks, a wall, a barrier concealing information rather than boxes containing it. What was it my mother'd said so glibly? "You don't keep books like these. They keep you." Glib or not, the truth of her words was apparent as I contemplated the tens of thousands of volumes that defined the basement of Stammers Hall far more than the pillars and arches and bolts of gray-green Jesus light. Just standing among them reminded me of all the history I'd spent the past year escaping, or avoiding, and when I forced myself to venture deeper in I couldn't help but think it wasn't *my* will that pressed me forward but the Stammerers', and their refusal to abandon a project until they'd seen it through, even if it destroyed them.

A laugh emerged from the shadows, followed by a pair of small, dark-robed figures. They fell silent when they saw me, or, rather, stifled their laughter into giggles as they headed upstairs, arms draped across each other's shoulders, faces bent together in gleeful conspiracy. But they couldn't have been older than twelve, and I doubted they had the patience to plan a tryst in an alcove of Stammers Hall, let alone the foresight. Their presence was a reminder, though, that if the crypts weren't exactly a thoroughfare, they weren't nearly as deserted as the rest stop. The trash cans by the reading tables were littered with paper, a book truck held perhaps a dozen volumes waiting to be reshelved. People did come down here, and not just to fuck.

The thought came to me out of the blue. Potter's Field! I would look it up! I'd find out whether it had begun life as mill or barn, whether it had done time as inn or whorehouse. And I'd have the perfect excuse if someone asked me what I was looking for down here, just in case they weren't looking for the same thing I was.

Say what you will about the Academy, the masters could index like nobody's business. I found no fewer than sixty-seven cards for our address, nearly all of which referenced the *Current*, the county weekly. The citations were unevenly divided between the letters section, where, once or twice a year, a building referred to as "Varnings Mill" or "Mrs. Varnings Rooms" was denounced as a "den of iniquity" and "house of ill fame";

and a series of articles that ran more or less monthly from 1866 to 1871. "Series" isn't exactly the right word, or "article," since, judging from the transcribed headlines ("Bedford Forrest to Grace Aug. 27 Lost Cause Picnic"; "Ladies Auxiliary Raises $143.23 for Vesture Fund"), the pieces seemed to be nothing more than the minutes of a fraternal organization that held its meetings in what was by then referred to as "the Chapterhouse," which name was only settled on after the organization's "Titan Emeritus" declined to lend his name to the building. "Stammers House crowns Inverna," he was quoted as saying, "and I should pity the gentleman who rode three miles beyond town only to find that his destination lay at the hither end of High Street. And I never affix my name to something unless I own it."

Fredrick Varnings had been a foreman at Stammers Copper. He left the company in 1844, as the reserves were drying up, and with "the Master's blessing" purchased a tract of land on the east side of the White Woman, where he built a sawmill that struggled along until 1866 (Marcus had his own mill, which dominated local business, and which calls into question the "blessing" he gave Varnings). The point was mooted, however, when the spring flood receded to reveal that the creek had jumped its banks and the main channel now flowed more than a half mile to the west. As it happens, Fredrick didn't live to see this, having died three years earlier defending Vicksburg, along with both his sons, but his wife, an apparently resourceful matron named RoBertha, was able to transform the building into a boarding-house, which, if the letters to the editor are to be believed, was in fact a brothel, and a busy one. One letter, written by a "Mrs. Col. Victor Maginnis CSA (widowed)," declared that no fewer than nine girls lived in a state of "godless degredation" in the building, though another, signed by someone who referred to herself only as "Dassy," said that she and "her unmarried sisters" were employed by Stammers Coal at tasks that require "a feminine touch" (props to Dassy if the double entendre was intentional) and, further, that they spent more money on fabric—"and not just muslin!"—at Lyn's Dry Goods than did most of "the wives on Stammers Hill." There were no reports of either raids or arrests concerned with the building, which suggests that Mrs. Varnings's boarders served the needs—read: the men—of Stammers Coal, if not Marcus himself, and also Henry, Seth, and William, his three sons, and Hugh, Chester, Wiley, Beau, and Broward, his five surviving grandsons, whose names all appear regularly in the minutes of the organization mentioned earlier. This group mustered between thirty and fifty members for its monthly meeting, but as I read through the articles it became clear that most of the members frequented Mrs. Varnings's establishment far more often—so often that, in 1869, when RoBertha broke her hip and moved to Mobile to live with her sister's family, a "Brotherhood" of five patrons purchased the property. The negotiations hit a hiccup when the prospective buyers discovered that "the girls were not included in the price," but went ahead with the transaction, and after being gently rebuffed by Marcus, settled on "Chapterhouse" as the building's new name. It's unclear whether Dassy and her sisters stayed after RoBertha's departure. On the one hand, there were no more letters to the editor after June 1869; on the other, there were accounts of a weeklong party to celebrate the purchase, and, a year later, an anniversary so well-attended and lasting so long that "the Slurry behind the house ran thick with Night Soil, such that a Boar fell in and was drowned."

This is not my family, I told myself as I continued to read. And in fact the new owners' names were never mentioned, neither in the *Current* nor in the property records or surveryors' maps housed in the crypt's collection, so for all I know Henry, Seth, William, Hugh, Chester, Wiley, Beau, and/or Broward weren't among the "Brotherhood" who purchased the building. The denomination pointed up the fact that families are made as often as born. That, despite the tale told by skin, by the mine or by the masters and slaves of the antebellum South (or the masters and novices of the Academy), genes are as often the victims of heritage as its transmitter. Nor was the name of the organization to which the Brotherhood belonged ever mentioned. It was always the "Marcuse Chapter," and its minutes were little more than a list of votes on the dates and times of various gatherings ("Dexys Hollow, after moonrise"), candidate endorsements (the Marcuse Chapter initially supported former South Carolina governor James Orr in the presidential campaign of 1868, and, after he was eliminated, begrudgingly switched its allegiance to embattled incumbent Andrew Johnson, whose most favorable quality was that he had said that individual states should be allowed to decide whether and how to amend their suffrage laws in the wake of reunification), and various pieces of legislation (the chapter supported the Anti-Vagrancy Act of 1866 and the Convict Lease Program the following year; it opposed the Fourteenth and Fifteenth Amendments). These are not my people, I told myself as I flipped through page after page of an ideology so pervasive that it didn't need to be acknowledged, let alone named. But our bond ran deeper than blood. The "blessing" Marcus had given to Fredrick's mill had extended to RoBertha's brothel, and if his name didn't hang above the Chapterhouse's door, his money still paid the wages with which the Brotherhood had bought it, and his and his sons' and grandsons' names dominated the chapter's rolls. If their individual yeas and nays weren't recorded, it was only because the organization's resolutions nearly always passed by acclamation.

None of that mattered, I told myself. I was my own person. My last name didn't make me a racist any more than my first made me a traitor, or (if you take my mother's view) a savior, a sleeper agent in God's secret employ. But no amount of denial could stave off the sense of familiarity—of kinship—as I read about a "Mr. Berry of Bayse Street (Wye)" who had, according to the *Current's* Nov. 20, 1870 issue, demanded compensation for the destruction of a "well-grown beech" on his property. The tree had burned down when several "pots of tar" were tipped onto it during the course of a "picnic and shivaree," depriving Berry and his family of the tree's "nuts, shade, and eventual use in construction, cabinetry, and fuel." The Marcuse Chapter didn't dispute Berry's account of the fire, but did question the condition of the tree, which was gleefully described as "withered," "skeletal," "all but dead," "unfit for kindling," "sicklier than a five-year-old pit pony," and most certainly not worth the $500 Berry was asking in compensation. I told myself that there were any number of reasons why you might bring tar and goose-down and "thirty feet of coarse Manila rope" to a picnic, or why that picnic would be held under the light of the full moon. It was only when I read the words of someone named Franz Schole, who was quoted as saying that "the nigger hanging from Berry's tree wasn't worth $500," that I could no longer deny *which* organization's Marcuse Chapter, under the aegis of its Titan Emeritus and his sons and grandsons, was publishing its minutes in the local paper (which, as it happened, was owned by said Titan). Which organization's local branch, thanks to the largesse of a Brotherhood that almost certainly included one or two or ten Stammerses among its extended clan, had met for five years in the house now occupied by me and my mother. Which organization's members had raped black prostitutes and burned crosses and hung black men and women and dumped gallons of shit and piss into the slurry behind the house. It was their white supremacist bowels that had filled in the brick pit, not the creek, and it was from their white supremacist bowels that the dill and strawberries that had so enraptured my mother had sprung, and of course the fifty-two pots she'd made since we moved into the Field, by which I mean Varnings Mill, by which I mean Mrs. Varnings Rooms, by which I mean the Chapterhouse of the Marcuse Branch of the Ku Klux Klan. In their identicality my mother's pots were as anonymous as Klan hoods, if for opposite reasons. The point of pulling a hood over your face isn't to negate identity but to universalize it. A hood doesn't say, "I am no one." It says, "I am anyone." It says, "I am everyone." My mother's pots were no more made of Klan shit than I was a member of the posse that had burned down Mr. Berry's beech while lynching a black man whose name was nowhere mentioned in the *Current*'s pages. But if this wasn't what made us, what was?

"You're late. Rush hour's between four and six."

My mind was so absorbed by the image of my mother digging up blocks of shit and fashioning them into million-dollar vases that I didn't turn the left side of my face away when I looked up, or pull my hair over it. The voice was male and youthful and I expected a novice, was surprised when a beige custodial uniform greeted me instead of a black robe, surprised again when I recognized the face atop the zipped-up collar as Lovett Reid. I knew nothing about Reid other than that he was in upper sixth like I was, but the uniform instantly told me he was a legacy: only townies were required to pay for their education, and at least part of their tuition had to come from wages they earned at tasks that, however else you defined them, would have once been performed by slaves.

"Rush hour?"

Reid glanced down the table. "I hope you're not planning on leaving these papers out for some poor twobie to reshelve."

Eight leatherbound volumes, each containing half a year of the *Current*, lay on the table. Each volume measured two feet by three, was four inches thick and weighed thirty-five pounds, and would in fact be difficult for a nine-year-old to reshelve, especially since they'd come from the neglected upper tier of their crypt.

Reid nodded at the volume in front of me. "Family history?"

I looked down at the open page, a quarter of which was taken up with a single engraved photograph. I don't know how to describe it. What I mean is, I don't know whether to start with the horror and move on to the banality, or open with the bucolia, then blindside you with the brutality. The image depicted the "picnic and shivaree" on Mr. Berry's farm. The picnic looked like a picnic, albeit a moonlit one—blankets and baskets, pitchers and plates—with perhaps fifty white faces turned toward the camera, men in flat caps, women in bonnets, children with ribbons in their hair, all staring not so much solemnly as fixedly, so their faces wouldn't blur, but still managing to communicate the light-hearted nature of the gathering. The shivaree looked like a lynching. The face of the man hanging from the tree, which lay on its side on his feathered shoulder like an egg in its nest, was as sharp as that of the picnickers, but the laces of his boots, the only item of clothing he was wearing, were slightly blurry, suggesting that a light breeze had blown that night. "A photograph taken Nov. 12 appears to contradict Mr. Berry's description of the Beech tree on his property," was the full caption. The beech tree did in fact look rather past its prime.

I looked up. The stiff collar of Reid's uniform bit into his Adam's apple, and I couldn't help but think that it was the same color as "coarse Manila rope." My eyes followed the zipper down to where it disappeared between his thighs. I know what you think I was thinking about, but what I was actually thinking about was the White Woman's spring—its stops and starts, its water, soiled and scrubbed, the mystery of its disappearance and the capriciousness of its return. Which is maybe just another way of saying that I was thinking about what you think I was thinking about, but not in the way you think I was thinking about it.

I looked back at the picture, tried to turn my head to parallel the face of the hanged man's, but my neck wouldn't bend that far. "I don't think I'm related to him. I'm pretty sure that's the quilt on my bed though," I pointed, "which probably makes that woman my great-great-great-great grandma."

"Shit," Reid breathed, like a kid who's just jerked off to a faceless video only to realize that the anonymous penis and vagina are in fact connected to his father and mother's bodies.

"Hey!" I said then. "Is there a john down here?"

A long pause. Then: "Shit," Reid said again.

It was only when he ran the fingernails of his left hand up and down his zipper like a nickel on a washboard that I realized he was wearing latex gloves. There was a broom in his other hand. He held it like a lazy hunter holds his rifle, at the bottom of his arm, its length balanced on two curled fingers, and as he led me deeper into the crypts I had to fight the urge to grab it, to make a lewd joke or gesture or just fall on my knees and start sucking. We passed through one crypt after another, turned right so many times I thought he was leading me in circles to fuck with me, but at last a closed door appeared at the end of a short hallway, or vestibule really, cut right into the foundation stone. Reid leaned his mop against a damp wall of polished graywacke, then pushed the door open and reached into the darkness and pulled light out of the ether. Even after I saw the pull chain swinging in the air I still couldn't shake an image of Zeus atop Olympus, summoning a thunderbolt to smite mankind. I am his creation, I told myself. I exist to praise him.

When I squeezed past him I couldn't help but press against his uniform. Reid didn't lean into my touch, didn't retreat either. Beneath the beige cambric his body was muscled and taut and his penis was already erect. His eyes stared stonily down at mine. He was only an inch or two taller than me, but broader, thicker, and all of this added to the sense of bigness, so that I felt as though he were looking down on me like one of the figures in the friezes in the pediments in Stammers Hall's facade. In the allegory of education, Fabulinus touches his rod to the lips of a kneeling boy, conferring the gift of speech on him, while Minerva and Apollo look on, affirming that the words that come from the blessed child's mouth will be both learned and wise. I exist at his whim, I said to myself. I am his slave.

"Judas Stammers," Reid said, as if he'd never once connected the name with a person.

P-please, I said, and though I can remember stuttering, I can't remember if I spoke out loud.

Did he let me strip? Or did he make me? Was I ever actually naked? He put his hands under my robe, guided my arms from the sleeves, then unbuttoned my shirt and slipped it off me. He palmed the back of a sneaker and pulled it off without untying it, then the sock, then unshod the other foot, and then his hands were opening my belt, my pants, pushing them down, pulling them off. He was kneeling now, and looking up at me. I couldn't have looked any different—my robe was still on, I could feel the broadcloth against my skin—but I'd never felt more naked. Never, until he peeled the latex gloves from his hands and tossed them aside and rubbed his hands together and smiled up at me.

He slipped his hands under my robe and ran a finger up each side of my body, ankles to armpits, over shoulders, down to wrists. The powder in the gloves left his fingers dry and smooth, and as they chalked my outline I felt a layer of space growing between me and the wool I held up like a tentpole. Felt as though I were sheltering beneath a tent that grew larger and larger until I stood at the center of a circus ring, lights beaming at me from every direction, blinding me from seeing the bleachers that I knew lay on the other side of the coruscating blankness while the ringmaster displayed me for all to see. Reid ran his hands over my chest, ribs, waist. He cupped my ass, fingers laddering over each other deep within the cleft, then wrung his clasped hands down one leg and the other as if squeezing me dry. He pressed his right hand flat against my stomach and began rubbing it in a circular motion, so firmly that I would've fallen backwards if he hadn't steadied me with his left hand against the small of my back. Then he was punching me in the chest, lightly, with the side of his fist rather than the knuckles, but firmly—not to hurt, I mean, though I could feel my heart bouncing around my rib cage, but as if testing the solidity of the body holding up its Academy wool—and as his hands continued to explore, to push and prod, rub and knead, to pinch tenderly, as though feeling for a join between two pieces of fabric, or roughly, as though trying to separate the plies of a plastic bag, I realized he was less interested in my body than in trying to tell if there was any difference between the way my birthmark felt and the rest of my skin. Knew when he thought he'd found the border, and then when he doubted himself. Understood that when his fingers darted to the left side of my body it was to be sure they were touching purple skin, or again on the right, when he pinched the pale. There was a measured movement as his hands finger-walked toward each other, palpating my ribs like a treasure hunter searching for hollow spaces in a wall, but each time his hands met in the middle of my body I could tell he hadn't been able to spot when he'd crossed from one side to the other, and the funny thing was I couldn't either. I couldn't feel any difference between the two halves of my body whose tectonic faults had plagued me for all of my seventeen years. Couldn't imagine my skin as anything but a solid, uniform casing, colorless, uncolored, erased, a sounding board for the fingers that played over it in continuous arpeggios and glissandos.

His face was still aimed at mine, his eyes soft as his focus turned to what lay beneath my robe, but when his wandering fingers brushed against my erect penis his eyes sharpened, then his smile, and before I knew what was happening he was lifting my robe, I expected his face to disappear beneath it but instead mine did, as he threw the robe over my head and wrapped it around me turban style, except that it covered not just my hair but my entire head in two, then three, then four layers of fabric, until the dim light in the room was completely extinguished and I was shrouded in . . . darkness is what I want to write, but that wouldn't be quite honest, because the word that came to mind was "blackness." He's choking me, I thought. He's going to lynch me, and my hand curled around my penis as if it might give me ballast. Do it, I thought. Twist tighter and tighter until it's my neck you're twisting, not fabric. Twist until my head spits free from my shoulders and falls on the ground like an overripe berry. With each revolution of Reid's hands I felt a perfect blackness enveloping me, not colorless, not dark, like the oblivion of a moonless midnight, but a solid layer, like glaze or whitewash or—

"No."

Reid leaned over me. He had opened the front of his coveralls and his abdomen pressed into mine from his chest down to his penis, which settled in the crack of my ass like a gondola sliding into its berth. His words were the kindest anyone had ever spoken to me.

"You okay, Stammers?"

I am perfect, I told myself in my colorless coccoon. I am pure.

I reached back and opened my ass and pulled him between my buttocks, athwart the hole rather than into it, then squeezed my ass closed.

Reid groaned. He began to slide himself up and down, slowly at first, then faster, he held me by the hips and pulled me closer to him and I could feel his knees bending and his cock sliding down until just the tip was between my ass cheeks, and then he was standing again, aiming his cock, and then he was inside me.

I worried about lube for half a second but either he'd put something on or I was too keyed up to feel anything other than the
sensation of Lovett Reid sliding all the way into me until his
hipbones touched my ass and he lay himself over me again,
wrapped his arms around mine and squeezed my chest so tightly
I thought I was going to pop him out like a cork and I bit down
on a mouthful of robe as though I could hold him in that way. I
am a lump of coal, I told myself. I am a diamond.

"That—is—the—*fuck*."

I moaned and bent forward and my forehead came down
hard on the tank of the toilet whose existence I'd forgotten. Reid
put his hands on the side of my head and grabbed fistfuls of
fabric and I felt the tug in my mouth like reins against a bit. I
imagined that I caught a whiff of shit and I wondered if it was
me or the toilet bowl, but when I inhaled all I smelled was wool
and my own breath. I wondered if Reid was the person who had
cleaned it. I wondered if he could clean me. I am a dray horse, I
told myself. I am a palfrey. I am a gelding.

The robe had come unwound by the time he shot, spilled off
my head in a hollow sagging funnel, and when I stood up it fell
down my shoulders. Reid had already zipped up, and when I
pushed my arms through the sleeves it was if nothing had happened. I farted.

Reid laughed, then tossed me my pants. "I don't suppose I'll
ever see something like that again," he said, and walked out of
the room.

But to my surprise he was still waiting when I walked out five
minutes later. He stood in the middle of a crypt whose shelves I
hadn't noticed were empty when we walked through it the first
time. The fir planks sagged as though the books they'd held had

been especially heavy, but they were completely bare save for a handwritten label pinned to one shelf. "Contents removed, March 32, 1995." I would tell you that the date rang a bell but I don't want to sound coy. I knew exactly what day that was.

"I didn't know anything ever left this library," I said, which was as close as I could come to asking the question that was actually on my mind.

"Seriously?" Reid said, even as I looked around the empty shelves and noticed that here and there a plank was missing along with the books. Although it wasn't really "here and there." It was six. Six planks were missing.

"These were Gaius Stammers's books? Your uncle?" Reid said when I continued to look at the six gaps in the shelving. I wondered how she'd gotten them out and why she'd chosen the six she'd taken. Had she moved the books or somehow slipped them free without disturbing the boxes atop them? Were they the planks I was conceived on, or just the easiest ones to grab?

"Gaius Stammers," Reid said. "Your mother's brother? He disappeared when he was a kid."

I looked at the label again. March 32, 1995. The spring we moved to the Field. The spring my mother disappeared for four months and my father's books showed up to watch over me in her absence. I had the sense of myself as a person who's been walking a path so long and tortured and walled in on all sides that he doesn't realize he's walking a circle, and then I remembered that this was the terminal point of the "Parable of the Man Lost in the Snow." Except it wasn't snow I'd been walking in. It was shit. It had always and only been shit.

The first rule of the parable is that any question phrased concretely and completely will be answered to the full extent of

the knowledge of the master administering the lesson. I sum-
moned a breath.

"What happened to him? To them, I mean. To the books."

Reid shrugged. "I guess he died? The library got a request to
send them to his next of kin."

"My mother?" I said, which question the masters would have
scoffed at as a feint.

"What? No!" Reid laughed, as though I were putting him on.
"I guess he had a kid. A son. Out there," he waved a hand at the
whole world as though it were a bit of dust he was brushing from
his thigh. "Oh, man!" he said then, an awe-struck smile curling
up one side of his mouth. "If your uncle hadn't run off that kid'd
be in charge of this whole place. But instead it's you. That is
some fucked-up shit."

I don't know, maybe he didn't say "fucked-up shit." Maybe
he said "duct-taped ship" and it was just my ears playing tricks
on me again.

6

In his weight room, a.k.a. the loft over his dad's work shed, Reid told me his maroon nickname was Bosky "'cause—ta-da!—my ass is hairy as a forest!" To a bunch of smooth-bottomed teenagers it probably looked pretty bushy, but, though numerous, the hairs lay on his ass in discrete ticks, reminding me more of Marcus's shaky sketches of his newly planted pines than the gnarled masts bristling across the craggy hemispheres of Aventine and Caelian, Capitoline and Esquiline, Palatine, Quirinal, and Viminal. One time a man I was sucking off in the rest stop pulled his dick away and whirled his ass in its place, cheeks pulled wide, tea-dyed flesh spiraling into pink shadows. The two plies of the wall were separated by less than an inch, which as it turned out was pretty much exactly how much tongue stuck out of my mouth. Even with my nose mashed against paint-flecked rusty steel I could do little more than trace the outline of the wrinkled rosebud on the other side. But I could still tell that the odor coming off it—out of it—was different from the air in the stall. Sharp rather than rotten, alive rather than dead. A flower in the soil as opposed to one in a vase. Reid's ass didn't smell like much of anything (he'd gone for a run before his shift in the crypts, showered right after) but with the hairs of his ass tickling my nose and his sphincter pulsing around my tongue I could definitely taste . . . something. Telluric, minerally, metallic. "Steely" popped into my head, then "irony," and I burst out laughing. Before he went to bed I asked him to tie me to the weight bench. Reid rolled his eyes. "Dude, it's cool, no one comes out here. Stay as long as you want." But I didn't want to stay. I wanted him to keep me.

MY MOTHER SAID once that the act of making something from clay, giving it form, breathing life into it, was the closest a human being came to duplicating God's creation of Adam. My mother. The woman who gave me life. I think it's not unfair to say that she valued her bowls more highly than she did her son. Not just the mass of them, but *each one of them*, a sorority of 174 Eves—174 Liliths really—from whose ranks I was excluded because I was a one-off, maybe, or because my flaws reflected badly on her craftsmanship. Despite what it says on her Wikipedia page Dixie Stammers didn't have a "Ph.D. in pottery." Didn't know the difference between Cherokee and Cheyenne, Aztec and Inca, Inuit and Yaghan. I'm thinking of their pottery, but the statement applies equally to the people. She'd acquired techniques but not the cultural realities that produced them and gave them local meaning. All she knew was what she knew: that Native Americans had made perfectly round pots without the wheel. She'd picked up a factoid (literally, if you bought her story about the funerary casket at the Met) and immersed herself in it so deeply it became aesthetic, ethic, and *raison d'être*. "Think about it, Jude. It's not just that they didn't have potter's wheels. They didn't have *the* wheel." She always said it that way—"*the wheel*"—her voice as pedagogically stilted as Sydney Poitier's in *To Sir, with Love*. "I mean, the pots must've *rolled*, right? They must've seen them *rolling*. And yet they never saw the potential. Must've seen the tendency of round things to, you know, *roll* as a drawback, and instead of making axles or flattening them out they made really fancy bases to keep them from weeble-wobbling away."

In fact Native Americans did have the wheel, although for various reasons they never put it to much practical use. And of course there were thousands of examples of Native Americans' transformative acts, the shaping and vitrification of clay into cooking, carrying, and sacred vessels being a case in point. But Dixie Stammers practiced what she preached. Though it might sound like she was calling Native Americans stupid, in her mind she was paying them a compliment. Their insistence on seeing objects as *what they were* rather than *what they could be* enabled them to create perfectly round vessels for aesthetic rather than utilitarian reasons. It wasn't a lack of imagination. It was focus—purity—and part of me wonders if she looked at her brother with this same clarity of vision, of intent. Wonders, too, if that's why Guy ran. Not from the Academy, I mean, but from her. He was a weak boy, she always said, susceptible to powerful person-alities, and he knew it. Knew that he couldn't help but fall into the role of yes-man and boot-licker. At the time I assumed she meant to the Stammerers, but in hindsight her words apply to herself as much as her father, his father, every one of those stick-up-the-ass Southerners and Scotchmen going all the way back to Marcus. And of course she was a Stammerer too. It must've been clear by age ten or eleven that she was the family genius, the family giant. Certainly it was to my grandfather, who after discovering that she'd attended nearly as many classes as Gaius chopped off her brother's hair so they'd no longer resemble one another. Her *brother's* hair, mind you: because it was only her brother he could control. (To be fair, he told my mother to cut hers, and she just flipped him off.) "It was the first time I ever thought of Guy as a boy," she told me when she relayed this story, smiling one of those wistful smiles that makes me shudder to remember. "I guess that's another way of saying it was the first time I thought of myself as a girl. Physically, I mean, as opposed to socially or politically, or however the feminists would put it." In fact her first impulse had been to cut her hair too, so she could keep going to classes. "I *liked* feeling like a boy." But as she contemplated Guy's shaved scalp she realized there were other ways to find out what boys felt like. ("B-U-one T but," as she said on that other occasion, though it's clear now I hadn't sunk nearly as far into the sewer as she had.) They were thirteen then. In a few months he'd take off and in five years he'd be back, to finally give her what she wanted, only to disappear for good when he realized it wasn't him Dixie desired, but his body. His manhood, and the privilege of primogeniture that came with it. The ability to receive and to bequeath. It's no mistake, after all, that the dispersal of one's property after death is called a will. But the laws of the polis are a poor reflection of the laws of physics. Instead of an heir, my mother got me.

REID HATED THE Academy. His dad made him go. Mr. Reid owned a filling station where the interstate crossed the Post Road at the foot of Wye, a last-exit-for-twenty-seven-miles kind of place, pretty much every car that went by topped off. "Nigger barely finished eighth grade and he clears a quarter mil per annum. *Clears.* I don't know why he thinks I'll do better just because I can read fucking *Latin.*" He lifted weights for two hours every night, not because he loved his body but because he hated the other novices, who looked down at him as a dilettante even though he'd advanced apace with the Foundry boys and stood ready to graduate with them in June. When he checked himself in the mirror he saw only imperfection, frailty. He flexed until the veins stood out in his neck and thighs, punched himself in the chest like he wanted to roquet his heart out of his ribs. He whipped his shirt off, then his pants, then his underwear. "Grow, you fucking faggot, grow!" His sweat made a bloody mirror of the red vinyl that covered his gym equipment. "Lick it up, bitch." He guffawed when I pushed my tongue the length of his weight bench. "I meant *me*, doofus," he said, reaiming my mouth at his balls. He fucked like he was trying to kill with his dick. He put his hand around my throat and squeezed so hard I saw spots (afterwards I found them around my throat, or at least the parts that weren't already purple), palmed my face and leaned on it till I thought my nose would break, or my skull. But after he was done he pulled me down on the floor, nestled my head on the pillow of his left biceps while his right hand traced the median line of my birthmark. It was the seam that fascinated him more than the birthmark itself, the high tide of its reach. His fingertips skimmed the border like a low-flying shorebird scavenging for snails and crabs, and when he found a hint of a raised lip he paused, pinched at it with two fingers or nudged under it with the edge of a nail, as if it might suddenly fold back and reveal the unblemished skin beneath or, who knows, maybe the works that gave it color, minuscule dwarves powdering amethyst or garnet and mixing it with my blood to dye it purple. He flicked my dick back and forth as though it were a wood sample whose genus he was trying to identify by grain, color, density, slipped two pinched fingers into my ass and opened them like a forceps—slightly, probably no more than half an inch, but I found myself imagining a light shining out of the crevice from a miner lost deep inside the shaft. I felt a breath of air, cool against the friction-warmed walls of my rectum, imagined the light flickering, going out. "Is it true your mom made you shit in her pots when you were growing up?" "She still does," I giggled, and Reid smacked me in the nuts. "Don't fuck with me, nigger." Then, in a voice whose lack of malice made it that much more painful: "I could stare at that face all day."

WITHIN A YEAR of Marcus's death a third of the faculty—eleven of twenty-nine—had deserted the school. They were scientists, after all, not academics. They didn't want to teach. They wanted to discover and make, register patents, and collect royalties. And if they did want to teach, they didn't want to teach freed slaves, or the sons of slaves, or any other black people. Then, too, instruction was challenging when half the student body was illiterate and the rest could parse little more than a bill of lading. I'm pretty sure most of the founding masters only made it through the first decade because they were too afraid of Marcus to quit.

At the same time, however, Master van Hooyster, who took over as chief arborist after Master Castell Davis absconded in 1900, believed that rote memorization by *students who didn't understand what they were learning* was precisely the way to discourage the kind of "extension" that he, like Marcus, considered an impediment to true knowledge. Master van Hooyster had suffered a brain injury when he was eight ("Ice hockey on the Mohawk—dangerous stuff") that left him with what appears to have been agnosic alexia, which is to say, he could write words, and recognize them when they were spoken aloud, but couldn't read a letter, let alone a word or sentence, including sentences he himself had just put on paper. He compensated for this handicap by developing a memory so prodigious that he had all of Linnaeus by heart by age twelve. He could recite full entries from the *Encyclopædia Britannica* with no more than a page number or phrase as prompt and identify the location of any of the conservancy's 261,079 trees (the tally was his own, and no one ever attempted to prove him wrong) from one of Master Castell Davis's five- or seven- or nine-year-old sketches. Master van Hooyster didn't allow slate and chalk in his classes, and instituted the program of mnemonic proficiency that persists in the recitations required to pass between forms. Literacy, he liked to joke, was an obstacle to the natural sciences (although he'd also admit that, failing an audience with Theophrastus or Avicenna, he was dependent upon a succession of head boys who read to him for two hours every evening before tucking him in).

Nevertheless most of the first novices did learn to read by the time they left the school, and in 1902, when Hugh lowered the age of admission from fifteen to five, he brought in a team of a dozen "basics masters" to teach a fairly standard core curriculum, albeit in less than standard fashion. Newly christened first-formers were taught letters and words but weren't allowed to pass to second form (or, more to the point, read sentences) until they'd demonstrated an active vocabulary of twenty thousand words. Painting lessons were given not from life but from memory, and the upper third take all their art classes blindfolded to boot, and aren't allowed to pass into fourth form until they've executed a recognizable depiction of one of sixty "foundation trees" in the conservancy, as well as a randomly assigned facade of Stammers Hall and a self-portrait. Gaius (by which I mean my mother) notoriously drew his (by which I mean her) blindfold into his (her) upper fourth picture, and gave up art after discovering that he (she) wasn't the first novice (sister of a novice) (incestuous brother-fucker) to do so.

More relevantly, three of Hugh's basics masters were themselves Academy graduates, and all but one of the twelve was black, which appointment led to the defection of nine more masters. Hugh seems to have anticipated this, and within three years all nine positions had been filled by alumni, a trend that continued until the last of the original masters, Winfred Pieg (who was in fact referred to as Master Winnipeg), retired in 1926, at which point all forty-four members of the faculty were Academy graduates, and remained so until the turn of the millennium. None was what you'd call a scholar. Certainly they were proficient. Could, depending on their field, recite the Old Testament in its original Hebrew and Aramaic or build a model of Brunelleschi's dome in 1:50 scale from homemade bricks or execute a technically perfect rendition of the Chaconne from Bach's Partita No. 2 on a violin they'd constructed themselves, which in addition to harvesting and shaping the spruce for the soundboard, maple for the ribs, ebony for the pegs, and rosewood for the chinrest also required slaughtering a sheep for the strings and several rabbits for glue and mixing up six ounces of varnish from the resin of *K. lacca*, a colony of which survived on the grove of jujube trees Great Grandpa Marcus had planted in 1857, under the mistaken belief (apparently occasioned by the doubled "jew" syllables of the tree's name) that their fruit was the manna of Exodus. Marcus was said to have liked his pickled.

But however impressive or esoteric these practices seemed to outsiders, they were less knowledge than the regurgitation of the autist or brainwashed. If you'd asked Master Ngugi how Plato defined wisdom in the *Apology*, his answer would be the same as his predecessor Master Arrowleaf's, and Master Noklindt's, Master Smith's, and Master Unferth's before them, each of whom would have replied, "I neither know nor think that I know." Which is of course Socrates's answer—or, rather, one of several that Plato tells us Socrates gave his accusers. If you pressed them, they'd have said, "I am called wise, for my hearers always imagine that I myself possess the wisdom that I find wanting in others." And again: "He, O men, is the wisest, who, like Socrates, knows that his wisdom is in truth worth nothing." If you've read the *Apology*, you know they could've kept this up all day, and at almost any other educational institution such gnomism would have been an impediment to advancement. But Academy pedagogy was steeped in Marcus's mines, or more accurately Marcus's miner's soul, which, like the soul of the critic (as opposed to the soul of the artist) seeks to reveal rather than invent, to amass rather than create. The masters took Marcus's "From nothing, take nothing, make nothing" to mean that the secrets of the universe will never be amalgamated by the collective efforts of generations of scientists and/or philosophers. That, rather, the nature of reality is already manifest, and we have only to look to see it. Looking is meant in its physical sense: with the feet, to bring you closer to distant objects, and the hands, to remove obstruction, and only latterly with the eyes, to observe dimension and duration, chroma and texture. Cognition, such as it is, is rooted in recognition rather than synthesis, and further exploration or invention, far from increasing our understanding of the world, only piles more dirt atop it.

   And note that I didn't write "our understanding of our *place in the world.*" To the Academy way of thinking, this is the first wrong turn: not the creation of art or the accretions of culture, nor even the metaphysical isolation of consciousness from the body that houses it and the material universe of which that body is a constituent part—i.e., the transubstantiating soul—but *consciousness itself*, which the Academy sees not as the kernel of selfhood but mere projection of language. A kind of seigniorage, no more immanent—no more valuable—than the image of Caesar's face stamped on a few grams of silver; no more us than the actor is Antigone or Hamlet.

   It's against God's nature to lie, Socrates tells us in the *Apology*; and "to God," Heraclitus taught, "all things are fair and good and right, but men hold some things wrong and some right." Of Heraclitus, Socrates was said to have judged, "The parts I understand are excellent. I think the parts I don't understand are excellent too, but it would take a Delian pearl diver to get to the bottom of them." At the very least, though, we can infer that *division itself must be untrue*, and that the way to return to grace is not by making more judgments, more divisions, but by giving them up. A more practical person might point out that this isn't the only thing that distinguishes humans from their creator. We need to eat, for example, and piss and shit, and foul weather has this nasty habit of killing us if we can't find shelter, and so perhaps our concerns are more tangible than

God's. But as with their notion of change, the masters respond with the on-high view, namely, that the kinds of divisions we make between edible food and poison, or friend and foe, aren't the ontological hierarchies with which Heraclitus is concerned. To outsiders, the Academy's educational program was nothing *but* division and classification: the isolation of a forest into its individual pines and oaks, a tree into its bark, branches, leaves, and sap, its hierarchy of genus, class, kingdom. (A much-repeated charge ran that if a novice was asked to account for the Great Wall of China he would have gotten stuck computing the number of bricks and blocks in the structure, and never gotten around to the Hsiung-nu, or the Ch'in for that matter. The apparent contradiction between doxa and praxis irked people like the critic who discovered my mother, who wrote: "Lake Academy's illusion of ahistorical holism is rooted in a fantasy of eternal infancy, cupidic yet carnally innocent lips clamped to the maternal teat from which milk pours forth like the springs of Mt. Helicon, and blissfully ignorant of the soiled nappies in which they wallow." The critic grew up in Colorado Springs and her use of "nappies" is about as authentic as my use of "dunno" and "prolly," by which I mean that the contradiction was hers rather than the masters', who, for all their rigidity and renunciation, were neither monists or nihilists. They never went so far as to say that change was impossible à la Parmenides, or motion an illusion per Zeno. They argued only that change is part of space and time as a foreleg is part of a running horse, and to focus on one leg at the expense of the other three—and the thorax that connects them, the head and neck, the mane and tail and the turf it runs on—is to stare at nothing at all, because the animal will have long since escaped you.

Which is to say: time passes. Even if we were confined to Plato's cave we'd still sense its progress in changes to our own body—sweat, gray hair, rickets, what have you. As it happens, the masters also rejected the distinction between the world of shadows and the world of forms, or, more specifically, reposited the material world as the real world, whereas the world of forms, far from being a divine or eternal reality, was just Plato's invention, or humanity's, a *folie à tout* made all but irresistible by thousands of years of cultural accumulation. You could argue that this makes God the human invention *ne plus ultra*, the collective fantasy that raised us out of our animal state and gave us a conception of past and future as well as present—something to learn from, something to live for—and thus reject the Heraclitean premise upon which the argument rests. The masters wouldn't have disagreed. But they'd have also said that metaphysics is as misleading as the object of its contemplation, and places human beings in a false relationship with time and, even more, with matter. As Marcus's resurrection of the Magic Mountains and the White Woman Creek demonstrated, any attempt to unwrite history only creates more history, and not even the masters were idealistic enough to think culture could be "corrected," let alone perfected. Instead they opted out. On January 1, 1900, the Academy announced "the end of history," and in a move that suggests they were aware of the performative nature of their declaration, backdated the development to "March 32, 1896," a.k.a. April 1, which in addition to being All Fools Day, was also the day of Great Grandpa Marcus's revelation. Though history might continue to pass outside the school and the conservancy, within Marcuse the masters and their charges wouldn't deign to notice it. The lamps would remain oil- or gaslit, heat would come from coal or wood. Horsepower would be measured in Percherons and Clydesdales rather than watts. Sentences would be Jamesian rather than Joycean, the psyche a single mechanism whose parts worked in harmony rather than Freud's bickering triumvirate.

There remained the problem of physics, of course, by which I mean not the discrepancy between the Newtonian and Einsteinian universes, but the more tangible manifestations of hunger and weather, desire and decay. Deciding not to read a book written after April 1, 1896, is one thing, or eschewing technologies developed after that date, but the body still needs to be fed and clothed and sated, and these needs can't be met without carefully coordinated activity, both individual and collective. The masters' response was to tie these activities to the gardens behind Stammers Hall in a regimen that, superficially at least, resembles the environmental movement of the second half of the twentieth century and presupposes more contemporary notions of sustainablity and bioregionalism, which gave it an unanticipated (and unwanted) relevance at the dawn of the Internet age, before it was abruptly snuffed out. Novices grew all their own food, animal as well as vegetable, made their own shoes from leather they flensed and tanned and robes from wool they sheared, carded, and wove, their paper, pens, and ink, their brushes and paint, their dishes, their sports equipment, their weapons. To emphasize the transitory nature of all these objects, they were referred to as "intervals," and, even more importantly, were destroyed after whatever lesson or technique they were meant to teach had been concluded—although not destroyed, of course, but reused or returned to the earth in a neverending cycle, from the paper on which the novices had recorded their lessons to their food, which ended up as night soil in the fields in which their next meals were growing. Furniture and books were passed from one class to the next, but all originated in the Academy's workshops, and when they wore out they were repaired and replaced there as well, including the dishes they cooked and ate with, metal pots as well as ceramic plates and bowls (though my mother always insisted that she didn't learn pottery at the school).

But even more important than the frugality with which their biological needs were met was the care with which they maintained everything else in as unchanging a state as possible, i.e., Stammers Hall and the other buildings on campus, and of course the vast folly of the gardens, from the eidetic replantings of tens of thousands of annuals each year to the individualized care regimens for thousands more trees. For twelve years the novices fertilized, mulched, pruned, and braced the trees each according to its individual need. They pored over them from root collar to crown edge in search of gypsy moths and ash borers and longhorn beetles, released nonnative insects to facilitate pollenation of dozens of exotic species, and snipped flowers from same because their pollen is poisonous to local bees. When a disease did take root or when a tree succumbed to age, it was removed in the dead of night, every log carted to the woodshop, every leaf and fleck of sawdust raked and mulched, the root bole dug up, and the fallen tree replaced with a substitute whose trunk and limbs had been trained for the previous three or four years to mimic the decedent as closely as possible. It's not that the gardens were held up as some kind of ideal. Quite the opposite: as "Botanica Balbi" suggests, everyone knew the gardens were as ridiculous an example of profligacy as could be imagined. Yet *they were there*, and to attempt to replace them with something "better" would only be a different form of self-indulgence. The trick wasn't in thinking you could perfect the world, but in realizing that the world cared not a whit for the changes men make to it. That, in fact, the things we create are only material simulacra for an internal malaise that can no more be cured by treating the symptoms than syphilis can be eradicated by rubbing balm on a chancre. Change itself—particularly biological change, the aging of bodies and growth of trees—couldn't be halted, but it could be subsumed in ritual, freeing the mind to go within, wherein lay the only answers to the questions it was constantly asking itself. Like most acts of self-abnegation that look to outsiders like self-absorption, Academy practice was one of those things that only had meaning in the doing. The critic who discovered my mother went so far as to say that her potting technique owed a lot to Academy regimen. For once I can't disagree with her, yet the only comparison that ever really resonated with me was to the Vedic practice of transcending the flesh by honing it into a fluid invisibility that appears effortless to observers, but in fact requires total concentration to pull off. The masters took this off the yoga mat, as it were, and extended it into all of life. And whatever else you could say about their ideas, you couldn't deny the effectiveness of their methods. In the hundred years the Academy existed after the masters declared the end of history, no novice—not even the most harried townie—failed to graduate. Thirty-two students came in each year as four- or five-year-old individuals and, despite their secret maroon societies and TV sets hidden in the attic of the Foundry and clandestrine trips to the arcade in Wye, emerged twelve years later as identical in their relationship to the material universe as Marcus's mountains and my mother's pots. In lieu of a diploma, the masters placed a coal pebble in each graduate's palm. The pebbles were the masters' only acknowledgment of the futility of their project, the only thing they allowed to leave the conservancy while it was under their stewardship—thirty-two pebbles and thirty-two novices a year, who spun out into the void like samaras, to wither or grow as they would.

THE ONLY MAKEUP in Reid's house belonged to his mom. I don't think she was into blackface as much as she was, you know, black. (For that matter, I don't think Reid thought he was disguising me as a black person as much as he was trying to cover up my birthmark: no matter how much he enjoyed fucking me, he was still savvy enough to know that it wouldn't do to be seen in public with Judas Stammers.) Still, the finished product seemed to amuse him no end. "All you need is some red lips and 'Mammy' on the squeezebox," he said after troweling cinnamon-colored paste across my face and neck. His voice wavered on "squeezebox," you could tell he'd just thrown it in for effect. He offered to uncover the mirror but I turned him down. This kind of masquerade only worked if you didn't know what you looked like—if you could believe yourself not just unrecognizable but someone else. He dressed me in shiny red tear-away sweatpants and a white satin basketball jersey that hung to my knees. The word "RODMAN" was emblazoned across the back in red letters. I assumed it was a double entendre, was disappointed to learn it was merely someone's name. At any rate Reid wore jeans and an untucked buttondown, so I should be forgiven for thinking the outfit was a joke at my expense. He dapped my fist. "Yo, homie, let's roll." Speaking of clichés: the ground floor of the shed was taken up by a 1968 Sedan DeVille convertible, the big-gest car I'd ever seen. When Reid whipped the cover off I whistled. I called it "cherry" but, like Reid's "squeezebox," I was parroting the script of a movie I'd never actually seen. Reid laughed, told me the car was ersatz from wheels to windshield, no more authentic than the Ship of Theseus. The drive into Mar-cuse took forty-five minutes instead of the usual fifteen because we followed the interstate around the northern border of the conservancy instead of taking the Post Road straight in. (In a total failure of theory of mind I thought Reid didn't want to drive by Potter's Field lest my mother spot me, but he was just avoiding his dad's filling station. "If he saw me in his Caddy he'd shoot me. If he realized it was a white boy with me—shit.") I missed our first pass up High Street because I was blowing him, but after we looped around the upper gardens we headed back toward the Foundry, and as we drove past the Browns' bakery I made eye contact with Mr. Brown through the open door of his shop. His stare took in me, the jersey, the car, and before he turned back to his counter he gave me what Reid called "the bona fide Negro nod." I caught a glimpse of myself in the shiny windows of the bakery, barely recognized the suety George Hamilton schmear that smiled back. It was only then that I realized that Reid had, intentionally or no, made a minstrel out of me. Though who knows, maybe I'd always been one, and I'd just been waiting for the maquillage. "Look at me, Mammy," I mouthed. "Don't you know me? I'm your little baby."

I ONLY HEARD my mother use the words "gangue" and "goaf" once each. The first, and clearly rehearsed, instance occurred in *Three by Stammers,* in a scene filmed at least a week before she actually sat down at her work table, when she dismissed the film, the money, and indeed everything said about her pots as gangue: something that had to be removed in order to make them visible. The second and equally self-conscious use occurred almost a year later, after she'd begun churning out pots at the rate of two or three a week from the clay she dug from the pit behind the house. A prospective buyer was starting to annoy her, and in a pique she suddenly declared that he was a fool to spend money on one of her pots. They were nothing but goaf, she said. It was the land from which they were dug that was the jewel, the commodity, "the only thing that would endure" (which line the buyer smugly repeated at trial as evidence that she knew the second series of pots was going to implode before she sold them for tens of millions of dollars). The implication was that the pots existed intact in the dirt and my mother wasn't making them as much as revealing them. I suspect she hadn't thought her analogy through that far—nuance was never her strong suit—but even so, there's a symmetry to the two statements, both of which posit culture as superfluous. The grave-sized pits she left in the earth were indistinguishable from the pots themselves, gaping tears in the fabric of the world, and both pots and holes were of a piece with the destruction Marcus had inflicted on the same land a century and a half before. "Man is explicable by nothing less than all his history" Emerson wrote right around the time Marcus was buying the Tsistuyi, and if that's true then it follows that nature is only nature in the absence, not just of human presence, but human traces. Thus the conservancy is no more a mountain range than a rood screen is a forest or a Ferrari the seam of taconite from which its iron was extracted and smelted into steel. Perhaps nothing on earth qualifies as nature any more, save for the planet's gravitational pull and the ions that bombard it from space, and the inevitability of death. But if that's true how did we get here, and was it where we intended to go? Or is it a case of a local civilization gone global, depleting natural resources like the Rapa Nui Polynesians and Icelandic Greenlanders, until all that's left is gangue and goaf, and not even memory to regret whatever bad decisions brought us to this pass?

Anthropologists speculate that the earliest notion of an aesthetic sense seems to have been tied to the idea of mimicry. Excavation of *Homo erectus* sites finds a proliferation of tools and containers each of which shows a high degree of consistency in its execution. The sameness doesn't appear to be dependent upon the shape of the materials from which they were crafted: a fuzz-barked larch branch and a smooth ovoid flint were both transformed into the same trapezoidal wedge, sharp on one side, softly rounded at the other. It may be that the minds of *Homo erectus* were so simple that having seen a palm-sized wedge work as an implement for flaying skin from flesh and flesh from bone, they believed the tool's power was dependent not just on its edge but on every aspect of its shape, and sought to reproduce it as closely as possible. Given the immense periods of time over which the same shapes continually appear, however, this suggests a remarkably steep learning curve, and my mother sided with those interpreters of proto-human remains who argued that the tools' makers produced the same shapes over and over for the simple reason that they *liked* them—liked the shape itself, and also, and more importantly to my mother, liked the fact that the individual objects *resembled each other*. Contemporary aesthetic sensibility focuses on distinction, on individuality and the aura of uniqueness. To my mother it was a case of forest for the trees. "Take a step back, let your eyes go soft, forget about what's written on the placards," she says in a section of *Three by Stammers* that follows her on a walk through the Met's painting halls, Old Masters to Abstract Expressionism in three minutes flat. "I mean, it's all just canvas and pigment, canvas and pigment. Do you think a Bushman sees the difference between Turner and Rothko? For that matter, can you tell the difference between Ibo war drumming and a Navajo prayer for rain?"

Sometimes I try to imagine it. The origin of consciousness. The evolution of language. Modern man existed for a hundred thousand years before he began to perform mental functions that people like you and me would recognize as thinking. For a hundred thousand years—a period twenty times longer than that between the building of the Pyramids and the fall of the Twin Towers—men and women did little more than pull fruit and berries from trees and pick bugs from the ground, gnaw shreds of meat and marrow from abandoned carcasses killed by animals that were faster or stronger than they were. One hundred thousand years. It beggars the imagination to contemplate such a vast span of time, yet it's irresistible not to. To shrink millennia down to ticks of the second hand like a wire model of the solar system collecting dust on a high shelf. By which I mean that I know I'm telling a story, but isn't that what consciousness is? The substitution of sensory data for a mental picture? Isn't that how language works? Through symbol and metaphor? To not tell the story would be to not be human. But to mistake the story for the world is, somehow, to not be alive.

So. A troupe of naked, tiny humans curled up in a hollow, sister-wives and uncle-fathers, bodies sooted over, matted hair bunched in uneven clumps around faces and groins, only the fingers clean, from licking the juice of whatever they'd eaten, fruit, greens, the rare piece of meat from some animal they'd killed or whose carcass they'd found. When did they start crawling away from where they slept to relieve themselves? When did they teach their children to do the same? When did they realize that fire could do more than burn? Could warm too, if you didn't get too close, and keep predators at bay. Flickering light glimmers on intertwined legs and arms, torsos pressed up against each other for warmth, strips of stiffened animal skin knotted over shoulders and stomachs, all surrounded by a darkness as solid as the land, and indistinguishable from it. There's *here*, the amorphous dome of orange light, and *not-here*, the vast blackness that's everywhere and everything else. Was this the first distinction we learned to make, more profound even than the distinction between self and other, friend and foe? On some sleepless night when a storm or an animal's roars vibrated through the dark did we feel that it was safer to be *here* rather than *there*? In the light. With the pack. When a child crawled fearlessly out of the circle did we make some kind of warning grunt or wave our arms instead of just dragging it back? And these grunts—and yips and clicks and moans and sighs. When did we begin to string them together like abaci, quipu? Juxtaposition as conjunction, as grammar. *Big—fear—pain. Eat—lots—full. Come—hold—mmmm.* Comparisons would have come before names, I think, *this better that* before *berries better leaves*, names of things before names of people. *Antelope. Lion. Cave. Water.*

Once the names were in place and synced up with that first distinction between *here* and *not-here* we would have been able to describe things not visible to the listener. *Over hill. Many hunters.* We would have been able to make suggestions. *Attack!* *Sshh!* And then, and then . . . ! And then, somehow, we started talking about things we'd never seen. Of course we'd have learned to conjecture thousands of years earlier: tracks and spoor and bones mean that this or that animal had passed by. But when did this gave way to invention? To the idea of forces animating this or that event, spirits, gods? And when, finally, did it give way to art?

Because this was the miracle of humanity: that we could make something and, liking what we'd created, make it again, not like a bird fashioning the same nest every year by dint of genetic programming, but out of study, selection, conscious manipulation—above all, desire. What had my mother done but take this behavior to its logical end: identicality. The absolute imposition of consciousness on nature. If life is change, then the perfect indistinguishable sameness of my mother's pots stood as simultaneous embodiment and refutation of death itself. But it wasn't miraculous—not to her. It was just a question of paying attention to what her fingers and eyes told her. Anyone could do what she did, she said, which is why she didn't call herself an artist. An artist needed to be in possession of a singular ability coupled with a singular sensibility, and my mother claimed she had neither: the shape of her pots wasn't simple because of some minimalist or essentialist aesthetic: it was simple because simple was what was called for. Her techniques were even more derivative and duplicable. Women had made pots in the same manner as she did for thousands of years; had used them to carry water and food and other mundane items of daily life, and no one made a fuss over them, let alone handed over kings' ransoms to claim them. If her contemporaries didn't duplicate her pots, it's not because they *couldn't* but because they *didn't want to.* Something else was more important to them, and they chose to pay attention to that instead. It was just a choice, possibly even a smart one. The world didn't need my mother's pots, after all, and she was only able to make them because she had enough money that she didn't need to take a job more useful to society. That people paid her for them was just another layer of irony. That didn't mean she wouldn't take their money, but she'd have never presumed to ask for it.

But these are reflections colored (to use a loaded word) by hindsight. At the time all I thought was that my life was gangue and goaf to my mother's, a feeling that's reemerged often as I attempt to write this account, in which I no longer know if my story is trying to reveal itself in the context of hers, or if in fact she is struggling to be seen through the tint of my birthmark. "Gangue," we call it, as if it had no other name until it came into proximity with something precious, something someone wanted, when of course it had had its own name all along: graywacke, silica; not a son but a boy. And "goaf," as though its continued existence were defined by absence. But would I still have been me, had I not been Dixie and Gaius Stammers's son?

THE MAKEUP WAS still in situ on day three, peach and purple sandbars peeking through the muddy smear after a night spent biting pillow, but all Reid did was add lipstick and blush and mascara and screw one of his mother's blonde wigs over my head like a swim cap. Her lingerie was waaaaay too big for me, but I knotted the garter belt in back (after I figured out what it was) and it held up the wrinkly pantyhose well enough. The bra just looked stupid though, and I ditched it before stepping into a sleeveless velvet minidress as though it were a pair of coveralls. "You know how to tuck?" Reid asked. Before I could ask him what he meant he spun me around so my back faced him, reached between my legs, pulled my penis and testicles toward him, smushed them into the crack of my ass. While he was back there he used clothespins to cinch the dress to my figure and, from the front at least, in the mirror, I looked liked the bride of Frankenstein, brown(ish) head on white body, one purple arm thrown in for good measure. He came in for a kiss but I jumped back. "You bastard!" I said in a voice less draggy than faggy. "Trying to kiss me with that hussy's perfume on your clothes!" "Um . . . ?" Reid leaned in again. I tried to slap him but he batted my hand away. "Bitch, please." "Can't you at least pretend to hate me?" I pleaded. "Tell you what," Reid said. "You can pretend I hate you while I pretend your ass is a vagina." I told him to call me Dixie but he didn't get it until I called him Gaius. "Fuck me like you're my long-lost brother!" He hung off me like a mountain climber dangling from a piton. "That's like your uncle, isn't it?" "I'm not sure," I said. "Is he still your uncle when he's also your—" "Dude," Reid cut me off. "You are *full* of shit." I thought he meant my words but he was showing his Academy training: he meant my ass. Seventeen-year-old physiology being what it is, he went ahead and finished (and give the boy his due: he made sure I did too) but then he walked me to the shower and, after washing himself, went at me with a loofah that left the right side of my body as florid as the left, and made me think of long-ago days when I had lovingly, hatefully, scrubbed the clay from my mother's smock in a sinkful of lye. "You just figure it out?" he said as he threw his mother's soiled clothes in a garbage bag, "when I told you about the books?" "Do I seem like the kind of boy who's always known his dad was his mother's brother?" Reid shrugged. "It would explain a lot of things." He gathered up my clothes, handed them to me. "But, you know, if I fuck you again I'm pretty sure I'm gonna go Jeffrey Dahmer on that face." I gave him a full left profile. "Would that be so bad?" From the corner of my eye I saw Reid's nose wrinkle like he could still smell me. "Yeah, dude, it's been real." "Yeah, well," I said. "I was gonna have to go home sometime."

I'D ONLY BEEN gone three days, but I half expected the house to be gone too—collapsed from age like the gardener's shed, or maybe just disappeared, like the phantasm of our imagination it had always been. But the bricks had endured my absence just as they'd endured Marcus's presence, their walls as straight as they were when he'd walked between them. They'd been baked until the moisture had been driven from them, then baked some more, so that they would never admit the White Woman's floodwaters again. They'd been cut from the earth, leaving a muddy hollow scar behind, and stacked and cornered and roofed around an even bigger emptiness, and the emptiness had filled up with people and their things but above all with their ideas, and the scar had filled with shit.

I didn't find her immediately. I didn't find her for several hours in fact. I didn't go looking for her because I didn't realize she was missing. She'd left before, after all, just like the White Woman, but unlike the White Woman she'd made it clear she'd always return, and after I waded through the puddled grass of our front yard to the house and found the first floor empty, and the second, I retreated to the third, where I went through book after book after book looking for a single word in my father's

hand, but the only thing I found was an underlined passage in
Electra.

Electra: And where is his poor body's resting place?
Orestes: Nowhere. Seek not the living with the dead.

Let's say I heard the splashing outside just as I finished reading the passage, or maybe after I'd thrown the book across the
room, or after I'd ripped the offending page out and used it to
wipe my ass. Let's say I had a premonition that I knew what I'd
see when I looked down. None of that's true but it makes for a
better story. Some version of it anyway. Maybe not one I can
come up with, but mine wasn't the kind of life conducive to
imagination. I don't mean the Academy indoctrination to which
I was subjected for twelve years. I mean my face. My mother, my
town, the view from my window. Though she claimed to despise
her family, my mother had nevertheless followed in their footsteps in one regard: she thought of objects as totems. This isn't
the same thing as saying she thought of them as metaphors, yet
to an outside observer the effect was identical. Everything in our
lives was so steeped in over-ripe associations that it became, if
not invisible, then normalized. Even I, who sometimes thought
I hated my mother, was blind to it 99 percent of the time, and it
was only every once in a while, when something knocked me out
of my orbit, that I saw just how over the top it was. Over the top,
but not unbelievable in the way that word is often misused,
because what was so fantastic about our house, about the Academy and Marcuse and the Magic Mountains, was how *believable*
it all was, when you traced its evolution step by step, from the
hundreds of thousands of years of erosion that formed the

Tennessee Valley and the peoples who migrated across land and sea to settle there, right down to the founding of the Academy and the misstep that took my mother's life. My history, my world, by which I mean the movement of trillions and trillions of atoms over the course of thousands and thousands of years, was a series of mistakes and misapprehensions, each of which made subsequent events that much more inevitable, no matter what the Academy teaches about the potential of chance. By which I mean that the world as I knew it was weird enough already, and nothing I could invent could top the sight of my mother submerged in a pool of soupy mud, only her head visible, and only just, her hair plastered to her scalp, her face smeared, even her teeth stained brown, as if she had drunk the stuff that drowned her.

"Mom!" I yelled as I ran out the back door.

The brown cracked across her eyelids. They opened halfway, weighted down by mud.

"Stay back," she whispered as I ran toward her; then: "Judas!" she gasped as I slipped sternum-deep into the muck. The cold shocked me immobile, but after a moment I continued trudging forward. "Stop!" my mother said, and if it had been a command I would have ignored her. But it was a plea, to providence as much as to me, a mother's desperate wish for her child to survive, and it cut through my own panic long enough to make me realize that if I continued to wade forward I would only end up as trapped as her. The whole pit seemed to have collapsed. It was nothing but quicksand, a mere six feet deep, but that was still three inches taller than me and four taller than my mother, and there was no treading this ooze. I couldn't have been two feet away from solid ground but it seemed to take an hour to backpedal my way there and drag myself onto the reeds, and even longer before I could summon the energy to stand again. My sodden freezing clothes hung off me like iron chains. They seemed to weigh a thousand pounds as I ran back into the house and grabbed one of the phragmites ropes my mother had braided two years ago, ran back outside and tossed it to her. My aim was true. The rope landed right on her arm, which bulged beneath the mud like a waterlogged tree branch. But her arm didn't move.

"Mom! Grab the rope!"

Only then did I see that her eyes had closed. They opened again, less than before. Her face was expressionless, too cold to move and too covered by mud to reveal if it did, but something gleamed in her eyes. I want to call it pride, though it could have just been mirth.

"What is that shit all over your face?" she said, and laughed a little wet laugh.

I shook the mud off my left hand and brought it to my face. It came away smeared brown—brown and purple—and I remembered the makeup Reed had painted me with yesterday afternoon. This can't be the last thing my mother sees before she leaves this world, I thought. This can't be the last thing I show her.

"It's not shit," I said, and my mother stared at me skeptically, as if I was the type of boy who might in fact smear shit on his face, and then gave me the tiniest of nods. The movement seemed to knock her mud-caked eyelids closed. They didn't open again.

"Mom, please," I begged in a hoarse whisper. "*Please*. Grab the rope."

There was nothing for a long moment. Then her eyelids parted and her lips twitched into a smile.

"I was only waiting for you," she said, and then she let go of whatever she was holding on to, and slipped beneath the surface.

The cause of death was ruled hypothermia. The coroner estimated that she'd been in 55-degree water for more than thirty-six hours. Her hands and feet died before the rest of her did; they'd have started to rot by the time I found her if the cold that killed her hadn't also staved off the start of decay. A half dozen people found the need to tell me it was a miracle she was still alive when I showed up. At the time I didn't think "miracle" was quite the right word, but now: who knows? Dixie Stammers's entire life was a case of mind over matter, so why not her death too?

When the mud dried I excavated the pit and found that a narrow zigzagging path of solider earth had held together as the rest of the pit collapsed into the holes my mother had dug over the course of three years. She'd managed to walk this tightrope, no doubt from memory, to the middle of the pit before it gave way beneath her weight. The shovel that she'd brought to dig clay had fallen only a few feet from her reach; her cubit-sized crate is what had enabled her to keep her head above water. Dried, the silt that had washed in with the flood brushed away like sand from a swimmer's skin, leaving behind the compacted night soil and the outlines of my mother's trenches like the ruins of an ancient city unearthed by archaelogists. Claw marks were scored clearly into the wall where she slipped in. Whatever led her to try to harvest clay that day, she hadn't abandoned herself to her fate. Not at the beginning anyway. She had tried to get out—a fact that mattered mostly to me and to the insurance adjusters, who ruled it a case of death by misadventure rather than suicide. Which is to say: her annuities were paid in full.

Not that it changed anything. When the second batch of pots began to fall apart their buyers demanded their money back. It's a betrayal of everything my mother stood for—every lesson she learned from Marcus Stammers and every value she passed on to me—to say that her pots only existed *because she believed in them*, and when she no longer existed to perceive them, they simply ceased to be. And yet I held them in my hands as they crumbled. Pots that, a day earlier, had held just over three liters of water now dissolved like dried sand beneath the tap; that had pinged their perfect C-sharp now, at the flick of a fingernail, sighed into dust. Sometimes all you had to do was look at one in its softly lit case and it collapsed beneath the weight of your stare like a wallflower desperate for attention, yet even more afraid of it, and the odor of hydrogen sulfide that seeped into the room after each self-immolation smelled like nothing so much as shame. When the existence of the shattered pots on the second floor came out, the courts ruled that my mother had knowingly sold a defective product and I would have to return their buyers' money. By then dozens of the pots had been resold at auction, many for two or three times what had originally been paid for them, and the claims far outstripped what had been taken in. It turned out the same corporate entity Marcus had set up a hundred years ago to fund the Academy and the conservancy also handled the sale of all the pots, whose money had kept the Academy going for the past half decade. Consequently both were seized and sold, to a mining company that had long before concluded that the most efficient way to extract the coal underneath them was through three spiraled pits each of which will eventually rival the largest open mines in the world. The novices were placed in foster care in cities as far away as Houston and Atlanta and Detroit and Spokane. The drilling started immediately. Within a month the White Woman had stopped flowing again.

Long before we moved to the Field my mother spoke rhapsodically about a vast cavern in the middle of the earth where the creek's waters collected after they deadended against Inverna's base. Depending on her mood (or who knows, maybe mine), this cistern was the source of the world's oceans or—rainbow covenant be damned—waiting to explode in a second planet-consuming flood. She stopped telling me these stories when I was ten or eleven and began assaulting her with half-understood citations from books I encountered in Master Darkholme-Smith's natural history lectures, but I have to confess that of all her romanticized explanations for natural phenomena, this one never quite relinquished its hold on me. Because, I mean, where did the water *come from*? Where did it *go*? It surged from the ground all year round with tidal force. In spring the Lake's shores never rose by more than two or three inches, no matter how severe the flooding was further upstream. The water simply returned to the earth as inexorably as it sprang forth. Even in winter, when an ice cap as thick as Marcus's paving cubits lidded the spring and novices skated on the Lake seventeen miles away, the water continued to flow beneath its frozen surface, which groaned whale song against the seething current yet never cracked. And unlike life, which forms from nothing and disappears just as absolutely, matter can't just cease to be. The water has to be *somewhere*. And so I watch for its return on the 216 acres that remain to me thanks to the bequest of an uncle and a father I never met—a proof that there's a world out there, beyond my conception of it, beyond the Stammerses's and the Academy's. I walk out my back door like Marcus did all those years ago, I stare for hours at the dark gash zigzagging through blackened, withered reeds. I'd like to pass off my watching as an act of hope, but the truth is I don't think I could conceive of a life that wasn't built around watching. Waiting. I'm just not sure it's the water I'm waiting for.

II

Parable of the Man
Lost in the Snow

The "Parable of the Man Lost in the Snow" always begins the same way: a group of novices asks a master to tell them the story. Strict guidelines regulate their interaction: the novices can only ask questions; the master must not extend, guide, or otherwise volunteer information about which the novices do not specifically inquire. Thus the parable's first lesson is almost always to illustrate the difference between a request, whose goal is the performance of an action (i.e., telling a story) and an interrogative, whose object is the revelation of information (i.e., the *contents* of that story):

Q: Do you know the "Parable of the Man Lost in the Snow"?
A: Yes.

And then again:

Q: Will you tell me the "Parable of the Man Lost in the Snow"?
A: Yes.

Many an ambitious fourth- or fifth-former has dashed his boat against the rocks of frustration in an attempt to convince a taciturn master that his (increasingly plaintive) queries, which call for nothing more than confirmation or denial, are in fact appeals for the master to disclose what he knows. Since the master can respond only to what was put to him, the novice will be stymied by the same "Yes" until he arrives at the correct formula:

Q: What is the "Parable of the Man Lost in the Snow"?
A: A man lost in the snow came upon a set of footprints, which he followed in the belief that they would lead him to safety. But the trail the man had found was in fact his own, and as such could only lead him in a circle. The man trod this circle over and over, wearing a deep trench in the snow. By the time he discovered his error he was trapped. And so he had to choose: continue walking, or surrender to the snow?

Because the interrogatory process can be quite attenuated, there are, by custom if not actual rule, at least three and at most seven novices in any session in which the parable is told. Although novices can request to hear the parable at any time during their tenure at the Academy, most wait until fifth form, by which point they will have completed basic instruction in logic and rhetoric, which teaches them to start from what is known—i.e., the "Parable of the Man Lost in the Snow"—and build upon that information, rather than hypothesizing one or a dozen premises or conclusions in an attempt to leapfrog directly to the choice indicated by the parable's final line. When a hound is given a scent, or an investigator is shown a body in a vacant lot, they do not set off randomly in the blind hope that they will pick up the trail. Rather, they walk in a slowly widening circle until they find a sign of the person or thing they hunt. To wit:

Q: What was the man doing at the time he became lost?
A: The man was taking shelter from a snowstorm.

Q: What was the nature of the man's shelter?
A: The man erected a conical frame of spruce branches over which the snow fell, forming an insulating layer.

Q: How much snow fell?
A: The snow fell in variegated drifts, most of which were significantly taller than the man's head.

And so information accrues, neither linearly nor quickly, but here and there, in bits and pieces, and with much wasted effort. But eventually a situation takes shape:

The man had been tracking a herd of caribou for much of a day when he noted dark clouds on the horizon. Although it was early in the season, he was far enough from his tribe's encampment that even a mild snowfall could prove fatal if he did not prepare. He used his axe (stone wedged into a wooden haft) to sever branches from a spruce, and, after clearing a small area of what little snow was already on the ground, lashed the branches together to create a lean-to whose inner cavity was about as tall as he was. He piled a thick layer of needled boughs over this frame, weaving the outermost branches together to add strength to the structure; he left only a small opening at the top to release the smoke from the fire he would build, and a shallow entrance positioned to the lee of what he could now see was going to be a substantial snowstorm. He lined the floor with such stones as he could find and pry loose from the frozen ground, covering them with thick branches cushioned with soft twigs and repeatedly stepping or laying his full weight on this platform to make sure it could support him. Normally he would have excavated a trench beneath the entrance to act as an air sink, but the ground was too hard and he had neither the time nor tools to work it, so a raised platform was necessary to protect the man from the frigid drafts that would settle at the base of his shelter. Once the snow began to fall—or, rather, once it began to fall in earnest, for a few flakes were already whirling out of the sky, batted about by gusts of wind that presaged a major gale—it would coat the spruce framework, forming a thick shell, and the heat from even a tiny fire would be enough to keep him warm. But not even a raging fire would raise the temperature of the floor of a shelter erected on the surface of the land, and, despite the fact that the low platform was only as high as the top of the man's boots, it made his chances of surviving the storm much greater.

The man left a small hollow in the platform's center in which to build a fire, lining it with the largest stones he could find, both to protect his platform from the flames and to project as much heat as possible. While he had been procuring live boughs for his shelter, he had also gathered dry wood as fuel, and he brought as much of this into his shelter as possible, piling the rest outside the entrance and covering it with needled branches to shield it from the worst of the snow. The wind was steady and the snow fell in sharp diagonals, stinging his forehead and cheeks. He would have liked to gather more fuel, but he had exhausted the nearby supply and visibility was falling rapidly; he was unsure he would be able to find his way back if he wandered farther afield. He retreated into his lean-to, sparking a fire and fueling it with logs from outside the entrance, saving the wood inside for later, when the opening might be blocked with snow. Wind whistled through the shelter's walls, which, though thick enough to obscure the last of the light, did little to impede the stiff gale bearing the storm ever nearer. The lean-to shook when the wind gusted, and several times the man ventured out to tighten the lattice that held it together, until eventually the snow had formed a layer on the windward side that both blocked the wind and weighted his shelter down.

After that there was nothing to do but maintain the fire and make sure the smoke hole in the roof did not close. The man used the longest of his arrows for this task, standing on the platform and swirling the darted end inside the narrow shaft. The shelter warmed quickly, and the man removed his anorak (the master is quick to point out that this is his word, and not necessarily the man's) and, as the temperature rose higher, his trousers as well. He left his boots on, and tied the sleeves of his anorak around his waist so that the body of the coat protected his buttocks when he sat down, but other than that he was naked, his skin glistening with sweat in the firelight. He slept sometimes, or sucked on a piece of seal blubber, or chewed a bit of snow to relieve his thirst. He stoked his fire with wood he pulled from outside for as long as he could continue to pass through the entrance, and then, after it became filled with snow, from the store inside; he poked and swirled his arrow around the smoke hole. When morning came he pulled a few branches from the frame of his shelter in order to make a pair of snowshoes. By that point there was little danger of his shelter collapsing. The innermost layer of snow had melted and refrozen several times as it interacted with the heat of the fire and the coldness of the open air, forming a layer of ice that supported much of the weight of the snow atop it. From the most pliable branches the man shaved strips of bark. Then, selecting a branch about as thick as his thumb, he bent it into an arched frame and wove the strips of bark across the open space, forming a lattice. The snowshoe was about three times as wide as his foot and twice as long, and, owing to the materials from which it was constructed, would probably not last a day. But it might make the difference between survival and death, and after he made the first snowshoe he made a second, and reinforced both with extra lengths of bark.

His firewood ran low. If he used it all before the storm was over he would have to leave his shelter. He attempted to burn branches from the frame, but the green wood threatened to put his fire out; and when it did catch flame it produced such copious amounts of smoke that the man thought he might suffocate, especially as his smoke hole had narrowed to an ice-edged tube longer than his arm and hardly as wide. The wind had lessened by the time he was down to his last piece of firewood, though the snow was still falling. He put the final log on the fire, donned his anorak and trousers, lashed his snowshoes to his boots with more strips of bark. He sucked on a piece of blubber, cleared his smoke hole one final time. When the fire was nothing more than a few dim coals, he began to dig out. More snow had fallen than the man had realized, and he had not only to excavate the entrance, but also to pack the snow into a ramp that would allow him to ascend to its surface. It took a long time to do this, owing to the depth of the snow and the near darkness in which he worked, as well as the fact that the fresh snowflakes were brittle as chips of stone, and similarly devoid of adhesiveness. But eventually he broke through to blinding morning light, and soon after that he stood on his snowshoes atop the powder. He looked down the angled chute and saw that the snow was significantly taller than he was. Since the entrance was located on the shelter's lee side, it was unlikely that this was merely drift; more probable, in fact, that the accumulated snow was shallower here than elsewhere, as his shelter would have acted as a windbreak.

Although perhaps not, for the massive snowfall had reshaped the land. Or, rather, robbed it of shape: what had been an undulating terrain of low hills and shallow valleys dotted with individual spruces and firs had smoothed into a vast glittering plain rippling away in every direction. Hollows had been filled in and hills graded until they were little more than dimples and bumps. The only dark spots—stripes really—were the shadows cast by the undulating drifts, which painted the land like the back of a skunk. Only the sun was in its familiar place, obscured behind a thin, even layer of cloud from which scattered flakes still fell, and it was this the man used to navigate. He was a day's walk from his tribe's encampment. The snow impeded his progress, but he believed that if he traveled through the day and night he could reach it. Certainly the snowshoes aided his journey, though they were awkward and taxing. Because they were framed with a single piece of bent wood, they were wider than they should have been, which forced the man to walk with his legs splayed far apart, and they lacked an upturned tip, and scooped up large amounts of snow unless he lifted his foot directly off the ground before moving it forward. Still, by the time the sun reached its zenith the beginning of the man's trail had long since disappeared behind him. The snow had stopped falling, although the wind remained strong, and when it gusted it raised incandescent phantoms that arced and dove like breaching whales.

Sometime in the afternoon the lattice began to loosen on one of the shoes; not long afterward it gave way completely. He tried to repair it but the strips of bark fell apart in his hands and, since one snowshoe is no better than no snowshoe, the man cut the second frame off his boot and started forward again. With his first step he sank to his thigh in the fresh powder, and he realized he would have to dig a path as he walked. He retrieved the intact snowshoe and used it to shovel snow from in front of his legs, and in this way he progressed, slower than before, but steadily, until the second snowshoe unraveled around dusk. Then there was nothing the man could do but labor forward as best he could, pushing the snow from his thighs with gloved hands and lifting each leg with the high-kneed step of a wading heron. He sweated inside his layers of fur, relieved his hunger with the pieces of seal left in his pouch. When his mouth was dry there was the snow all around him.

It was nearly dark when he came upon the trail. By then he was no longer sure he was heading toward his tribe's encampment. Certain landmarks he had expected—a hillface that should have been visible above even this snowfall, the forest in which he had found the caribou's track—had failed to materialize. The trail came from the left, angling back in the direction from which he had just walked, and led to his right, southwest of his current trajectory. The man knew other members of his tribe had ventured out the day before, some to hunt, others to gather wood, stones, mussels. It was his hope that the trail had been made by a fellow tribesman or –woman who, like him, had gotten caught in the storm, and was perhaps surer of the way back to camp than he was. Additionally, the walker, though not equipped with snowshoes, had managed to wear something of a path through the snow, which would make the man's progress easier. The light was falling rapidly and so was his strength. Nothing but unbroken snow lay in the direction in which he had been heading. The man decided to follow the new path. As he merged with it, he did not despair.

LIKE THE PARABLE'S protagonist, the novices stand at a crossroads, the point at which the man ceases to be a Paleolithic ancestor and transforms into an allegorical hero. The next step he takes will complete the first revolution of the circular path he has unknowingly traveled; the step after that will begin to wear the trench into the snow that seals his fate, forcing him to confront one of the existential dilemmas at the core of civilization:

persevere despite the absence of hope, or give up and forfeit what it means to be human?

Questions remain, however: have the novices gone back far enough? And is the path they have excavated the right path, or is it, like the one the man now sets off on, a false lead? Narrative tenets point toward an exploration of the next leg of the man's journey, but few novices choose to pursue it at this juncture. Rather, they backtrack, checking for missed signs. Unlike the man, they have the luxury of time.

Indeed, time is built into the lesson, as it takes a dozen or more meetings for even a large group to assemble the narrative framework of the parable. Sessions may last many hours or be over in a few minutes, depending on the master's schedule or mood or his assessment of the novices' progress. On occasion a member of the group will miss a session, and it is up to the others to fill him in. These conversations are instructive in their own way, as the novices who received the information directly from the master quarrel over what was said, accusing their peers of misremembering or, worse, misinterpreting—by which they mean simply interpreting—what they heard. Sometimes a day or two passes between meetings; sometimes weeks go by. These intervals are considered as instructive as the meetings themselves, because the downtime gives the novices opportunity to contemplate what they have learned. The world of the man lost in the snow grows in their imaginations until, as one novice once put it, "It comes to life inside your head." The novices feel as though they have a three-dimensional view of the man: from all around him, from the sky, from beneath the snow and frozen ground. But later, as more time elapses and more information is learned, "You come to live inside the story," according to the same novice. Instead of looking at the man, the novices see his world through his eyes. They understand the decisions he made subjectively rather than through storytelling's omniscience. This limits the scope of their knowledge, but makes it more personal. Their empty stomachs spasm, their thighs and calves burn with the labor of their march. Sweat freezes on their eyebrows and drapes their cheeks like tinsel.

It's usually at this point that some empathetic novice, trying to find a kinship with the man lost in the snow—which is to say, trying to make the man more like him—seeks the flaw in the man's reasoning:

Q: Had the man encountered any other paths since he became lost in the snow?
A: No.

Q: And had the man seen anyone else since he became lost?
A: No.

Q: Had he been keeping watch for other people as he walked?
A: Yes.

Q: Then would it not be logical to conclude that the path in front of him was his own, given that, if there was another person in the snow, the man would have had ample opportunity to see him or her?
A: Yes.

The novice feels an initial sense of elation: exposing a flaw in logic is, after all, a primary goal of the traditional dialogues from which the "Parable of the Man Lost in the Snow" derives its format. But what has been learned by ascertaining something that was obvious from the beginning? Is the man lost in the snow stupid? Ignorant? Desperate? Too weary to think correctly? None of this matters, nor is it even ascertainable. Often two people choose the same course of action, one by true reasoning, the other by false. Yet if either fails or succeeds, it is not because of acumen (or lack thereof), but *because of the action taken*. And, of course, sometimes there is no right answer. No solution. Sometimes a person's fate is beyond his or her control. Thus the group is back where it started: with the man at the juncture where he failed to recognize his own footprints and chose to follow them. Although perhaps they have learned a valuable lesson: their task is not to pass judgment on the man, nor to attempt to figure out what he *should* do when he realizes he is trapped in a trench worn by his own passage. Only what he *will* do.

But the previous line of inquiry reflects a wakening curiosity about a different aspect of the parable's protagonist. Humanity is distinguished by its ability to reason, but also by its ability to feel, and the novices, having explored the logical aspects of the man's predicament, now turn to the psychological. Initially their goal is to humanize the subject of the parable, but as their questions progress they discover that what they are really trying to do is assess his humanity. The story's historical moment cannot be pinpointed. The master tells the novices that the man counts the years but does not number them; he says that if calendars exist at the time the incident occurs, they are unknown to the man and his tribe. The presence of clothing and compound tools locates the story well after the Upper Paleolithic Revolution of fifty thousand years ago, the so-called "Great Leap Forward" that saw the emergence of language, symbolic thinking, and other characteristics of behaviorally modern *Homo sapiens*. The hafted axe and snowshoe are the most distinct temporal markers, since both are believed to have been invented no later than six thousand years ago—some four thousand years after the end of the last Ice Age, a geological event, and the Stone Age, an historical one. But such tools were still widely used by subarctic peoples at the end of the nineteenth century, and even into the twentieth, and the only thing the novices know for sure is that the parable's protagonist is, anatomically and anthropologically, "modern." But how modern? How like the young men who are evaluating his actions is he? And, perhaps more to the point, how different?

The novices return to the beginning of the narrative, when they found the man trailing a herd of caribou. They make an exploratory inquiry:

Q: Was the man a hunter?
A: No.

The response surprises the novices. They parse the master:

Q: But the man had been trailing a herd of caribou, armed with a bow and arrows? His intention was to kill one or more of them?
A: Yes.

Q: In other words, he was hunting them?
A: Yes.

Q: How, then, was the man not a hunter?
A: The man hunted, but he neither identified himself nor was identified by his tribe as a hunter.

Q: So he performed multiple tasks in his society?
A: Yes.

The master's response tends to elicit an *a-ha!* moment in at least one of the novices.

Q: Had the man been hunting when he first found the caribou's trail?
A: No.

Q: What had he been doing?
A: He had been gathering firewood.

Q: Of his own volition? Or had the task been assigned to him?
A: He had been asked to do so by his tribe.

Here is the first glimmer of psychology the story has offered—or, at any rate, that the novices recognize. (The novices do not count the lack of despair the man felt as he merged with the second path, for it seems to them that, whether the path was his own or not, the man was clearly doomed. Night was falling and there was no sign of his tribe. The snow was deeper than he was tall, and he had been walking all day, and was two days without a proper meal. Any rational person—any person the novices recognized *as* a person—would have despaired.) Eagerly they probe this new lead. They learn that it was late in the hunting season, and the man's tribe had not laid in the usual store of provisions. They made a small group, numbering just twenty-six souls, and, owing to a confluence of accidents, illness, and skirmishes with other tribes, women outnumbered men, and children made up over half the group. Most of the adults would probably survive the winter, with some degree of privation— possibly extreme, if the season was long or harsh—but one or two children would surely die. The days were shortening rapidly, and during the lengthening nights the man could not help but think of the boreal darkness ahead. It would be his first winter as a married man. His uncle had drowned that summer, and the man had agreed to take on his aunt and her daughter. The man had done this partly out of filial duty—the man's father was long dead, and his uncle had served as head of household since the man was a child—and partly out of a desire to take his first sexual partner. There were no other available women in his tribe, and if he did not take his aunt he would have to wait until the beginning of the next hunting season, when his tribe would encounter other groups and he could attempt to barter for or steal a woman. Additionally, taking his aunt gave him a claim on her daughter, who was not far from puberty, meaning that in a few years the man could be the head of a large household, with sons to provide meat for him in his old age. But that was all in the future. For now, it was his responsibility to provide for his wife and cousin, now stepdaughter, which is why, when he encountered the caribou's trail, he decided to follow it: firewood can be had all winter, but the caribou and other ruminants would retreat farther south than the man's tribe was free to travel.

The track was crisp in the patchy snow, suggesting the herd had been by recently. The man assumed it had passed through earlier that morning on its way to shelter in the nearby forest. He was wrong about that: the day, like the past several, was cold and windless, meaning there had been nothing to disturb the trail left by the caribou, which had passed through the previous night, on their way through the forest to forage in the tundra beyond. The man realized this as soon as he emerged on the far side of the forest and saw that the caribou's trail disappeared into the vastness of the tundra. By that time, however, it was no longer possible for him to complete his assigned duty— chopping firewood, an onerous task—and return to his tribe's encampment before nightfall, so he decided to press on in the hope the he would come upon the herd sheltering in the lee of one low hill or another. He knew that people would worry when he failed to return that evening, but he knew too that if he returned with one or even two caribou pulled on a sledge behind him, he would be hailed for the days of hunger he would save the tribe during the coming winter. Later, when the storm appeared, he knew that would no longer happen, but after he had taken refuge inside his lean-to he comforted himself with the skill and speed with which he had erected it. It was better to come back with meat than with firewood, certainly, but it was also better to come back alive than not at all, for the addition or subtraction of a single able-bodied adult could make the difference in the survival of the tribe's youngest members. Still, it was bitterly cold before the snow accumulated enough to insulate his shelter, and each time the wind gusted the man was terrified that the flimsy frame he had thrown together would be torn apart. Snow sifted through the boughs and sputtered on his fire. His supply of fuel was not as large as it should have been.

As the snow began to accumulate, though, as the perilous shaking quieted and his shelter warmed up, he grew calmer, and he selected the longest arrow from his quiver to clear his smoke hole. This arrow had always brought him luck: unlike most projectiles, which are broken or lost during the course of a hunt, this one had come back to him more times than he could remember. It had pierced the sides of innumerable deer, caribou, elk, and moose; also hares, foxes, wolves, and, on three different occasions, bear. So successful had this arrow been that the man had taken to trimming the other arrows in his quiver so that this was always the longest, and the first he reached for, and he fletched it with two white feathers from a snowy owl and a black one from a corvid—rare feathers, normally reserved for ceremonial uses—so that it would stand out in a downed beast from those of the other men in his tribe. When the arrowhead needed to be replaced he used only amber chert, the stone from which its first head had been fashioned, and when the shaft grew brittle he replaced it with tamarack, a deciduous wood significantly more scarce at that latitude than spruce or fir, but much more durable. So dear was the arrow that the man hesitated before using it to clear his smoke hole. The half-melted snow would dampen the coil of dried gut that bound the head to the shaft, softening it, and possibly weaken the wood as well. He decided to use it anyway: when he got back to his tribe, he could replace the binding if need be; the wood; the head. His luck would hold.

The snow thickened atop the lean-to. The stones lining his firepit grew hotter and spread their heat to the stones supporting his platform. Even after he removed his anorak and trousers he was still drowsily warm, and he dozed off and on, a sliver of blubber softening between his bottom teeth and lip, his nose filled with the spicy scent of a handful of needles he had tossed on the fire. The storm had become an invisible hum from which he had made himself safe. He had harnessed it like the northern tribes, using its own force to protect him. He looked forward to telling his tribe of his resourcefulness. He imagined his wife's cries of relief when he showed up alive. He had never taken much notice of her before his uncle died, or at any rate had never considered her as a wife. During the winter the family slept in one room. He had heard the sounds of her coupling with his uncle and smelled the mineral odor of her fertility; had been present when two of her three children were born. But though she was only a few years older than he was, he always thought of her as a member of his parents' generation. Her belly was stout and her breasts softened from the children she had borne and suckled. Her face, though smooth and open, had been solemn since her two oldest children had died in a famine five winters earlier. Even when he agreed to take her on he was thinking more of her daughter than of her, and he suspected his aunt understood his motivation because, their first night as husband and wife, she slid her pallet next to his and positioned herself with her back to him before pulling her daughter into her belly and folding an arm around her. But during the night he awakened to fingers on his body. He must have turned toward her in his sleep, and now her broad soft back pressed against his chest, and the curve of her buttocks filled the hollow of his groin. He did not understand what was happening until she lifted her leg and deftly pulled him inside her. He had not expected it to be as warm as it was, as soft and welcoming, and, stunned by the sensation, so entirely foreign that it did not, that first time, register as pleasure, his body stiffened like uncured leather. His wife rocked her hips back and forth; it was over almost as soon as it began. His hidden ejaculation took him by surprise, and when he called out it was as much in confusion—fear, really—as anything else. From farther down the room he heard a quiet laugh. "You are a man now," his mother said. "Now go back to sleep."

Later he learned that his wife had eased his passage with a smear of rendered fat. At first this disappointed him. He had thought the electric smoothness a natural thing, perhaps even a blessing of marriage. But he came to appreciate her thoughtfulness, as when she served him the biggest piece of meat or instructed her daughter to remove his boots and rub his feet when he returned from the forest or the sea. As his aunt she had heckled him with the other women, belittling the hare he brought back for not being a deer, a deer for not being a moose, a moose for not being a bear. But as his wife she defended him, chasing away even his mother from his kills until she had cut out the choicest meats for him, the tenderloin, the haunch, the liver. She never faced him when they coupled or engaged in any of the play that he had seen her enjoy with his uncle, but she never denied him either, and was often more conscious of his physical state than he was; that first night's awakening was repeated so often that he came to think of it as part of sleep. Indeed, he was erect now, and he dribbled a bit of blubber into his hand and curled it around his penis. It was his first time masturbating, although he was aware of the practice, and he tried to imitate the speed of his wife's hips, the soft even pressure of her flesh around his. But it was the image in his head that most compelled him. He had fantasized before. He had just never been aware he was doing it, because he had been coupling with his wife at the same time, and it was she he thought of. He was surprised by the power of the mental image. Not so much by its vividness—he had nothing against which to compare it—as its potency, its ability to excite him, and he reached fruition almost as quickly as he did with his wife.

Afterwards he lay still, his eyes closed, contemplating what had just happened. The image in his head had not been a memory. Although it was similar to things he had done, it was wholly new, and he found himself wondering if his wife had entered his mind, like an arrow piercing the eye of a fox, or if he had built her there, the arrow crafted from wood and stone and feathers. But no, he thought. The image in his head was not his wife, just as the fur of his clothing was no longer caribou or seal. A transformation had taken place. Something had been lost, but something had been made too. Or perhaps something had been revealed—the part of his wife that was not contained by her flesh. Her spirit, yes, but he had always believed the spirit remained in the body until the body died. Now he understood that it could go out into the world while the flesh yet lived. Could his spirit do the same thing? It seemed improbable that it could not, but how did it work? Was it a directed action, like throwing a harpoon or calling a dog, or did it happen of its own accord, like blinking against blackflies or flinching from a flame? He thought of the caribou whose trail he had followed. There was no evidence to suggest they had passed by recently. He had been aware of the stillness of the weather; knew very well that the tracks could have been older than they appeared. But he had wanted to return to his tribe—to his family, to his wife—with meat rather than wood, and it was this vision he had trailed, not the herd, which in his mind was not composed of animals but of so many servings of food. But without that vision—without spirit venturing into the world—what was there? Spirit saw the arrowhead inside the piece of stone, the waterproof boots in a seal's skin, the bow in a curved tree branch. Spirit saw the tree and the seal and the stone even—without spirit the world was undifferentiated. The world did not recognize animal or plant nor make a distinction between earth and sea and sky. It was spirit that broke the world into pieces and saw how those pieces could be recombined to make new things, that named the pieces, and the new things made from them, and in so doing left a piece of itself behind, as his wife had left the feeling of her body in his flesh, so that the gift of her touch would always be with him.

A drop of water fell on his skin then. All his senses concentrated on the spot of bitter, burning coldness, so that it seemed as if it was his thought—his spirit—that warmed the water until it became indistinguishable from the sweat rolling off his body. Another drop. He threw his spirit at the frigid corona, obliterating it. Another drop. Another. Another. A sheath of ice was trying to form around him but his spirit glowed like a coal, melting it. But a part of him wanted to let the ice take him. It would protect him, he told himself. From what? From the snow. From the—

With a start, he remembered where he was. He shook himself awake, sucking in air, but could not take a full breath. His smoke hole had filled with snow. He grabbed his lucky arrow and stood unsteadily, supporting himself on the frame of his shelter. He jabbed the arrow into the icy hole. Snow fell into his fire, sizzling there, creating even more smoke, but the hole remained blocked beyond the reach of his arrowhead. He jabbed and swirled, the arrowhead scratching audibly against the ice that lined the shaft, but it remained blocked. He tried to jump and crashed through his platform to the frigid air beneath. He grabbed his bow and aimed up the narrow tube. Taut sinew twanged, the arrow disappeared. Smoke continued to fill his shelter. The man was reaching for a second arrow when a fist-sized clump of snow fell into the fire, and a shaft of silver light appeared. The smoke hole had opened. The sun had come up. The man stared at the circle of blue-gray sky far above him, sucking in air, but then just waiting—waiting for his lucky arrow to reappear. He waited a long time, but all that came down his smoke hole were snowflakes, dancing and dying in the shaft of light. When, finally, he was convinced his arrow was not coming back, he stripped a few branches from the frame of his shelter, and began to make a pair of snowshoes for the long walk home.

THE RAMPED TUNNEL, the labored strides.

The infinity of white, the phantoms of marauding whales.

The falling light and the realization that he was lost.

The step that completes the circle. The step that starts its eternal revolution.

The novices revisit each stage of the man's journey. Their focus this time is not on logistics but on state of mind—above all on this notion of spirit, which they sense is intrinsic to the parable's resolution.

But when they quiz the master, he tells them that the man's sudden awakening had all but wiped the idea from his memory. Further, the master says, he cannot rule out the possibility that the man's reverie was nothing more than an hallucination borne of oxygen deprivation. The novices have done their work too well, he says: their syncretic approach has created a seamless linguistic version of what, for the man, was a fractured progression of images and emotions of which he remembers only vague, conflicting premonitions: a disquieting sense that the world is not what it appears tempered by a comforting oneness with everything around him. Now, as he labors against the snow, he no longer thinks of *his* spirit, a finite or contingent entity, but merely spirit, a universal intention permeating all living and nonliving things, a metaphysics fully in line with his tribe's beliefs.

To the resolutely materialist novices, the familiar animism of the man's tribe seems a kind of deistic translation of the contemporary idea of culture, whereas the more idiosyncratic notion from the man's dream, of a personal spirit, seems like a pre-psychological attempt to recognize one's own consciousness —culture being shared ideas, consciousness being the mediator between external information and the individual. Long before they approach the parable, the novices will have rejected the dichotomy that posits culture as all human activity that is not biological or, in the more common, though even less precise, term, natural. It will have been drummed into them that human beings are animals like any other; their brains, while capable of prodigious feats of mentation compared to other species, are still biological organs, and as such any activity they engage in, any thought they produce, is inherently natural. The novices define culture instead as any mental activity that classifies the world— divides its unity and gives the pieces names—as well as any physical action that stems from those classifications. On this they agree. What divides them is culture's relationship to consciousness, with some claiming that consciousness is anterior to culture, while others argue that culture not only comes before consciousness but is a necessary cause of it. But how can you share ideas, the former ask, without first *having* ideas? To which the latter respond: the emphasis should be on *sharing* rather than on ideas. After all, many if not most animals demonstrate the ability to teach and learn without possessing consciousness, at least not in the ratiocinating form possessed by human beings.

In the end anthropology carries the day: before *Homo sapiens* developed the sorts of mental functions contemporary human beings would recognize as consciousness, our behavior was instinctual and genetic, including our ability to learn. There was no speech with which an idea could be communicated, no logic, no metaphor. Nevertheless behaviors *did* accumulate from generation to generation, and in a manner distinct from other species; were assimilated at a younger age and progressed further until, over the course of thousands of years, human beings began to engage with mental symbols of the world as well as with the world itself. It is likely that the interaction with this collective store of information led to the development of the construct of the self—another mental symbol—as people came to require a mediator between their bodies and the increasingly complex behaviors available to them. But this mediator was itself a collective development. No one stood up one day and said "I"; "I am"; "I am I"; "I am that I am." The development was gradual and species-wide. But when it was complete—or, at any rate, when it had reached a certain threshold—humanity had created a mode of being that separated it from other animals. It had become the creature that *thinks* of itself rather than *is* itself. This is not to say that previous generations lacked a sense of themselves as discrete beings, only that they spent no time wondering what that meant—what the self was, and if and how it was distinct from the flesh and blood and bone of the body. But once a person starts talking about "myself" a split occurs. There is a physical entity that is the self and a mental entity in search of it. This split is the ultimate origin of the Oedipus narrative: we hunt for something that is us, never suspecting that the only way to find it is to stop looking. To realize that the search is what is preventing us from finding it.

So. The self. A mental construct that says "I," but is in fact saying—is only capable of saying—"we." An infinite we, comprising all who have gone before and will come after; a unifying we, slipping the bonds of biology and time; but a we that obliterates the individuality whose illusion it fosters. Is this the crisis at the heart of the parable? Was the man led astray by culture's inability to reconcile the world with an idea of it, rather than by his own poor judgment? And if so, can culture save him? Or, failing that, can it predict how he will respond to his situation?

A sense of unease has grown in the novices during these latter discussions. Because they have spent so much time exploring the ways in which the man is like them, they inevitably find themselves asking if their own selves are collectively created—if consciousness, which they have always thought of as oceanic in its drift and swell, is nothing more than a runnel in the narrow flume of culture. They feel tantalizingly close to completing the parable, which has occupied most of their first year in fifth form, yet are frightened of the conclusions they might reach, of the implications their work may have for their own lives—their own selves. But narrative moves in only one direction, and, tentatively, they begin to parse the relationship between culture and consciousness as it exists in the parable's hero.

The novices start by asking the master if the man could have had the same thoughts about spirit had he been awake and in an oxygen-rich environment. The master dismisses the question. The parable is not a quantum state: there is only what is and what is not. The novices ask if the man has a name, and the master tells them that the man has had several names, some concurrently, some successively, for himself, for his wife and stepdaughter and tribe, but that these names are similar to the words he uses for plants and animals and landmarks, characterizing the things to which they refer by virtue of appearance, behavior, or relationality rather than some innate identity. He called his wife one name before she married his uncle, for example, another when she was his aunt, and a third when he married her, just as he has different names for a seal in the water and a seal on dry land, a caribou when it is alive and a caribou after he has killed it. The novices ask if the man thought of himself as an individual—if he thought of his wife and stepdaughter, his mother and the other members of his tribe, as individuals. The master tells them that, though the man does not have the word "individual," he recognizes that he and the people around him are separate beings, but only in the sense that a single step is a component of walking or running: it's not that one cannot say where one stride ends and the next begins, but if you take the time to wonder you'll probably end up falling on your face. The novices ask, finally, if the man is capable of reasoned as opposed to rote response to stimuli. The master tells the novices that in the early stages of the famine that claimed his future wife's two oldest children, the man shared food with his niece and nephew, but later, when a mouthful of blubber was the difference between survival and death, he turned a deaf ear to their pleas. Moreover, the master tells them, the man's uncle and aunt did the same, eating such food as there was in front of their dying children, although his aunt continued to nurse her youngest daughter, which is why the girl survived. And when the older girl and boy did succumb, the family said prayers to return their spirits to the gods, then consumed their flesh. They did not ask themselves if they should perform these actions, let alone why; they did not regard their actions as choices. Is this reason? Instinct? Training? Because the people of the man's tribe did not ask themselves these questions, the master cannot answer them. All he can say is that similar actions had been performed by people who came before the man's tribe, and would continue to be performed by people who came after, right down to the present day.

Which demands the question (the novices whisper among themselves, outside of their sessions with the master): perhaps they should not be asking if the *man* is capable of independent thought. Perhaps they should be asking if *they* are. Think about it: by the time they came to the Academy as five-year-olds, they had assimilated almost 150,000 years of cultural production. They knew how to speak, for one thing, something that took ancient humans a hundred millennia to figure out, and had at least a rudimentary understanding of reading and writing, which took another 45,000 years or so to emerge. "Or so": 5,000 years glossed over in four letters. How could a single mind could jump so ingrained a track! More believable that thought, shaped by language and directed inexorably toward speech, would race through the channel previous generations had excavated for it, and the closest it could come to freedom would be a quivering or writhing in its course, like a hose twitching when a spigot is opened and water fills it. Seen in this light, William James's dictum that the first characteristic of consciousness is its "absolute insulation" from all others, the "irreducible pluralism" of minds, seems not just false but an inversion of the case, with some or all thought—or, more likely, some part of all thought—being shared among all members of an established group, not through telepathy or genetics but through culture. But is this "course" the novices keep invoking—this track, this channel, this hose—pointed toward a single end, or is it part of an irrigation system watering a vast area? Is humanity still wandering the vast snowy plain, as it were, still capable of directing its fate, or has it fallen into the same trap as the man?

And of course culture's pervasiveness goes far beyond language. The novices understand rhythm, pitch, melody, and harmony, for example, and make sense of what they hear based on these suppositions; they can look at pictures in a variety of styles, from fingerpainting to photographs, from trompe l'oeil to collage, and not only do they recognize the images there, but they see the world in terms of these modes. They can work all of the simple machines and combine them to make more complex tools. They understand doorknobs, light switches, keyboards. They navigate fluidly between hundreds of systems, operating bicycles and telephones and phonographs, and, despite Academy proscriptions, televisions and automobiles and computers. Then there are the institutions, the classrooms and corporations and governmental bodies not even an Academy man can wholly escape, individually monumental but together forming a mechanism whose complexity is beyond the capacity not just of any one person but of any group to comprehend fully—*even a group composed of all its members*. And this is not just how we live now. It is how we have always lived. To acknowledge it is not to protest. It is to admit that it is what makes us possible. As a species we are not herd but hive. We cannot even conceive of ourselves as individuals. When we attempt to, all we are really calling to mind is an idea—"the individual"—created over the course of what is, in the long view, a handful of generations. We see ourselves as isolated beings in a vast field of snow, when in fact we are more akin to the snowflakes falling from the clouds: fleetingly discrete before being subsumed into that from which we came.

AND SO, APPREHENSIVE but determined, the novices push toward the parable's climax.

They ask first how the man failed to recognize his own footsteps. The master tells them that the man's trail was long enough that he could not see its end: he saw one set of footsteps behind him, which he recognized as his own because they terminated at his feet, and another set before him, which stretched off in either direction farther than he could see. Thus there was no visible evidence linking the path behind him with the one before him. And, since he believed he had been walking in a straight line, no logical evidence either.

The novices nod. They cannot disagree with the man's assessment, based on the facts as he understood them.

The novices ask why the man did not go in the direction from which the steps came rather than the direction in which they led. Someone from his village could have ventured out in the snow— perhaps to look for him? The master tells them that the man knew no one would have left the encampment while the snow was so deep, and certainly not in a northerly direction, or to look for someone who almost surely had perished in the storm. Further, the wind was picking up and the light was fading. The beginning of the trail was already starting to be obscured, and would likely disappear before the man would have reached its origin. Thus his best bet was to try to catch up to the person who had made the trail.

The novices look at one another. Yes, they agree. They would have done the same thing, given the circumstances. Indeed, they could have done nothing else.

The novices ask how the man did not realize he was walking in a circle, and the master reminds them: the wind was picking up, the light fading. The snow had obscured any landmarks. By the time the man had circled back to where he first intersected his own trail, the older fork, if it was still there, was no longer visible. Initially the man was confused by the deepening path in the snow, the presence of not one but several sets of footprints. Then he realized he must be getting closer to his or another tribe's encampment. Indeed, it appeared as though dozens of people had walked this trail, and all in the same direction, and the man came to believe that he had crossed the trail of some tribe or other heading south in response to the snowstorm. Plus the deepening trench protected him from the wind, and the packed snow made walking less arduous, so that he felt he could go on longer. The sky was clearing, the moon rising. The man told himself he could go all night if he needed to.

Yes, the novices agree. The man could go all night. He could go forever, and still get nowhere.

Finally the novices ask how the man discovered he was

walking in a circle. The master tells them that at some point during the night the man heard voices ahead of him in the trench. Among them he heard his wife's voice, bemoaning his loss, begging to be allowed to look for her husband, and he called out to tell her that he was right behind. But the voice that answered was his uncle's, and he knew then that the sounds he was hearing did not emanate from human mouths, but from the spirit world. His uncle told the man that it was not far now. That if he pushed on he would find what he was looking for, which was not fire, shelter, food, but his tribe. Death was inevitable, his uncle reminded him, whether it happened today or twenty years from now. But if the man continued to push on he would not die like an animal. The man got up when he heard these words. He did not remember falling. He pulled an arrow from his quiver and stabbed it into the wall of the trench. He left this mark not for himself—he did not yet suspect he was walking in a circle—but for those who would come after. He wanted them to know he had made it this far. It was not his lucky arrow, obviously—his lucky arrow had cleared his smoke hole, saving him from suffocating—and as the man walked on a part of him could not help but think of the second arrow as unlucky. And so, in a way, it was, because after he left it behind it fell to the ground and the man walked over it who knew how many times as he continued to wear his trench deeper and deeper in the snow. By now the voice the man was following was that of his unborn child. He had not known his wife was pregnant until his daughter's voice came to him to thank him for the gift of life, and to comfort him with the knowledge that the tribe would take responsibility for her as he had taken responsibility for her mother when his uncle died. They were one tribe, she reminded him. They would provide for her and teach her to provide for her children, and she would teach them to provide for themselves. His daughter told him: it was not his arrow that was lucky. He had made his own luck, she told him, by crafting the arrow of the finest materials and taking extra care when using it and above all by trusting the arrow with a piece of his spirit. It was his spirit that came back to him, even when the arrow did not.

The man felt something snap beneath his boot. He bent over, felt around in the darkness. He came up with his arrow, broken in two pieces.

And here one novice always jumps to his feet:

Q: Which arrow?
A: Which arrow?

Q: Was it the arrow he had stabbed in the side of the trench? Or was it his lucky arrow?
A: Why does it matter?

Q: If it was his lucky arrow, it could be a sign.
A: A sign of?

The novice falls silent. He cannot bring himself to invoke providence.

A: It was not his lucky arrow.

The novices heave a collective sigh. All of them know the next question, but none of them wants to ask it.

Q: Did the man keep walking, or did he surrender to the snow?
A: What do you think?

The novices look at each other. Is this the end of the parable? Or have they not reached it yet?

Q: Does it matter what we think?
A: What you think has determined the course of the parable.

The novices ponder the master's words. A light flickers somewhere in their minds, so dimly that they are not even sure what sparks it. They perceive this light as understanding, yet it feels more like hope.

Q: Are you saying that the parable isn't the same for every group?
A: Given the virtual impossibility of two groups of novices asking exactly the same questions in exactly the same order, let alone *every* group of novices asking exactly the same questions in exactly the same order, the functional answer to your question is no, it's not. But that does not preclude the possibility that two or more groups of novices may explore the parable in exactly the same way, assuming the master gives exactly the same answers to their questions.

Q: Then is the parable dependent on the questions put to the master? If, for example, we had never asked about the device the man used to clean his smoke hole, would his lucky arrow have been mentioned?

A: To the first question, the answer is yes. To the second, no.

Q: Are the events of the parable the same at every telling, regardless of the order in which they are revealed?

A: No.

Q: Is the master required to give the same answers to the same questions every time he tells the parable?

A: No.

Q: By what criteria does the master choose what answers he gives?

A: The master gives the answers the novices' questions presuppose.

Q: So you created the parable—the man—in our image?

A: No. You did.

Q: So the parable's final question is not what would the man do but . . . what would *we* do?

Q: Or, rather, what have we already done?

Q: What couldn't we stop ourselves from doing? What were we destined to do?

This, almost always, from the novice who had invoked the divine.

A: Imagine a wall of bricks made of ice, each of which contains a light that turns on when a pebble of coal strikes it. It is nighttime. Nothing is visible. You throw a pebble. A light comes on. When you throw the next pebble you aim as close to the first as possible. Another light comes on. You throw handfuls of pebbles in an effort to speed the process, but here's the rub: hit a brick once and its light turns on. Hit it again and the light goes off. Working one pebble at a time, you light up brick after brick. A shape begins to reveal itself. It is a curve. You cast your pebbles wider in an attempt to determine the scale of the object. It is bigger than it at first appeared. Very big, in fact. In fact, it surrounds you on all sides. It is a circle. You throw more parables— pebbles, I mean—seeking to fill in the dark places. The distance between you and the wall is great, your aim less than perfect. As a result some bricks remain dark for a long time, even though they are surrounded by light, and some that are lit go dark again when you hit them a second time. You fritter away time and energy trying to illuminate isolated bricks even though all the evidence suggests they are nothing more than stretchers in the third or fourth or fortieth course of the wall that surrounds you. As you work your way up the wall you notice that it curves in at the top. Indeed, it seems to form a dome, the top of which is at the farthest edge of your range. The shape is clear now. You understand that all you are doing is illuminating something whose name you already know.

Say it. Say the word out loud. Say: "iglu."

Now: ask yourself why you threw that first pebble.